All ☞

"Readers will love the main character's charm and wit and the many twists and turns of the plot." —*Debbie's Book Bag*

"An entertaining read, and I look forward to the next installment in the series." —*Cozy Crimes*

"Well plotted with interesting, likable characters, *All Sales Fatal* is a nice balance between cozy amateur sleuth and police procedural." —*The Mystery Reader*

"Fun, well-paced mystery that keeps readers guessing." —*Fresh Fiction*

"An enjoyable investigative tale starring a dedicated heroine. In some ways Grandpa Atherton steals the show of this fast-paced whodunit as he and his granddaughter team up as mall sleuths." —*Genre Go Round Reviews*

PRAISE FOR

Die Buying

"[A] wonderful start to a new series with likable characters, lots of humor, and a swift-moving story that will grab anyone who has ever stepped foot in a mall . . . I'm adding *Die Buying* to my cozy favorites for the year—even though I hate to shop." —*AnnArbor.com*

"One hell of a great novel! This novel will crack you up with DiSilverio's humor and razor's-edge wit. A great book to curl up with over the weekend. You won't be able to put it down." —*Suspense Magazine*

"DiSilverio has a hit on her hands with this debut series . . . Charming, fun, and refreshing." —*Seattle Post-Intelligencer*

"Laura DiSilverio has come up with a unique hook whereby she reels in her readers . . . I'm eager to read the next installment in this offbeat series." —*Mystery Scene*

Berkley Prime Crime titles by Laura DiSilverio

DIE BUYING
ALL SALES FATAL
MALLED TO DEATH

Malled to Death

Laura DiSilverio

BERKLEY PRIME CRIME, NEW YORK

THE BERKLEY PUBLISHING GROUP
Published by the Penguin Group
Penguin Group (USA) Inc.
375 Hudson Street, New York, New York 10014, USA

USA / Canada / UK / Ireland / Australia / New Zealand / India / South Africa / China

Penguin Books Ltd., Registered Offices: 80 Strand, London WC2R 0RL, England
For more information about the Penguin Group, visit penguin.com.

MALLED TO DEATH

A Berkley Prime Crime Book / published by arrangement with the author

Berkley Prime Crime Books are published by The Berkley Publishing Group.
BERKLEY® PRIME CRIME and the PRIME CRIME logo are
trademarks of Penguin Group (USA) Inc.

For information, address: The Berkley Publishing Group,
a division of Penguin Group (USA) Inc.,
375 Hudson Street, New York, New York 10014.

ISBN: 978-0-425-25191-1

PUBLISHING HISTORY
Berkley Prime Crime mass-market edition / April 2013

PRINTED IN THE UNITED STATES OF AMERICA

10   9   8   7   6   5   4   3   2   1

Cover illustration by Ben Perini.
Cover design by Rita Frangie.
Interior text design by Laura K. Corless.

ALWAYS LEARNING   **PEARSON**

For Amy Sagendorf—
new friend, true friend.

One

...

Anya Vale clutched the world's ugliest dog to her chest and let loose with the scream that paid her bills.

I winced. Normally, a scream like that would have me Segwaying at top speed toward its source, riding to the rescue, as it were. However, I knew Ms. Vale wasn't being raped or mugged, that she hadn't had her purse stolen, or tripped over a python near the food court fountain. Agatha, the fifteen-foot python, was safely ensconced in her enclosure at the Herpetology Hut, as far as I knew. No, Ms. Vale wasn't upset about reptiles, or a bad haircut from the mall's salon, or even the total on her black American Express card. She—

Anya Vale screamed again, this time ending with a sob.

"That's impressive," Joel whispered, his South Carolina accent tickling my ear. "Do you think it hurts her throat?"

It certainly hurt my ears, but I didn't tell Joel Rooney that. At twenty-three, he was the youngest of Fernglen

Galleria's security force members, and probably the nicest.
Before I could answer, another voice broke in.

"Cut!" the director yelled. "Not so shrill next time, hm?"
he said to Anya.

She whirled on him, inky hair flying, all pouty lips,
uptilted nose, enhanced boobs, and "I'm an A-list star" attitude. "It's the dry air in this mall, Van. It's killing my aller-
gies. You've got to do something about it." She flounced off
the set, the Chinese crested dog tucked under her arm looking back at me and Joel. The wispy hair atop its pointy head
flopped with every step Anya Vale took.

"C'mon," I urged Joel as the movie people started milling
about, doing whatever it is they do. Cameras and cables and
huge lights cluttered the corridor, and people scurried here
and there, adjusting boom mikes, checking the lighting, and
touching up makeup. Enough uniformed police officers
mingled with the grips and gaffers that the uninitiated might
think the mall had better security than Fort Knox. I knew
better: the "cops" were extras in *Mafia Mistress*. We left the
theater wing and headed toward the elevator that would take
us upstairs to the security office. A long table laden with
pastries, water, and fruit partially blocked access to the main
hall and Joel filched a cream cheese Danish as we passed.

"What does she think that Van guy can do about the air?"
Joel asked around a mouthful of flaky pastry. He kept pace
with me on the Segway, the two-wheeled electric vehicle I
usually rode when patrolling the mall. The leg injuries
inflicted on me by an IED when I was a military cop in
Afghanistan kept me from walking the miles of mall corridors and parking lot on foot.

"She probably expects him to get a humidifier installed,"
I said.

My tone must have been snarkier than I intended because

Joel gave me an uncertain look. "Don't you think it's fun that they're filming the movie here, EJ?"

No, I most certainly didn't think it was "fun" that my father, one of the top two or three action stars in Hollywood, had insisted on his newest cop thriller being filmed at Fernglen Galleria. He'd done it thinking that exposure to the glamour of the moviemaking world would convince me to hang up my mall cop uniform and join him at his production company, doing whatever producers did. I'm not sure anyone in Hollywood could supply a job description for a producer, but it didn't matter because I didn't want to be one even if it involved eating chocolate truffles for breakfast and lunching with Daniel Craig every day. My heart was in policing, and even though I'd been having trouble getting hired by a police department because of my partial disability, I wasn't going to sell out and return to L.A. where I'd grown up, and where the first prerequisite for being successful was having your brains sucked out. Or maybe that was second, after you got your boobs augmented. I never could remember.

"It makes it harder for us to do our job," I finally told Joel.

"Yeah, but look how many customers it's brought in," he said, gesturing to the unusually large crowd of shoppers present before noon on a Monday.

"Quigley's probably happier than a teenager with a cure for zits," I agreed. Nothing made the mall's operations manager, Curtis Quigley, happier than a mall full of shoppers. I'd once seen him outside on Black Friday, reveling in the full-to-capacity parking lot with cars circling, looking for a slot. He'd agreed to the film company using Fernglen because he hoped their presence would bring in crowds of people eager to gawk at Anya Vale or Ethan Jarrett. Once in the mall, he was convinced, they'd succumb to the lure of a new phone from RadioShack, or a cute terrier from the pet shop, or a mist-producing table fountain from Merlin's Cave.

"Speak of the devil," Joel muttered as we rounded the corner into the side hall where the mall's offices were safely hidden from public view. Curtis Quigley came toward us with that "I'm holding a quarter between my cheeks" walk that Joel could imitate to hilarious effect. Curtis had light brown hair swept off his high forehead and pomaded in place, a narrow face, and a nervous manner. He affected a faint British accent and suits—frequently referring to his tailor on Savile Row—and had a different set of cuff links for every day of the week.

"EJ," Curtis said. "I've been looking for you. Do you think Ethan"—he preened slightly, clearly flattered that my dad had asked him to call him by his first name—"would be willing to pose for a photo with some of the Figley and Boon higher-ups? And me," he added.

Figley and Boon, Incorporated, otherwise known as FBI, owned Fernglen Galleria and other malls around the country. "No clue," I said between gritted teeth. "You'll have to ask his publicist." This was the movie company's first day at Fernglen and my dad was already driving me crazy, even though he wasn't even here yet, as far as I knew. I pushed through the glass doors fronting the security office before Quigley could say anything more about Ethan.

A small, windowless room, the security office is dominated by the banks of monitors that display data from the security cameras, only about one-third of which actually work. Quigley and the former director of security, Captain Woskowicz, thought the cameras themselves were enough of a deterrent to shoplifters and vandals and didn't see the need to pay for more connectivity. The monitor screens were divided into quarters and someone got the job of watching the screens and serving as dispatcher each day. A couple of battered metal desks and filing cabinets made up the rest of the front office's decor. It smelled of coffee with an underlying hint of mildew from last week's plumbing leak (from a sink, thank heaven) in the bathroom next door. The boss's office was down a short hall, across from a storage room, and it wasn't mine, despite the fact that I'd interviewed for the job when Captain Woskowicz got murdered.

The new director of security emerged from the office as I settled into my chair. If the FBI hiring board had set out to find the anti-Woskowicz, they couldn't have done a better job. Dennis Woskowicz had been well over six feet tall, bald, and steroid-bulky with years of security experience of one kind or another. He'd also been surly, sexist, and a crook. Coco MacMillan was a twenty-something wannabe fashion designer who'd lucked into this job because her uncle chaired FBI's board of directors. A bubbly redhead, she'd undoubtedly been a high school cheerleader before getting her degree at some fashion institute and promptly joining the ranks of the degreed but unemployed. What she knew about security work would fit on one of Quigley's cuff links with room left over. She'd been on board a week and had spent most of that time designing new uniforms for the security staff.

If I come across as slightly bitter, it's because I am. With my time as an air force cop and the year-plus I'd spent at Fernglen, not to mention the leadership training and security seminars the military had sent me to, I had more knowledge about running a security force in my left pinkie than Coco MacMillan had in her entire designer-suited body. I tapped harder than necessary on the keyboard, trying to avoid interacting with my new boss. It didn't work.

"EJ and Joel," she greeted us with a wide smile that showed her dimples. "Come see what I've come up with."

Careful not to glance at Joel, who I knew would be rolling his eyes at having to admire yet another potential uniform design, I rose and followed her into her office. She'd shoved Woskowicz's heavy desk to one side and set a drafting table in its place. Vintage fashion posters covered the walls and a mannequin stood front and center, decked in dark red slacks and a ruffled white shirt—one of Coco's prototype uniforms. If you didn't know better, you'd think you had wandered into the headquarters of Diane von Fürstenberg or Gucci. Coco rushed to the high table and flung aside the top sheet. "Ta-da!"

I looked at the design and bit the inside of my cheek.

"Is that a hat?" Joel asked incredulously, stabbing at the pillbox-type hat secured under the chin with an elastic band. Wearing it would make us look like bellhops or an organ grinder's monkey.

"Absolutely!" Coco beamed. "Isn't it the cutest?"

I was partial to our black Smokey Bear hats and said so. They went nicely with our simple black uniform slacks and white shirts.

"But they're so yesterday," Coco said, "and they look too military. We want our security officers to look approachable and fashionable."

"How about competent and professional?" I suggested.

She wrinkled her little nose and giggled. "Oh, EJ, you are *too* funny."

Who was being funny? "You should show it to Mr. Quigley and get his opinion," I suggested. I hoped that if she bothered Quigley with a fashion drawing, he'd toss her out of his office and maybe fire her for wasting her time on sketches when she should be doing security work. Coco shooed us out so she could get on with her designing, and Joel and I straggled back to the front office.

"I'll quit if she tries to make me wear a hat like that," Joel muttered. "I've picked up lots of new clients. It might be time to see if I can make a go of my business."

Joel was a dog lover who had recently launched a dog training business, patronized mostly by his parents' friends.

"You can't quit over a hat," I said. "Not in this economy."

"I wouldn't quit over just any hat," he said, "but I would over that one."

I had to admit that the tiny pillbox hat perched on Joel's head of brown curls would look pretty awful, especially since he was a big guy, still twenty-five pounds overweight despite his recent attempts at diet and exercise.

"Who's quitting?" The jovial voice came from just inside the glass doors, and I looked over to see Ethan Jarrett standing there oozing charisma. I'd probably need to spot clean the carpet when he left. He looked no more than forty, despite being fifteen years older, and had good genes, a discreet plastic surgeon, and a great spray tan to thank. I had to admit he looked fit and handsome in the dark blue police uniform that was his costume for the movie.

"No one, Ethan," I told my dad.

He'd long ago insisted that Clint and I call him Ethan; "Dad" was too aging if your kids were over twelve, he maintained. I was grateful for that now, since it made it easier to hide the fact that he was my father. Only a handful of my co-workers knew we were related, as my name was Emma-Joy Ferris and he went by his first and middle names: Ethan Jarrett. When he'd first brought up the idea of filming his new movie at Fernglen, I'd insisted—okay, pleaded—that he not let on to any of the movie crew that I was his daughter. He'd been happy to comply, mostly because I looked my age—thirty-one—and even the most math-challenged fan could figure out that Ethan must be more than forty if he had a daughter as old as I was.

"What are you doing here?" I asked.

"Now, EJ, is that any way to welcome your fa—"

I shot him a look.

He waved it away. "Joel knows. I don't know why *you* want to hide our relationship, anyway."

Joel grinned. "How are you, Mr. Jarrett? I think it's way cool that you're filming *Mafia Mistress* here."

"How many times do I have to tell you it's 'Ethan'?" my dad asked, striding forward to shake hands with Joel. "I'm glad someone"—he gave me a look—"is pleased to have the movie company here."

"Lots of people are pleased," I said, unperturbed. "Curtis Quigley is probably your biggest fan." Before he could say more, I added, "But you can't pop into the security office on a daily basis, Ethan. People will suspect something." I had to admit it had amused me the time a reporter for a tabloid spotted us lunching and published the "news" of our affair, complete with grainy photo, but I didn't need that kind of gossip floating around my workplace. My father hadn't sued the paper, knowing that most fans were happier thinking their idol was cheating on his wife than knowing he had adult children. "Stars of your caliber don't trot around to the security office to ask questions, they send a minion."

"I'm fresh out of minions," Ethan said, flashing the smile that had landed him the title of World's Sexiest Man more often than Brad Pitt or George Clooney. "Delia quit to get married."

"I heard. I sent her and Rocco a present. Mom will find

you a new assistant soon." Mom was in charge of hiring most of Ethan's staff because he was apt to overlook checking references and credentials if he liked someone. Mom had started doing the interviewing and hiring after an assistant some twenty years back stole over a hundred thousand dollars from them. "In the meantime, I'm sure—"

High heels click-clacked behind me and the sound of something dropping preceded, "Ethan Jarrett! Ohmigod, ohmigod."

We turned to see Coco standing at the threshold where the main office meets the hall, surrounded by a litter of art pencils and pads, hands clapped to her cheeks. Her eyes opened wide. "Oh! I grew up watching you in *Roll Call*. I can't believe—"

Ethan stooped to pick up one of the pencils that had rolled to a stop against his shoe. I was too used to this sort of reaction to let it faze me, so I said, "Mr. Jarrett, this is Coco MacMillan, our director of security. Ms. MacMillan, Mr. Jarrett stopped by because . . ." I trailed off on purpose. He was the actor—let him come up with a plausible reason for his presence.

"Lovely to meet you, Coco," he said, making her flush an even deeper pink, if that was possible. "I dropped in because I received a letter that makes me uneasy and I thought I should let your officers know."

Good one, Ethan, I thought, as Coco said, "Oh, of course. A letter? Um, what kind of letter?" She pushed a red curl off her forehead and managed to look about as capable as a kitten of dealing with threats to the mall's security.

Ethan pulled a sheet of paper from the pocket of his police uniform. Unfolding it, he held it at arm's length—still too vain to wear reading glasses, I noted—and read, " 'Stop

making movies that glorify violence and capitalist material-
ism or we'll stop you.'" He lowered the page and looked at
us expectantly.

My brow puckered. He was serious. When he'd first mentioned a letter, I'd thought he was making it up to explain
being in the security office. "When did you get this, Eth—
Mr. Jarrett?" I moved in to read the letter as he held it out.
I didn't want to touch it and risk screwing up any fingerprints
that weren't already obliterated by Ethan handling it. I
scanned the page. No greeting, no signature, just like he
read it. Large-font black letters on a generic white page with
a black-and-white graphic of a knife dripping blood. Crossing to my desk, I pulled out a nine-by-twelve envelope and
held it open. Ethan slid the page in.

"This morning," he said. "It was in my trailer when I
came in, on the floor, as if it'd been pushed under the door."

Great. The stars' trailers, along with a makeup trailer
and various others, were parked in the mall parking lot. A
temporary chain-link fence ringed them, but it wouldn't stop
a curious Boy Scout from getting in, never mind someone
more determined.

"Do you get a lot of letters like that?" Coco asked.

Ethan gave her a wry smile. "A fair number. It comes
with the territory. Most of my fan mail is complimentary,
but every now and then I get a letter from someone who
doesn't like my movies or what they stand for. I don't let the
cowards who write anonymous letters intimidate me." He
stood straighter, as if he thought he really was a cop ready
to protect truth, justice, and the American way.

"That's so brave," Coco said.

"Very brave," I said briskly. "Let me walk you back to
the set, Mr. Jarrett, and ask you a few more questions on
the way."

"Good idea, EJ," Coco said. "We're responsible for Mr. Jarrett's safety while he's at Fernglen and I'd hate for anything to happen to him. You can be, like, his bodyguard."

I almost gagged and Joel choked back a laugh. "The movie company has its own security personnel," I reminded Coco. "I'm sure they're sufficient to protect Mr. Jarrett and the other cast members if they stay on the set."

And quit wandering around my mall, I added internally.

Two

. . .

I herded Ethan out of the security office before Coco could come up with some other harebrained idea.

"She's cute," Ethan observed.

He was apparently talking about Coco. I felt myself flush with anger. " 'Cute' doesn't cut it when you're talking about security," I bit out.

He chuckled. "Come on, EJ. We're talking about a sub-urban mall, not the front lines in Afghanistan. I'm sure she'll do fine." Belatedly recognizing, perhaps from my stiffness, my silence, or the way I wouldn't meet his eyes, that he'd offended me, he added, "Of course, she won't do near as good a job as you'd have done. Any idea why they didn't hire you?"

"Because this place is just like Hollywood. Cuteness and connections get you farther than competence." Not wanting to discuss it further, I asked, "Are you worried about this note, Ethan?"

"Hell, no," he said with a laugh. "I get bushels of mail every week and there's always something from a woman who wants to marry me and have my babies or a nutter who thinks my movies are undermining American's values or some such rot. I only brought it along because I thought you might find it amusing with that bit about 'capitalist material-ism,' because that must refer to the mall, don't you think? Frankly, I find the ones from lovelorn women much scarier than this. I've gotten a couple of 'love' letters—" He broke off with an artistic shudder.

We got into the elevator, and a pair of middle-aged women stopped their conversation to stare in awe at Ethan Jarrett. He gave them a smile that reduced them to pools of hormones. Neither had worked up the courage to ask for an autograph by the time we reached the ground floor, but I knew they'd be telling their families all about their encoun-ter with a movie star at dinner that night. They were so starstruck that they forgot to get off the elevator and the doors closed with them still inside.

"Don't you ever get tired of that?" I asked.

"Of what?"

I shook my head, smiling to myself. We arrived at the theater wing and the movie set moments later and I got in one last question. "Was the letter in an envelope?"

"Nope. It came like that."

A petite, fortyish woman with a black pageboy that swished at her jawline hustled toward us, clearly intent on reclaiming Ethan. A younger, ginger-haired woman with a clipboard followed in her wake, looking anxious.

"Ethan," the first woman said, "we need to talk about the script." She gave me a sharp-eyed glance that dismissed me. "I'm not happy with the action sequence in the fountain scene."

"I've been thinking about that, too, Bree," Ethan said. "Maybe if we played it more like we did the pool scene in *Random's Redemption*, only change it so—"

"They're ready for you in makeup, Mr. Jarrett," Clipboard Woman cut in. "Oh, and I put some tulips in your trailer because I know how you enjoy them. The peach-colored ones you like. And Van wants to see you right away. He said . . ."

The threesome moved out of earshot and I returned to the main part of the mall, stopping by the food court for a cup of coffee on my way back to the office. Fernglen Galleria is laid out in a big X, with the food court located on the ground floor where the four wings come together. Department stores anchored each wing, and kiosks selling everything from sunglasses to calendars to skin potions sprouted in the middle of the wide halls. Lots of glass in the roof gave the mall a light, airy feel, and encouraged the luxuriant hostas and ferns and other greenery in huge stone planters that inspired the mall's name. The plant service that keeps the greenery clipped back and watered must have visited recently, since the leaves glistened and the smell of wet earth rose from the containers. I inhaled it and felt myself relax. Somehow, I always ended up tense when Ethan was around.

As had become my habit recently, I patronized Legendary Lola Cookies, owned by mall newcomer Jay Callahan. I told myself it was because the aroma of fresh-baked peanut butter cookies was so appealing, but I was afraid it was because Jay Callahan was so appealing. Wearing a long-sleeved orange Lola's shirt that clashed with his dark auburn hair, he smiled as I approached. The tee shirt skimmed his hard chest muscles and biceps and was tucked into faded jeans that gave him a casual, boy-next-door sort of vibe.

A vibe mitigated by an air of watchful alertness and hazel eyes that seemed to take in everything around him.

"My favorite mall cop, doing her appointed rounds. 'Neither rain nor sleet nor—' "

"That's the postal service," I said, accepting a steaming cup of coffee and handing him cash. I sniffed the aromatic brew gratefully.

"Big doings this week, huh?" he said, nodding toward the theater end of the mall.

I twirled a forefinger. "Whoop-de-doo."

He laughed. "You don't sound excited about having a movie crew at Fernglen. Old hat to you, I guess."

Jay was one of the few mall employees who knew that Ethan Jarrett was my dad. He'd seen us together when Ethan dropped by the mall a few weeks back and assumed we were having a romantic relationship. Not wanting him to think I was involved with a married man—or any man, for that matter—I'd told him the truth.

"I didn't spend much time hanging around Ethan's sets when I was growing up," I said, sipping the coffee. "To give him credit, he did his best to keep Clint and me away from the acting world, said we needed to get a college education and make our own decisions about what we wanted to do with our lives. He and Mom thought it was too easy to get caught up in the trappings of stardom—they didn't want me or Clint becoming actors only because we wanted to be famous."

"I guess they got their wish, with one cop in the family and one investigative reporter. No one seeking the limelight."

"Former cop," I said morosely. I'd applied at—and been rejected by—over twenty police departments since getting injured and medically retired from the air force. Being a mall cop was a stopgap measure at best; I certainly didn't consider it real policing, even though I'd gotten to stick my nose into a couple of murder investigations since I'd been at Fernglen.

"How's the new director of security working out?" Jay asked, refusing to participate in my pity party.

I both liked and hated that about him. Would it have hurt him to say, "I'm sure you'll get on with a police department soon"?

"She's very nice," I said, looking at him over the rim of the mug.

"But she doesn't have a clue about the security business."

"I didn't say that."

"You didn't need to. It leaps to the eye. Pink shoes with five-inch platform heels, and lacy blouses don't add up to an image of lean, mean security professional. She doesn't know the first thing about surveillance systems, lockdown procedures, or self-defense and hand-to-hand combat."

I almost grinned. I'd suspected from the day Jay arrived a couple months back that he was more than the owner of a cookie franchise. His familiarity with the details of security work further confirmed my suspicions, which had been aroused by finding him staking out the garage at oh-dark-thirty on several occasions.

"To be fair," I said, even though I didn't want to be, "there's not a lot of call for krav maga or sharpshooting at Fernglen. She's more likely to need counseling skills for talking to parents of shoplifting teens or negotiating shift schedules with the security officers. Not that there's any evidence she's got any skills that don't involve bobbins and hemlines." My words sounded petty even to me, and I winced.

Jay took the half-empty mug from my hand to top it off,

his fingers brushing mine and lingering for a moment. "The job should have been yours." His hazel eyes met mine.

His words salved my wounded pride. "I'm not sure I really wanted it, anyway." That was true. Part of me had hesitated to apply for the job, worried that I'd get comfortable in it and stop trying to find a way back to the career field—policing—that I really felt called to.

"So quit with the dog-in-the-manger act, okay?"

I clunked my mug on the counter, sloshing coffee on the glass. Ow. Jay's tone was gentle, but his words stung. Was I being a bit dog-in-the-mangerish about the job? My pride had been injured when the hiring committee picked Coco over me, but hadn't I been the teensiest bit relieved? Yes. I couldn't keep blaming Coco MacMillan for landing a job I hadn't wanted wholeheartedly. Well, I could, but. I gave a rueful smile.

"How about—" Jay started, but yelling from deeper in the food court interrupted him.

"Now!" a man's voice demanded loudly. A loud crash followed, like a chair had been flung over. "I want it now!"

Exchanging a quick glance with Jay, I hurried toward the commotion, wishing, not for the first time, that the FBI board authorized us to carry a weapon more intimidating than pepper spray.

Three

. . .

I wove through the tables and chairs that clogged most of the real estate in the food court. It was set out in a horseshoe shape with Lola's on the outside edge opposite a pretzel vendor on the other side of the opening. Different fast-food places ringed the interior of the horseshoe, with picture windows at the far end looking out on a peaceful pasture that was shortly to become a golf resort called Olympus. Strong sunshine—a nice break from the gloomy gray skies we'd had the last week—poured through the windows and illuminated dried swish marks left by the janitor's mop. Only a few shoppers sipped coffees or munched bagels at the tables this early and all of them were staring at the man pounding on the counter of the burger place.

"I want a cheeseburger right now!"

A nervous-looking girl stood behind the counter, her blue-and-white-striped paper cap askew, and said, "Sir, we don't serve our lunch menu until eleven o'clock. If you could wait a few—"

"I'm hungry." The man was tall and bulky in a plaid lumberjack shirt and jeans. Brown stubble covered his scalp, the hair so short I could make out the livid scar behind his right ear even from this distance. He was young—maybe Joel's age—and I noticed he was shoeless, his feet covered only by thick gray socks. He pounded his fist on the Formica-topped counter again, jolting a metal straw dispenser off the edge; it clanked to the floor and spewed straws.

I approached from the man's left, righting the overturned chair, and said, "Jesse, what's up?" I made sure he could see me coming, didn't try to take him by surprise.

He turned to face me, confusion and anger on his once-handsome face. A burn scar stretched smooth and red over one temple and cheekbone, and no hair grew where his right eyebrow had been. Both eyes, luckily, had escaped damage when an IED blew up the army supply truck he'd been driving in eastern Afghanistan. Like me, he'd been medically retired from the military. Unlike me, he'd suffered a head injury—traumatic brain injury—that made it hard for him to concentrate and left him prey to mood swings; at least, that's what his father had told me a couple weeks ago when Jesse first turned up at the mall and caused a ruckus by splashing water out of the fountain onto passing shoppers. He'd said he was trying to stop them from burning and I'd wondered what kind of hellish memory he was reliving.

"EJ," the young man said now, recognizing me.

"Where's your dad?" I asked, scanning the area for signs of the elder Mr. Willard, who usually accompanied his son to the mall . . . and everywhere else, I suspected.

"I'm hungry," Jesse said again, single brow drawing in toward his nose.

"Hey, big guy, come have some cookies." The voice came from behind me and I realized Jay Callahan had followed me.

"I want a burger."

"We don't serve lunch until—"

I stopped the counter girl with a look.

"Peanut butter chocolate chunk, fresh out of the oven," Jay said. He smiled at the younger man. "Come on."

After another moment's thought, Jesse followed Jay toward Lola's, his heavy limp a reminder of how lucky I really was. "I'll find his father," I said in a low voice as Jay passed me. "Thanks."

Keying the radio attached near my left shoulder, I called Joel at the dispatch desk and got him to find the card Jesse's dad had given me when it became apparent Jesse, for whatever reason, was attracted to Fernglen. Other than the splashing incident, Jesse had been unobtrusive, occasionally wandering into shops, sometimes sitting for hours on one of the benches, usually near the fountain. I'd chatted with him several times, exchanging stories of our experiences in Afghanistan. He was funny when his head wasn't hurting, making me laugh with stories about a stray mutt his unit had adopted.

"He's not violent," Mr. Willard had assured me anxiously, his thin face drawn and gray, "but sometimes he gets agitated. It's the pain, and not being able to think the way he used to. Call me if there's any trouble." *Please don't call the police*, had been the unspoken subtext. I called the number Joel read off to me and heard relief in Willard's voice when I told him his son was in the food court.

"He left this morning before we were up," he said. "I've been looking all over for him. I'll be there in five."

"Great." I joined the two men where they sat at a table in front of Lola's, cookie crumbs gritting the slick surface. "Your dad's on his way," I told Jesse.

"He worries about me," he said, brown eyes somber. "Mom, too."

"It's their job," Jay said. "Parents get paid extra to worry, or so I've been told."

Jesse managed a half smile. "Yeah, well, they're supposed to get to stop worrying at some point, right? Like after a kid moves out on his own?"

I thought of how frantic my mom and dad had been when I'd first returned from Afghanistan, how my mom was at the hospital every day, how Ethan kept trying to get me to work for him where he could keep an eye on me and be sure no one was shooting at me. "I don't think parents ever quit worrying," I said.

"Crappy job, then," Jesse observed, and Jay cracked a laugh.

The men started talking sports and less than a minute later Mr. Willard hurried up, tan trench coat unbuttoned and flapping around his knees. "Jesse."

The younger man smiled, a flash of strong white teeth at odds with his ruined face. "Pop."

"Ready to go?"

"I suppose."

"How's your headache?" Mr. Willard asked as they walked away. Jesse answered in an angry tone, but I couldn't hear the words.

"That's tough," Jay said, looking after the pair.

"Makes me feel damn lucky," I agreed.

A flat *cra-ack* sounded, jerking our heads toward it.

"Gunshot," Jay said grimly.

I was already halfway down the hall.

Four

. . .

I **sprinted toward** the north end of the mall and the theater wing, wishing I had my Segway when my knee began to ache and jabbed spines of pain into my thigh and lower leg. As I ran, I keyed my radio to notify the office.

I expected to get Joel, but Coco's voice crackled through my radio. "Hello?" She cut off. Seconds later, her voice came again. "Stupid radio. I—Can you hear me?"

"This is Officer Ferris," I said, making a mental note to give Coco another lesson on radio operation. "I heard what sounded like a shot—"

"Yes. Joel—" She cut off again. Static followed, but I was pretty sure she said something about the police.

I spotted six or seven cops as I neared the theater wing and I picked up the pace, worried something serious had happened, until I realized they were the movie extras. The way they were milling around, one of them licking an ice cream cone, told me nothing tragic had occurred. Drawing a deep, exasperated breath, I passed them and limped into the hall. The first thing I saw was Ethan with his arm around a pretty young woman who was sobbing like her fiancé had told her he was becoming a priest and moving to Papua New Guinea. I scanned the area but didn't see anything resembling a threat. A few people were gathered around a handsome actor in a cop costume. Others, including Joel, watched Ethan comfort the distraught woman.

She had her face buried against his chest, and he stroked the glossy brown ringlets that fell in a mass to just below her shoulders. The sight made me prick with slight discomfort. "There, there, Zoë," he said. "It's not your fault."

The woman raised her head, doe eyes drenched with tears, and I saw she was a bit older than I had assumed from her slim build, maybe thirty-five.

"The weapons are my responsibility, Ethan," she said in a tear-roughened voice. "It *is* my fault, even if I didn't pull the trigger."

I beckoned to Joel and he scurried over, relief lighting his face.

"What happened?" I asked. "I heard a gunshot—"

"Me, too," he said enthusiastically, clearly excited by the opportunity to cope with an event more interesting than a shopper who couldn't locate her car. "I was on my way back to the office after visiting the men's room—" He caught my look and gave a sheepish smile. "Right. Concise. I heard what I thought was a gunshot and I phoned it in and hurried down here. Turns out it was a blank," he summed up. "One of the fake cops was messing with his gun and it went off."

I nodded. "What's wrong with her?" I jerked my head toward the woman in Ethan's arms.

Joel shrugged. "Dunno."

I approached Ethan and Zoë, who was now hiccupping

and blowing her nose under my father's direction. "I won't let them fire you, Zoë, so no more tears. Your face is getting blotchy."

She started to say something, but he put a finger against her lips and she shushed. I raised my brows. Noticing me, Ethan smiled without a hint of self-consciousness. Zoë gave me an assessing look from behind the curtain of ringlets that had fallen over her eyes, said, "Thanks, Ethan," and walked toward the exit. Before Ethan could say anything, there was commotion at the far end of the hall, where doors led to the parking lot, and two police officers burst into the building. It took me a moment to realize they were real Vernonville PD officers. Any shopper with a cell phone, startled by the shots, could have called them, I realized.

"We had a report of shots fired," said the first cop, a strong-looking blonde. Her eyes scanned the crowd and landed on Ethan. "Are you Ethan Jarrett?" Awestruck fan voice momentarily replaced her cop voice.

Rolling my eyes, I told Joel to corral a couple of the production company's security men, identifiable by their black polo shirts, khaki slacks, and the wraparound sunglasses they had pushed atop their heads or hanging from lanyards around their necks, and keep curious shoppers from crowding into the hall. I approached the VPD officers, introduced myself, and explained the situation as I understood it. A couple of movie people verified the story Joel had told me and a gun was produced for the cops' inspection. I left them to it, and cornered my father.

"Anything else I should know?" I asked.

He shook his head. There was a wet spot on his shoulder from the woman's tears. "It was an accident, EJ, like I told Zoë. She blames herself because she's the props person and the gun shouldn't have been fired, even though it was only loaded with blanks."

"Who fired the gun?"

Ethan pointed toward the actor I'd noticed earlier, now leaning against the wall like he wished he could sink through it. "I don't know his name."

"He was aiming at Ethan," a new voice said.

I turned to see the skinny woman with the clipboard who had greeted my dad earlier. Ginger-colored hair hung lankly to her narrow shoulders and was held back by an Alice band. Hazel eyes made a striking contrast to her pale, lightly freckled skin. She would have been plain, in a mousy sort of way, if it weren't for her eyes. Worry sounded in her voice as she repeated, "He almost hit Ethan."

I remembered a news story about an actor being killed on a movie set back in the '90s by the wadding discharged by a gun loaded with blanks. Most people didn't realize that there was actually a discharge when a blank fired, and it could be lethal at short range.

"Is that true?" I looked from Ethan to the actor against the wall. He was gnawing on a fingernail and looked more like he should've been cast in a Disney movie than a cop thriller.

"It was an accident," Ethan said firmly, giving the woman a look.

She rolled her lips inward, but didn't argue. "Can I get you anything, Ethan? A Pellegrino? Maybe a sandwich. I had the caterers stock the roasted portabellas you like."

Before Ethan could answer, the director, Van Something, I vaguely recalled, clapped his hands and began to restore order to the set with the help of a tall, bald, black man who seemed to be acting as a stage manager. The movie company's public relations woman was talking to the cops and shepherding them gently toward the empty storefront where the producers had set up an office. Figuring there was nothing more for me to do, I crooked a finger at Joel, who was chatting with a pretty extra in a cop uniform, and we left.

"It looks like fun," he said, as we left the chaos of the movie set behind us.

"What does?"

"Making movies."

It struck me as nothing short of torture: hours of waiting around to film a scene, hours spent sitting still as a cactus while people plastered your face with gook and fussed with your hair, a lifetime spent worrying about every ounce or wrinkle or gray hair that might limit your appeal and, thus, your employability. I didn't say any of that. "Ethan seems to enjoy it."

"He's nice," Joel said, shortening his longer stride to stay with me. "It was good of him to try and make that props woman feel better."

"He *is* nice," I agreed. Despite Ethan's obsession with fame and appearance and the like, he was a kind man. Even when he most exasperated me, I didn't lose sight of how lucky I was to have him as a father. His interaction with Zoë, though, had seemed like more than casual kindness; it felt like he knew her pretty well. I was being silly, I told myself, biting the inside of my cheek. He'd probably worked with her before and they were friends. As far as I knew, Ethan had always been faithful to my mom, despite tabloid stories suggesting otherwise. Recently, papers had begun writing stories about my parents' long-lasting marriage in a town where divorces followed weddings about as quickly as sitcom cancellations followed low ratings, and I'd felt proud of them.

When the elevator brought us to the second floor, I told Joel to return to the security office to brief Coco on the incident, and I headed to Merlin's Cave. My friend Kyra Valentine had taken over the store for a year while her aunt Harmony, who owned the shop, took a sabbatical in Nepal or Kathmandu or some such. Merlin's Cave sold a variety of magic-related items, as well as New Agey stuff, books on spiritualism of all sorts, herbal teas, table fountains, mood lamps, and CDs by people I'd never heard of playing instruments I couldn't name.

"EJ! It's about time," Kyra greeted me as I came through the door. She strode toward me, making a funny tinkling sound.

A six-foot-tall black woman who was an Olympic track athlete, she had taken up roller derby a while back and was the last person I'd have pictured running a woo-woo store like Merlin's Cave. However, she was also a savvy marketer who was sincerely fond of her aunt Harmony, so she'd managed to adjust her style to fit her surroundings (and her customers' expectations). Today, she wore a gold lamé broomstick skirt, a white tee shirt printed with gold stars, and an ankle bracelet that was the source of the clinking. Her dark hair crinkled loose to her shoulders and I caught the flash of gold hoop earrings that could have encircled a softball.

A customer dithered between a couple of table fountains, and Kyra told her, "Let me know if I can help you," before dragging me behind the counter that stood toward the rear of the store. "Is it true that one of those movie people got shot?" she asked, keeping her voice low. "Not your dad, I hope."

I'd first met Kyra when I was eleven and we were in Vernonville to visit my grandma and grandpa Atherton, so she knew all about my family. "No one got shot," I said, with an exasperated huff. Einstein thought light was the speediest thing in the universe, but gossip put light to shame. "An extra goofing around with his prop fired a blank."

"Is that all?"

"You'd prefer a terrorist invasion? Blood, gore, and dead bodies littering the corridors?"

Kyra pretended to consider it, pursing her full lips. "I guess not. There's nothing romantic about terrorists. Maybe a jewelry store heist or a sophisticated ring of art thieves."

"Right. They'd be here to steal the quarter-carat diamond rings and tennis bracelets, or the Thomas Kinkade prints from the frame store." It's not like Fernglen had a Tiffany's; we had three jewelry stores and a framing store that sold prints and a handful of original canvases by local artists. "I suppose you think Brad Pitt would be part of the gang. You've watched too many *Ocean's* movies."

"I was thinking more along the lines of Pierce Brosnan," Kyra admitted. "He was yummy in *The Thomas Crown Affair*." She shivered dramatically.

I eyed her, catching a note of discontent beneath her banter. "You're bored with the store, aren't you?" I said after a moment.

She gave me a rueful look. "Does it show?" Without waiting for an answer, she batted at a stars-and-moon mobile over the cash register, setting it whirling. "I love Aunt Harmony and I want to help her out, but being cooped up in this . . . this *cave* is driving me batty. I don't know how I'll last a year."

"Why don't you hire someone to help part-time?" I asked. "Then you wouldn't have to spend so many hours here."

Before agreeing to help her aunt, Kyra had sold the rights to a software program she'd created. It did something to help coaches and event planners schedule sporting tournaments and competitions and she'd made a mint on it. The company that had bought the rights had also paid her to consult, and before coming to Fernglen she'd been on the road a lot, so I could understand why being confined to the shop made her antsy.

"The store doesn't make enough to hire someone else," she said. "In fact, I don't know how Aunt Harmony saved enough for her trip."

"You could hire someone out of your own pocket, if you wanted to, couldn't you?"

She turned to me with an arrested look. "I could," she said slowly. "Aunt Harmony wouldn't have to know I was using my own money." She gave me a sudden squeeze. "EJ, you're a genius."

"Excuse me," the customer said, holding up a tiered fountain still plugged into the wall. Water sloshed to the carpeted floor. "Can I use Kool-Aid in this instead of water?"

I got off shift at three and stopped by the Y to swim on my way home. We work staggered shifts at the mall to ensure the most coverage during the mall's busy times, and I was almost always on days, which meant I worked from seven a.m. to three p.m. Swimming flushed the day's tension from my muscles, and I was feeling pleasantly relaxed when I parked my Miata in front of the patio home I'd bought when I moved to Vernonville over a year ago.

As I got out of the car, my knee collapsed under me and I sprawled on the ground. Damn it! This was my knee's way of showing me it objected to the sprinting I'd done earlier in response to the gunshot. Pushing aside the niggling worry that my leg wasn't getting stronger, I pushed to my hands and knees and found myself face to face with a large rust-colored cat with a mangled ear and shortened tail.

"Mrrow?"

Fubar wasn't used to finding me at his level. "Hi, cat," I said, patting him. He purred for two nanoseconds before trotting to the front door and letting it be known he'd like his personal servant to open it. Never mind that he had a cat flap around back he could use anytime. Lurching to my feet, I continued to the door, unlocked it, and let Fubar in. He streaked past me, headed for the kitchen and his dinner bowl.

"You're welcome," I called after him. I picked up the mail dumped in the front hall and flipped through it, both disappointed and relieved to see there was nothing from any of the police departments I'd sent applications to recently. No news was good news, right? I considered my options for the evening. Try a new clam chowder recipe and play my guitar for a while? Spend time on the phone trying to locate the college kid who'd started tiling my kitchen floor to earn money for Spring Break but who might have been kidnapped in Cancún because I hadn't heard from him in weeks? I had decided on Option A, when my phone rang and Grandpa Atherton's voice boomed through the line.

My mom's dad, he'd been getting steadily louder the last few months and I wondered if his hearing was going. No surprise, if so, since he was in his eighties. A retired CIA operative, he managed to keep his hand in the spook world somehow. I suspected he was being paid under the table by any number of agencies who needed someone they could trust to plant listening devices, do surveillance, set off incendiaries, keep track of diplomats they didn't trust, and who knows what else. I didn't know about a lot of his off-the-books activities, which was probably just as well because the ones I heard about frequently involved ER visits or near-run escapes from the legitimate authorities.

"I heard there were shots fired at Fernglen today, Emma-Joy," he said, not bothering with any of the social niceties.

"Blanks," I said. "An accident."

"Still, sounds more exciting than the horseshoe tourney at my retirement complex. I was thinking I might come down tomorrow, check out the action."

I rolled my eyes, grateful he couldn't see me. As if the movie people being in the mall didn't make my life chaotic enough. "Just don't go tailing anyone," I said warningly. I'd more than once received complaints from shoppers who were worried that the businessman/homeless person/wheelchair-bound invalid—pick a disguise—was stalking them through the mall. I was convinced Grandpa must have flunked Surveillance 101 in spy school and he'd been trying to compensate with extra practice ever since.

"I've got to keep my skills up, Emma-Joy," he protested.

"Not in my mall you don't."

Five

. . .

I reported to work early on Tuesday because the movie people were shooting a chase scene that traversed a lot of mall acreage. The shoot was set to start at seven, with the hope that they'd have it wrapped by Fernglen's opening time at ten o'clock. Fat chance. Edgar Ambrose, the laconic black man who usually worked the night shift, hauled his bulk out of the chair in front of the monitors when I walked in.

"Yo, EJ."

"Anything interesting happen?" I asked.

"Nah." He lumbered toward the coffeemaker on the file cabinet and dumped out the used filter. He began to make a fresh pot and I arched my brows; usually, Edgar was out the door moments after his relief stepped into the office.

"Sticking around?"

"Yeah."

Understanding dawned. "You want to watch the filming."

He shot me a sheepish look from under heavy brows. "I always wanted to be an actor."

I stared at him. I'd never heard the man string together more than ten words and he wanted to be in a career field that required near constant verbal expression? Will wonders never cease, as my grandma used to say. "Well," I finally said, "we could probably use your help keeping the area clear."

"What I thought." Edgar nodded.

Joel and Coco arrived simultaneously moments later, and then most of the rest of the Fernglen Galleria security force showed up, including several officers who weren't on duty. Apparently, all of them had turned out in a spirit of altruistic volunteerism to help provide security for the movie company's shoot. I swept them with a cynical gaze, but Coco thanked them all for coming and shot me a helpless look.

I was tempted to let Coco sink on her own, but I realized her ineptitude could delay filming and cost the movie company big bucks, or create problems for the mall's merchants and shoppers. Taking charge, I assigned the officers to various parts of the mall, mostly to make sure that unauthorized people didn't get into the mall during the filming, and to cordon off the areas where the carefully choreographed chase scene would take place. We usually opened the building at four thirty for mall walkers, but we'd excluded them this morning. Despite that, there were a surprising number of people in the halls and I realized they were movie extras costumed as shoppers. Mounting my Segway, I glided toward the atrium, where the movie crew was setting up cameras and lights and other paraphernalia.

I had to admit I felt a glimmer of admiration for the sheer logistical undertaking of filming a movie. Whoever had coordinated the use of the mall; gotten the cameras, lights, props, and generators to Fernglen and positioned them; hired the dozens of actors and extras and made them up and costumed them; and arranged for food for the hordes involved in the production, deserved a lot of respect. I wondered if whoever it was had trained by planning an army invasion. Come to think of it, orchestrating a military invasion was probably easier because there'd be fewer egos involved.

I saw Ethan apparently discussing something in the script with Van, the director, and he waved. I gave him a cool nod meant to remind him that we didn't freaking know each other. For a man who pretended for a living, he had a lot of trouble pretending we'd never met. He flashed his famous smile at me, totally unrepentant, and three extras behind me—women, of course—sighed in unison. I wondered if Mom was around. She frequently showed up on Ethan's sets for lunch or to play a game of gin with him in his trailer between shots. She told me it never hurt to remind the starlets and extras and script girls that he was a married man.

"There are drawbacks to being married to a sex symbol, EJ," she'd told me once. She reflected for a moment. "Of course, there are undeniable benefits, too." Her veiled smile left me in no doubt of her meaning and I put my hands over my ears.

Now, I thought about how cozy Ethan had seemed with Zoë and wondered if she was one of the "drawbacks" Mom had referred to. The filming kicked off at five after seven, with Anya Vale the center of the action. Her character, a mobster's mistress about to turn state's evidence against her lover and his criminal associates, would be chased through the mall by a contract killer intent on shooting her. The scene included stuntmen and women pushed down escalators, bullets exploding plate glass windows, tumbling mannequins, and a body falling from a second-level bridge to the floor below. It was going to require several days' filming and lots of special effects and stunt coordination. If I'd written the script, the attractive but underestimated mall cop would have saved Anya Vale's character, running over the hit man with her Segway, or drowning him in the fountain, but the scriptwriters, in their clichéd way, had provided a police officer—Ethan's character—to rescue her.

Assistants in tee shirts emblazoned with the movie's title started clearing the set, and I rode the elevator to the top level and joined Joel where he stood at the railing, watching the action below. Today's filming was mostly taking place on and near the escalator. Someone yelled for quiet and a voice called, "Action!"

The fake shoppers started "shopping" and a business-suited man in a fedora caught my eye. He was strolling almost directly beneath us and I leaned forward for a better look. A glimpse of white hair peeping beneath the hat convinced me. Grandpa Atherton! How had he wangled his way into the movie? I wondered uneasily if he was on an "op."

A moment's consideration convinced me he couldn't be. It probably tickled his fancy to worm his way into the movie. I doubted he was a paid extra; somehow, he'd slipped in without the casting people or other extras noticing. I bit back a grin as he pretended to window shop at the lingerie store, where a headless mannequin wore a particularly risqué red and black corset and panties. I wondered if the store's owner had changed the display, hoping to get a little free advertising, or if the set designer had supplied the garments.

"This is so exciting," Joel whispered as Anya Vale ran into view from the far end of our level, sending hunted looks over her shoulder. She wore a designer suit that certainly hadn't been purchased in this mall, and her hair streamed like a dark cloud behind her as she ran. "Did you know she went to Princeton?" Joel whispered. "I read about it in *FANtastic Movie Mag.* She studied geology and got discovered in a Bloomingdale's in New York. *Random's Redemption* year before last was her first big break."

I merely nodded, watching as the star started down the escalator, frantically pushing past the shoppers that clogged it. A shot rang out, making Joel and me jump, until we realized it was a blank fired by the hit man who had suddenly appeared, gun extended in black-gloved hand. I recognized him as a character actor who frequently played heavies, but I couldn't bring his name to mind. A "shopper" tumbled over the side of the escalator, apparently shot, and landed on an inflated mat below. The stuntwoman bounced off the mat and gave a thumb and forefinger okay signal to someone I couldn't see. Anya screamed and I resisted the urge to cover my ears.

"She's got some lungs on her," Joel said.

I slid him a sideways look, but I didn't think he intended the double entendre.

The screaming went on and on and it took me a moment to realize it wasn't only Anya Vale screaming anymore.

Six

. . .

The sound came from the first floor, somewhere near the theater wing. Before the thought had even coalesced, I was zipping toward the elevator on my Segway, Joel jogging behind me. As I stabbed the button to descend to the first floor, an irritated voice yelled, "Cut!" and someone else asked, "What's that infernal racket?"

The screams had stopped by the time I exited the elevator on the first floor. Someone grabbed Joel to ask what was happening, but I kept going. The movie people were behind me, milling about and setting up for another take, apparently willing to forget about the screaming now that it wasn't messing up their shot anymore. I wasn't.

With the mall not open to customers, and the movie people clustered near the atrium, the halls at the north end of the mall were deserted. I glided silently down the Macy's wing, peering into darkened shop windows. Nothing seemed out of place. Barred by the closed grille at the Macy's

entrance, I turned around. Back in the main corridor, I was
heading to the theater wing when a choking sound came
from the narrow hall on my right, a spur that led only to
bathrooms, service corridors, and an emergency exit.

I had barely turned into the hall when the door to the
men's room burst open. A man in a green jacket appeared
and tripped over the yellow plastic "Closed for Cleaning"
sign sitting near the door, righting himself before he fell.
He looked around wildly—I'm not sure he even noticed
me—then lunged for the door at the end of the hall, hitting
the release bar and bolting into the parking lot. The sudden
burst of daylight in the hall was disconcerting, and I flung
my forearm up to shade my eyes. When they adjusted, I
started after the man, but stopped when I drew level with
the men's room. The sun illuminated a smudged handprint
beside the door. It glimmered red.

Damn. I didn't want it to be blood. Drawing closer, I
confirmed my worst fears and shut my eyes for a split second, then snapped them open. Was the man who'd run out
injured? Should I chase after him? Or, maybe someone still
in the restroom was hurt and needed help. I couldn't ignore
the possibility. Dismounting the Segway, I pushed into the
bathroom, automatically using my shoulder to nudge the
door open rather than contaminate what might turn out to
be a crime scene with my fingerprints. The door yielded
with a slight *skreee*.

I didn't see anything alarming. A bank of urinals
reminded me I was in a men's room. The scent of bleach
burned my nostrils. My gaze swept the sinks—no blood, no
injured shopper collapsed beneath them. I turned toward
the four stalls and saw blood spatter on the floor. It wasn't
much, I thought hopefully; it could have come from a nose-
bleed. The stall doors were shut, but I thought I heard the

ghost of a moan and lunged forward, all concern for possible crime scene forgotten, to push open the nearest door. Nothing. I banged the second door inward and saw a foot. It extended from beneath the adjacent stall. Breaths coming faster now, I pushed on the third door and immediately saw a body lying on its side in a semifetal position, blood from a stomach wound contained within the C shape formed by the woman's body.

I keyed my radio, but no one picked up in the security office. Everyone was watching the filming, I realized, fumbling for my cell phone. Coco had said she'd stay and cover the office and watch the monitors, but she wasn't answering the radio. I dialed 911 for an ambulance and leaned forward to feel for the woman's pulse. At first, I didn't detect one, but when I shifted my fingers on her neck, I felt the tiniest thread of life. I'd had enough buddy care training in the air force to know I needed to treat her for shock. I didn't know how long she'd been lying on the tiled floor, but she was cool to the touch and her skin matched the white ceramic of the toilet. Strands of rich brown hair partially obscured her face.

I yelled for help as I slipped out of my uniform jacket, a lightweight Windbreaker, and draped it over her upper body. I needed to elevate her feet, too, I knew, so I ripped nearly full rolls of toilet tissue from the rollers and propped her feet atop them. I felt helpless, like I was doing too little, too late. Her eyes were shut and I couldn't tell if her chest was rising and falling or not. Trying to decide if I should put pressure on the stomach wound, or if that would cause further damage, I was relieved to hear voices and footsteps in the hall.

"In here," I called. "Hurry!"

Joel stumbled through the door, skidding to a stop at the sight of me on the floor, tending the injured woman.

"Give me your jacket," I said, "and go outside to flag down the EMTs." Spotting Harold Wasserman, another of our officers, I told him to stand at the entrance to this side hall and make sure no one came this way. He left without a word.

I was tucking Joel's jacket around the woman's legs when running footsteps sounded outside the restroom and a couple of EMTs in navy blue uniforms burst through the door. Grateful to abandon my post to the experts, I backed out of the bathroom to give them room to work. It seemed like half an hour but was probably fewer than five minutes before they were wheeling her out on a gurney, IV flowing. I could tell from their grim expressions and their haste that the woman was in real trouble. To avoid the looky-loos gathered in the main hallway, the EMTs hurried the gurney out the service door that Joel was holding open, updating someone via their radios.

As the door swung shut, I collected myself and began to make a mental list. The police would be arriving any minute, alerted by the 911 operator, and they'd be unhappy to find hordes of people gawking at the crime scene. Harold had displayed some initiative and gotten a maintenance person to bring the stanchions we used to rope off lines for Santa photos or author autographs, and he, Joel, and I forced the crowd back by setting up the stanchions. I realized all the onlookers were movie people, extras, or technicians not involved in the scene currently being shot, and I was grateful that the mall wasn't open to regular customers.

The thought of shoppers brought Curtis Quigley to mind, and I knew I needed to let him know what was going on before the cops and reporters started arriving. He was not going to be happy that we had another "incident," as he would call it, that would reflect negatively on the mall. What with the reptile "liberation" from the Herpetology Hut that had garnered "snakes in the mall" publicity, and the murders of a local developer, a gangbanger, and two of our security personnel within the past couple months, Fernglen was getting a reputation as a dangerous place to shop.

Figuring that Joel and Harold could hold the fort, I headed for the administrative offices, planning to break the news to Quigley in person. As I rounded the corner into the main corridor, I bumped into someone turning into the hall. Strong hands steadied me by gripping my upper arms, and I looked up into a narrow face with an aquiline nose and fjord blue eyes. Nordic-blond hair was brushed back from a high brow and a resigned look settled on the handsome face as he recognized me.

"Officer Ferris. I might have known."

"Detective Helland. Known what?" I pulled away from his grasp, putting a couple of feet between us. I wasn't sure I liked Detective Anders Helland much, if at all, but something about him set me on edge in a not entirely unpleasant way.

"That you'd be mixed up in this. Do you realize I haven't investigated a single homicide in the last two months in which you weren't involved?"

"It's not a homicide," I said, refusing to let his tone irritate me. "She's still alive."

He shook his head. "Died on the way to the hospital. You haven't messed up the crime scene, I hope."

I stood, stunned and saddened, as he pushed past me to get to the men's room. "Don't go anywhere," he said over his shoulder.

Crime scene technicians trooped after him, as did two uniformed officers belaying black-and-yellow tape to cordon off the area officially. All I could think was that I'd failed the young woman by not finding her sooner, by not doing enough to keep her alive. The sensible part of me recognized that I'd done all I could do, but I felt wretched nonetheless.

"Emma-Joy, are you okay? What happened?"

I glanced up at Grandpa Atherton, concern shadowing his face. His fedora was tilted at a cocky angle and I stared past him, noticing other movie people milling around.

"Fine. Are you done filming?"

"Never mind that. Why is there blood on your shirt? Are you sure you're not hurt?"

I looked down to see the dried red streaks on my white uniform shirt. "Not me," I assured Grandpa. "Someone else. A woman. I found her in the men's room."

"Is she going to be o—"

I was shaking my head before he finished. "She died."

He eyed me closely. "Are you sure you're okay?"

Someone bellowed "Places!" and Grandpa looked over his shoulder.

"Go," I told him, making shooing motions. "I'm fine. I'll fill you in when you're done doing your Cary Grant shtick."

"I do look debonair, don't I?" he said with a grin, poking one finger under the fedora's brim to nudge it to a jauntier angle. "If I hadn't been recruited by the CIA, I could have made a go of it in Hollywood."

"It's never too late," I said, smiling for the first time since entering the bathroom.

With a two-fingered salute to the hat's brim, he headed back to the movie set, moving with the slouchy ease of a Rat Packer. Maybe the CIA's gain was the movie industry's loss, I thought with a small smile.

It vanished when a hand gripped my arm above my elbow and Helland's voice spoke from behind me. "Let's find a place to talk," he said. "I understand you found Ms. Winters."

I looked up at him. He topped my five-six by a good six or seven inches. "Was that her name?"

He nodded. "Yes. Zoë Winters."

Zoë! That was the name of the woman—

A gunshot broke into my thoughts and Ethan's voice yelled, "Gun!"

Seven

. . .

Detective Helland swept me behind him and drew his weapon. Every cop in the vicinity now had a gun in his or her hand. Two of them had started toward where Ethan's voice had come from. Terrified that some trigger-happy cop would shoot my dad, I grabbed Helland's wrist. He shook me off with a furious look.

"It's a movie," I said urgently. "They're filming a movie."

Helland lowered his weapon slightly. "You're sure?" His voice was tight.

I nodded so hard my chestnut hair swished around my face. "Absolutely. That was Ethan Jarrett."

He gave me an inscrutable look, told his team to stand down, and motioned me toward the set. He knew Ethan was my dad because my family had descended en masse on the hospital when Grandpa had been shot and I'd been concussed stopping a murderer a few weeks back.

"Why the hell are they filming a movie here?" Helland asked as we walked.

"Good question," I muttered.

A security man with his muscled arms crossed over his chest stopped us as we approached the set. "You can't—"

Detective Helland flashed his badge and shouldered past him.

"The woman—Zoë Winters," I said. "I'm pretty sure she worked for the movie company."

"Nice of you to mention it," he said, sarcasm lacing the words.

"I didn't know who it was until you said her name," I said, stung. "It's not like—"

Anya Vale screamed—I could pick out her piercing scream even if a troop of gibbons was howling—and Helland winced. "What was—"

"The heroine," I said, pointing to where the beautiful star was rushing down the escalator again. We watched as the stuntwoman dove over the edge and Ethan appeared, gun in hand, to charge up the down escalator after the hit man. The actor leveled his gun and fired at Ethan, who staggered as if hit and rolled backwards over the escalator's handrails to land on the inflated mat below.

"He does his own stunts?" Helland asked with a hint of admiration.

"Usually. My mom hates it." I started to tell him about the man I'd seen come out of the restroom, sure he'd want to find him for questioning, if nothing else. "I saw—"

"Who's in charge of this circus?" Helland cut me off.

I nodded my head at Van, sitting with his elbows propped on his knees, his feet tucked around the legs of the canvas chair he sat on. "DIRECTOR" was spelled out across the back in red letters.

Ethan rolled off the mat, ignoring hands outstretched to help him, and Van said, "Cut. Good fall, Ethan. Now we need—"

Before he could finish, Helland moved forward, somehow bypassing assistants and security people and stage managers who moved to stop him. He showed the director his badge, and gasps and whispers sounded from those close enough to see. Van peered at Helland's ID closely, as if to assure himself it wasn't a prop. "What's this—"

"I'm afraid you'll have to shut down for a while," Helland said. "There's been a homicide. We'll need to interview your cast and crew. You are?"

"Elias Vandelinde." He paused, as if waiting for Helland to comment on his movies or his Oscars or to ask for an autograph. When Helland merely lifted one brow, Van continued testily, "We have a schedule. And time is money. If another gangbanger got shot, it's nothing to do with—"

Clearly, Van's people had briefed him on recent events at the mall.

"It's not a gang member," Helland said in his level voice, "and I'm afraid you have no option but to cooperate."

"Who died?" a reedy voice called before Van could raise further objections.

Helland turned to survey the crowd, trying to identify the speaker. Before he could say anything, a woman's voice said, "Oh, my God, no! It's Zoë. It's Zoë, isn't it?" A woman pushed toward Helland, her eyes beseeching. In her early fifties maybe, she had gray-streaked brown hair corkscrewing to her shoulders, wire-rimmed glasses over anxious eyes, and wore a loose-fitting dress that partially disguised an extra twenty or thirty pounds. "She should be here, but she's not. Tell me it's not Zoë."

When Helland didn't respond, she burst into noisy tears and covered her face with her hands. I wondered who she was and how she knew the victim was Zoë, when Helland hadn't even mentioned the victim's gender. Helland looked at me, a slightly harassed expression on his usually impassive face, and said, "I need a room for interviews, and also someplace to corral these people while they're waiting for us to talk to them. Also—"

"Security camera footage, our patrol schedules, and a corned beef sandwich," I finished for him, letting a hint of sarcasm color the final words. He'd once asked me to fetch him a sandwich. I hadn't done it, but the memory still annoyed me. "I know the drill."

"With mustard."

"In your dreams."

He gave me the lifted brow and I thought I caught the tiniest hint of a smile. Was he baiting me? I wasn't sure the man had a sense of humor, but every now and then he surprised me with a look or comment that hinted that he wasn't as humor-free as he appeared. Maybe he even laughed uncontrollably at Three Stooges movies, like most of the men I knew. I started to tell him once again about the man I'd seen leaving the bathroom, but he turned away as uniformed cops came forward and began taking people's names and contact information. With the movie cops in dark navy uniforms, and the VPD officers in a slightly lighter blue uniform, it looked like a cop convention had landed at the mall. The Keystone Kops, I thought, hoping all the police, real and faux, kept their weapons holstered for the duration.

"Tell me there hasn't been another . . . incident, EJ," Curtis Quigley pleaded minutes later when I dropped by his office to give him a report. His British accent, which rumor had it he'd adopted during a semester abroad in college, was more noticeable when he was nervous. His assistant Pooja hadn't wanted to be the bearer of bad news, so Quigley was still in the dark when I arrived. He might not shoot messengers, but he whined at them a lot.

Quigley had perfected the head-in-the-sand approach to life; I'd bet his mother had had to slip medications into his apple juice to get him to swallow them. The unpalatable things in life went down better smeared with peanut butter or drowned in juice. Nothing was going to make murder go down easier. Quigley twiddled his cuff link, which flashed a pale orange when it caught the light. "Nothing . . . major has happened, has it?" he repeated.

"Um . . ."

He winced. "An accident of some sort?" he asked hopefully.

"Homicide."

Sinking into his chair, he heaved a put-upon sigh. "I don't understand. None of the other FBI malls has murder-of-the-month issues. Sure, some of them have gang problems, and one in Texas got blown up when the gas line ruptured, but my mall is the only one with dead bodies littering the place." He flapped his hands aimlessly, as if to show how widespread the bodies were. "Do you know how bad it looks at board meetings when I have a murder or two to report every quarter? 'Profits were down three point one percent for the first quarter,' " he said as if making a presentation, " 'and bodies were up two hundred percent.' " He ended on a bitter note.

"Only three of them were actually at the mall," I offered helpfully. "Weasel and Captain Woskowicz were killed off the premises, so technically—"

"You know I hate it when you get technical on me, EJ," he said querulously. He craned his neck to peer around me. "Where's Ms. MacMillan?"

I was hoping he'd overlook Coco's absence since I had no idea where she was. Certainly, as the director of security, she should have been updating Quigley. I was tempted to say, "Who knows?" but couldn't make myself throw her under the bus. "Since I found the body," I improvised, "she thought it was best that I fill you in."

"Hmph." He listened as I told him about finding Zoë in the restroom, about the cops' arrival, and about the kind of support we'd need to offer them.

"But they'll be out of here before we need to open, right?"

"No." I refused to sugarcoat the truth. "They may not even let us open." Although it felt like two days had passed, it had only been an hour and a bit since I'd walked into the restroom and found Zoë. It was still an hour until mall opening time . . . if the mall was going to open today.

Quigley made a strangled sound. "Not open! But it's Tuesday. A weekday. Malls are always open on Tuesdays. What will shoppers think?"

Quigley could have printed up one of those rubber bracelets with "WWST" on it, as that question pretty much drove his life.

"I'm calling the chief of police right now to make sure he understands that our priority at this mall is the customers," Quigley said. "If the police need to investigate, that's fine, but they can do so—discreetly—while the kind of commerce that made this country great takes place. It's the American worker's right to spend his—or her—hard-earned dollars any way and at any time he pleases that sets us apart from the Third World."

I wasn't sure that buying Victoria's Secret lingerie and

upscale kitchenware was what made this country great, but Quigley was clearly moved by his own speech. When he stabbed the intercom on his phone and asked Pooja to get him the chief of police, I made my escape.

I bumped into Coco MacMillan in the hall. She was clearly returning from somewhere since she dangled her car keys in one hand and her purse in the other. "Gosh, it seems busy around here," she observed brightly. "Are all those cop cars in the parking lot for the movie?"

"Not exactly." I gave her the same report I'd given Quigley, ending with, "You were watching the monitors, Ms. MacMillan. What did you see?"

She preceded me into the office, where Joel sat talking to Harold Wasserman. It looked like they were downloading the camera data for the police.

"Not two minutes after you all left, I remembered I had a dermatology appointment so I had to rush out. It took me months to get that appointment. I couldn't miss it!"

I felt helpless in the face of her . . . what? Naïveté? Lack of work ethic? General cluelessness? She was my boss—not the other way around—so I couldn't chew her out like I would have one of my airmen who did something similar. "There's got to be someone in the office all the time," I said in a nonaccusatory voice. At least, I thought it was nonaccusatory until she burst into tears.

I backed away.

"It's my fault that woman's dead, isn't it? She's dead because I wanted to get my t-tattoo removed!"

"What tat—" Joel started, but I shushed him with a look.

Patting Coco awkwardly on the back, I said, "It's not your fault. It's no one's fault but the murderer's. We don't know when she was attacked. It might have been long before we even came into work today."

"Like last night?" She looked up, eyes reddened and face tear-stained.

"Or even before that." I was thinking about the "Closed for Cleaning" sign and wondering if one of the janitorial staff had left it up, or whether the murderer had put it out to keep anyone from finding Zoë. "We won't know until after the autopsy's done." And probably not then, either, since "share" was a four-letter word as far as Detective Helland was concerned. He was about as likely to give me the results as he was to post them on YouTube.

"I'm terrible at this job," Coco said, blotting her eyes on a hankie Harold handed her.

"Yes, you are," I said. Both men glared at me, and Coco looked taken aback, but I went on, "Anyone would be who hadn't had any training or experience. But you don't have to stay terrible. You can learn."

"EJ could teach you," Joel piped up. "She's taught me everything I know about security work."

"There's a recommendation for you," Harold said drily, and we all laughed. In his sixties, Harold was retired from a career as an engineer and had turned to mall cop work only to avoid having to babysit his twin grandsons. The odor of cigarettes drifted off him and I figured he was between attempts to quit. He'd tried at least five times since I'd been at Fernglen.

Coco looked torn, as if she wanted to ask for help but thought it was beneath her dignity as the boss. I was darn glad I wasn't twenty-three anymore. Although, at her age, I'd been an air force cop for almost five years and had already done one tour in the sandbox, as we not-so-affectionately called Iraq and Afghanistan.

"Is there a book I could read?" she asked.

"*Mall Cops for Dummies*," Harold said. "I think they

made a movie out of it." Mustache twitching, he turned back
to the monitors.

"If you ever want to know something, just ask," I told Coco.

She sighed with relief, probably glad that I wasn't pushing. "Yeah, okay, thanks. Um, do we have to do anything
about this murder?"

"The police—"

On the words, the glass door swung open and Detective
Helland stepped in. His eyes swept the room before focusing
on me. "I need your statement," he said. "The back office?"
He started toward the director of security's office, which he
had used briefly following Captain Woskowicz's death.

"This is the new director of security," I said loudly, stopping him. "Coco MacMillan, meet Detective Helland."

Helland summed her up instantly, his gaze skimming her
black-and-white polka-dotted dress, the pink belt and shoes,
and her guileless face. He shot me a look but said only, "Nice
to meet you, Ms. MacMillan. Downstairs, then."

That was directed at me. Not wanting him to think I was at
his beck and call, I said, "I'll meet you there in five minutes."

He nodded and left.

"Well!" Coco said, apparently half offended, half
intrigued. "Is he always that . . . that abrupt?"

"Pretty much."

"There" was the empty storefront I'd arranged for him
and his team to use during the investigation. On the lower
level, it faced the main corridor, not too far from the utility
hall where I'd found Zoë. I noted with approval that the
maintenance staff had already set up tables and chairs as
I'd requested, and Helland's team had supplied computers

and peripherals. On the downside, the space was close to where the movie crew had set up and I imagined the frenetic comings and goings would be distracting. The place also reeked, I discovered, sneezing as I came through the door. It had most recently housed a perfume shop and, judging by the painfully floral scent that pervaded the room, some of the product line had been spilled on the carpet.

"If I smell like this when I go home tonight," Helland greeted me conversationally, "I'm going to come back and strangle you."

That startled a half laugh out of me that became a sneeze.

A uniformed policeman entered data at a computer in the far corner, but other than that we had the room to ourselves. Helland dragged a rolling chair forward with his foot and sat. He motioned me toward a padded, red-velvet-upholstered, thronelike chair I recognized as the one the mall provided for Santa at Christmas.

"Why did they bring this up?" I asked, sitting reluctantly. It was surprisingly comfy.

"I told them I wanted something more comfortable than metal folding chairs, and this is what I got. I thought maybe you'd had a hand in it."

"Not guilty." I raised my hands. Privately, I thought that a throne fit his lord-of-the-manor attitude.

Nodding, he got down to business, walking me through how I'd come to find Zoë in the bathroom. When I got to the part about seeing the man stumble out of the bathroom, he stopped me. "Did he say anything?"

"No, just ran to the end of the hall and out the door. I considered following him, but when I saw the blood . . ."

"You did the smart thing. What did he look like?"

I provided a description.

"That's very detailed," Helland said with a rare note of approval when I finished. "He shouldn't be hard to find. We—"

"I can do better than that," I interrupted him. "I can tell you his name."

Eight

. . .

Part of me was reluctant to turn Jesse Willard in, which is probably why I'd let Helland shut me up so easily when I'd tried to tell him about Jesse earlier. He was a fellow vet, trying to recover from injuries just like I was, and I hadn't sensed that he was violent in the way whoever had stabbed Zoë was violent. Unease niggled at me, though, and I knew I should have forced Helland to listen to me at the scene. I gave him Jesse's name and his dad's phone number, and told him what little I knew about the man. "Traumatic brain injury is tricky," I said. "I've known—"

"Thank you, Dr. Ferris," Helland said, snapping his notebook closed.

I glared at him.

"You should have given me his name immediately."

"I tried. You shut me up." I sprang to my feet.

Helland rose, too. "He could be halfway to Aruba or

Mexico City by now," he said. "If you'd told me sooner, we could have put a watch on the airports and bus terminals."

"He's recovering from his wounds. He's not well enough to be jetting around the world. I'll bet you next week's paycheck he's at home, scared to death."

"You'd better hope you're right."

The policeman in the corner gave us a covert stare, probably catching the tension in our slightly raised voices, and then went back to his typing. A civilian, maybe a movie extra, pushed at the shop door but retreated quickly when Helland glowered at him.

"Maybe Jesse stumbled over Zoë this morning," I said, trying to sound reasonable. "Someone stabbed her earlier— maybe even late yesterday or last night—and Jesse was unlucky enough to find her. He couldn't possibly have a motive for killing her . . . how would he even have known her?"

"As you've already pointed out, brain injuries are tricky." Helland wasn't giving an inch and I would have been frozen like an Ice Age mammoth if his eyes were the chilly ice rays they seemed.

"Do you know yet when she was stabbed?" I hoped that whenever it was, Jesse had an alibi.

"The autopsy's barely started," Helland said crushingly.

"When was the last time someone saw her alive?"

"Thank you for your—belated—help, Officer Ferris," Helland said, making it clear he was dismissing me. "Someone will give you a call when your statement's ready for signing."

I drew myself up to my full five foot six and sucked in a deep breath, prepared to tell him what I thought of his autocratic, condescending manner. Instead, I turned on my heel and swept out of the store. I was four shops away before my knee reminded me I'd forgotten the Segway and I had to go back for it. That did not improve my mood.

Joel's voice on the radio told me that Quigley had prevailed with the chief of police and the mall would be opening on schedule in fifteen minutes. The regular roster of mall cops was on duty, the rest having left now that the movie company had ceased filming for the day, at least at the mall. On impulse, I headed for the theater wing and the movie's production office. Maybe Ethan would be hanging around, or someone else I could talk to about Zoë. It wasn't my job to inquire about Zoë, I knew, but I told myself that having an "in" with the movie company, at least with Ethan, gave me an edge the police didn't have. If I learned something important, I would share it with Detective "Thank You for Your Belated Help" Helland, I told myself virtuously.

The black-polo-shirted security guard on duty greeted me with a nod and let me pass without question. About to poke my head into the production office, where I could see several people moving around, I turned the opposite way and glided past the movie theater's dark ticket window to the door that led to the parking lot. A bright April day sprang at me as I pushed the door open. Pale sunshine washed the mall's exterior, and a fresh breeze made me wish my Windbreaker hadn't gone in the ambulance with Zoë. I doubted I'd get it back.

My jacket was scant loss compared to the loss of a human life, I thought somberly, as I Segwayed into the parking lot which housed several long trailers that gleamed silver in the sunlight. A temporary chain-link fence cordoned them off from the rest of the parking lot, and another black-shirted guard kept the curious away from the one gate. Cars had started arriving in the lot as opening time approached, and people eyed the trailers, some stopping to stare or take pictures. I found Ethan's trailer by reading the names stenciled on the doors. His was directly across from Anya Vale's. The talented screamer emerged from her trailer as I knocked on Ethan's door, and she gave me a raised-brow look. The Chinese crested dog trailed her, venturing one sharp bark when he saw me. The puff at the end of his tail quivered.

I fought the urge to offer an explanation, and turned my back on her as Ethan opened the door with a pleased, "EJ!"

He caught my hand to pull me in, and the door clunked shut behind us. I'd been in similar trailers a few times before, when I'd visited my father on the set as a kid and a young teen, but it had been a while. I was struck anew by the degree of luxury that could be crammed into an aluminum tube on wheels. Granite and burled wood, high-end appliances in the kitchenette, leather-covered chairs and sofa, and a fifty-plus-inch television screen made the trailer feel like an exclusive men's club or den in a private mansion. A humidor and a wine cooler added to the impression. I knew the closed door to the rear hid a similarly appointed bedroom and bathroom.

"It's horrible the way you have to rough it on location," I said, smiling.

"I make do." He had changed out of his cop uniform and wore the kind of jeans that looked almost as good on Brett Favre in his commercials, and a movie-logo tee shirt. "I heard you found Zoë," he said, giving me a concerned look. "Are you okay?"

"I've been better," I admitted. I sank into a leather club chair that almost swallowed me in its cushy depths. "How about you? You knew her, after all."

"We worked a couple of films together," he said, tugging at one earlobe. "She was good at her job and a lot of fun."

How much fun? I wondered, surveying him from beneath half-lowered lids.

"Margot's devastated."

"Margot?"

"Her girlfriend."

Zoë was gay. I offered my dad an unspoken apology for having suspected there was more to his relationship with Zoë than friendship. An image of Zoë snuggled against Ethan's chest popped into my head and it occurred to me that she might have swung both ways. We sat in silence for a moment, and then I said, "I keep feeling like I should have done more."

"I heard she was stabbed?"

I nodded. "That's what it looked like. When did you last see her?"

He moved to a blender in which several kinds of fruit and ice sat waiting. Pouring in some brown powder and adding some crinkly green strands, he said, "I'm fixing a protein shake. Want one?"

"What's the green stuff?"

"Seaweed. I read that it's a great source of organic vitamins and omegas." Ethan had become a card-carrying health-food nut about five years back when a doctor took him to task for high cholesterol and borderline high blood pressure.

When I shook my head to decline the shake, he pulsed the blender for thirty seconds or so, poured the glop into a crystal goblet more suitable for a vintage cabernet, and joined me in the seating area.

"Zoë?" I prompted.

"Hm. She disappeared for a while after the gun incident, but I saw her later that afternoon—three-ish? Or four? We discussed what kind of gun I'd use for my backup, in the ankle holster. It's important in the scene where—never mind. Zoë doubled as the weapons master on this shoot, in addition to being the props master, which shouldn't have been a problem since the script doesn't call for any machine guns or rocket launchers or similar weapons. Just garden-variety nine mils and thirty-eights and the like. I'm wondering, though, if she was overtasked."

"What does a weapons master do?"

"Chooses and acquires the weapons for the shoot, issues them to the cast members immediately before shooting scenes that require them, and retrieves them when the scene is in the can. Sometimes the weapons master will do some training for the cast—teach them how to hold a saber at the right angle, say, or look realistic aiming a gun."

"So . . . was the incident yesterday really her fault? Was she in trouble over it?" I was wondering if there was any chance Zoë had stabbed herself, committed suicide. I hadn't seen a knife in the bathroom, but it could well have been underneath her.

Ethan shook his head. "No. She followed procedures. The idiot who fired the gun should have known better. He's been fired."

"Really?" I perked up. Could the actor have blamed Zoë for his firing? "What was his name?"

Ethan shrugged. "I don't know all the extras, EJ, or the actors with bit parts."

"Who would know his name, or where to find him?"

"The second AD." At my enquiring look, he added, "The second assistant director, Bree Spurrier. She's in charge of the extras." He took a long swallow of his health drink and gazed at me over the rim of the glass. "Why are you asking? I'm sure the police have already talked to her."

"I'm sure they have," I said, ducking the question. "Did Zoë have enemies that you know of? Were there any on-set feuds?"

Setting the goblet down with a clink, he reached across the table for my hand. "EJ—"

"Don't say it, Dad," I said, prying myself out of the chair. I wasn't up for another lecture on how much better suited I was to a life as a movie producer than a cop or security officer. "This murder happened in my mall and I've got a right to look into it." Detective Helland might not agree with that statement, but his druthers weren't driving my priorities.

"You haven't called me 'Dad' in years," Ethan said.

"Because you hate it."

With a half smile of acknowledgement, Ethan said, "I don't know about enemies—can't imagine Zoë having any—but you might talk to Margot. Margot Chelius. She'd know more about Zoë than anyone else. I think they've lived together the last eight or ten years." He described the woman who had broken down when she realized Zoë was the homicide victim.

"Thanks." I leaned down to kiss his forehead.

He caught my hand. "You know, you could take advantage of the production crew being here to learn more about what my company does. I could arrange for you to shadow—"

I yanked my hand away. "Ethan! How many times do I have to tell you I'm not interested in coming back to L.A.? I don't want to work in an industry that's all about make-believe, pretend, making a buck by catering to teenage boys' desires to see starlets chopped up in 3-D splendor, that discards women when the first wrinkle appears, and ignores the fact that there's *real* crime and *real* war happening in the world. I want to make a *difference*, not make movies. Why can't you respect that?"

He drew back, studying my face, his hurt expression making me regret lashing out. Still, it was about the hundredth time he'd tried to foist his career path on me and I was tired of the same conversation.

"It doesn't much sound like you respect what I do, either," he said quietly, turning away.

His words took me aback. I bit the inside of my cheek, not knowing what to say. Before I could think of something, he said, "I've got to run lines with Anya. I'll see you soon, hm?" He didn't turn around, but busied himself stowing his health drink ingredients back in the refrigerator.

I opened the door and clanked down the two metal steps to the parking lot. More people were around now and I nodded at a few I vaguely recognized, including the actor playing the hit man. I replayed the exchange with my dad in my mind, flinching at the knowledge that I'd hurt him. I thought about his quiet accusation. Was I contemptuous of his work? Maybe a little, I admitted. I wasn't denying that he worked hard—he put in long hours and frequently read scripts or did character research on weekends—but did I think his efforts were meaningless? I put the question aside to ponder later and tried to think of a way to apologize, even though I'd only dissed his chosen career this once, while he had tried over and over again to pry me away from the military and policing. I realized ruefully that this came pretty close to the "he started it" defense of a kindergartner.

With the mall now open, I pushed my Ethan troubles to the back corner of my mind and returned to my patrols after checking in with Joel. My morning ritual consisted of cruising the halls, chatting with shopkeepers and clerks, and generally checking to make sure that everything was as it should be. It bothered me slightly that I'd referred to Fernglen as "my" mall while talking with Ethan; I didn't want to be invested in the mall, didn't want to feel any attachment that would make it hard for me to shake the mall's dust from my feet if—*when*—I got an offer from a police department. I'd applied for two more jobs—one with the Kansas City PD and one with a Montana sheriff's office—last week, and I was keeping my fingers crossed that I'd get an interview.

Word of the murder had filtered through the mall community and I ducked a lot of questions about the victim and the circumstances from mall workers. I verified that the victim had been found in the downstairs men's room not far from the theater wing, figuring the crime scene tape gave that away anyway. When I ran into Fernando Guzman, one of our janitorial crew, I asked him what time he'd cleaned that bathroom yesterday.

His gray green uniform contrasted pleasingly with his tanned skin and brown eyes. "Before opening, like always, EJ," he said, hands clenching and unclenching on the rim of the gray rubber trash bin he was pushing. "The *policía* asked me the same thing and I told them I was done in there by eight thirty or nine."

"Did you leave the 'Closed' sign up?"

Fernando shook his head, black hair flopping across his brow. "No. I leaned it against the walls, under the sinks, *como siempre*."

So the murderer, or anyone else, could have set the sign out to keep men out of the restroom. "Thanks, Fernando."

"*De nada*." He shook his head. "There are too many deaths in this mall, EJ. My wife says it is an unlucky place. She wants me to find other work. I ask her where else I'm supposed to find a job in this economy? I am working on my college degree, but until I finish . . ."

He trailed off as if to say that any job was better than no job, even one in a mall with more homicides per annum than some small towns. "What are you studying, Fernando?"

"Literature. I want to teach high school."

"Better you than me." I gave a mock shudder. "Facing down a roomful of teenagers takes more courage than most any job I can think of."

Fernando laughed and I leaned forward to start the Segway, thinking about what he'd said. That led me to think about Jesse Willard, and I wondered if Helland had found the young vet at home. I hoped once again that he had an alibi for whatever the pertinent time turned out to be. On the thought, I spotted a woman I thought might be Margot Chelius slumped on a bench near The Bean Bonanza, the coffee kiosk. She held a cup in her hands and was staring into it as if expecting revelations to waft upward with the steam.

I glided to a halt beside her, but she didn't even look up until I said, "Margot Chelius?"

She raised her head and her eyes met mine, but there was a pause, like the gap between shouting into a canyon and waiting for the echo to come back, before she said, "Yes?"

Dismounting the Segway, I offered her my hand, saying, "I'm EJ Ferris. I found Zoë. I heard you were close and I wanted to tell you how sorry I am for your loss."

She shook my hand automatically, her grip as weak and dispirited as her expression. "Oh." She studied my face. "Was she really still alive when you found her?"

I nodded. "For a moment. I did what I could, but . . ."

"Did she say anything?"

"I think she was unconscious."

"Oh." She looked down into her coffee cup again, seeming to forget she still held my hand. I pulled it away gently and that brought her head up. "We fought, you know. Yesterday. The last words we said to each other were angry ones." Tears leaked from the corners of her eyes, fogging the lower half of her wire-rimmed glasses.

I joined her on the bench, not wanting to loom over her and intimidate her. "When was that?" I asked softly.

"Right before production wrapped for the day, about six. I'm the key costumer for this movie and I had just retrieved the police uniform from Tab Gentry, the poor kid who shot off the gun, when Zoë stopped by. She saw the uniform and made a remark about Tab being an idiot who deserved to get fired. I didn't know the kid well, but it was only an accident, after all, and I told her she was being too harsh. Well, that set her off and we argued. If you've got a significant other, you know how it is." She gave me a tired smile. "You start off disagreeing about one thing, and then you find yourselves squabbling about who didn't clean up the breakfast dishes or who feeds the cats more often. It was nothing, silliness."

Drinking half the coffee remaining in her cup, she looked up and said, "But it's the last memory I have of her."

"You weren't worried when she didn't come back to your hotel room last night?" I imagined the cast and crew were being housed in a nearby hotel since most of them weren't from this area. My mom and dad had rented a magnificent home near Mount Vernon, but I didn't imagine a props master and a key costumer—whatever that was—could afford similar accommodations.

"We didn't share a room," Margot said.

I flushed. "I'm so sorry. I heard that you . . . that you and she—"

"Oh, we were partners," Margot said, taking pity on my embarrassment, "but we liked our own space. We had

connecting rooms, but after our argument, I wasn't too surprised when Zoë didn't join me last night. I spent the evening
reading poetry—Do you know the poet Mary Oliver? She
writes such lovely, uplifting poems!—and then went to bed
early, maybe nine thirty or so."

Was she a shade too quick offering an alibi? Not that
reading poetry—alone—and sleeping—alone—made for
much of an alibi.

"I didn't hear the TV in Zoë's room, or hear her bumping
around at all, so I don't think she was back before I fell
asleep. Sometimes she did that," Margot said unhappily.
"Stayed out, chatted someone up at a bar, when we'd had
words. She was younger than I am," she added, "and so
much prettier. I knew other women came on to her sometimes, but I didn't say anything. I don't know if she ever . . .
She loved me, though. I never doubted that."

Rising, Margot let her cup fall into a nearby trash can.
She took a step away from me, then turned back, long skirt
flapping around her calves with the sharpness of her movement. "Find out who did this to her," she said, a muscle
jumping at the corner of her mouth. "She didn't deserve to
die like that, in pain, lying on a bathroom floor. No one does."

"The police—" I started.

"Them." She dismissed the police with a wave of her
hand. "You're a good listener. That counts for as much as
fingerprints and DNA testing and all the scientific bells and
whistles." She sighed and her momentary burst of resolve
and anger seemed to leak out of her. "Well, then."

Without a good-bye, she started down the hall toward
the production office, clogs slapping against her heels. I
watched her for a few moments, until enough shoppers
surged between us that I couldn't see her clearly.

Nine

. . .

After the morning's influx of security officers, the office seemed unusually quiet when I entered it minutes later. Joel sat alone at the dispatch desk. He hastily closed a magazine when I came in and pushed it aside. Coco was in her office, I assumed, from the faint noises drifting from that direction.

"What's that humming sound?" I asked, plunking the sub sandwiches I'd brought for lunch on the empty desk and sliding one to Joel.

"Thanks. Sewing machine," he said with an expressive look.

"Oh, no."

He nodded grimly. "Oh, yes."

If Coco was occupying herself by sewing up a uniform prototype when there'd been a murder in the mall, I was ready to give up on her. I unwrapped my sub and the delicious fragrance of pickles, vinegar, and tuna salad made me salivate. I bit into the sandwich, realizing I was starving. Joel started on his chips and for a short time only the sounds of crunching and chewing broke the silence.

"Is it true your father—Ethan—used to be a plumber?" Joel asked.

"Wherever did you hear that?"

Sheepishly, he drew out the magazine. Ethan smiled from the cover, his crisp hair overlaid with large type that read: *FANtastic Movie Mag.*

"You don't believe the garbage they print in there, do you?" I asked.

"So he wasn't a plumber?"

"I think he filled in for a sick friend at a home repair store for a week, and worked in the plumbing department," I said. "Believe me, you do not want Ethan messing with your plumbing." I had vague memories from when I was only three or four, before Ethan made it big, of him trying to hook up a dishwasher and flooding the kitchen, which meant we got to eat at Dairy Queen for two days in a row. I'd ridden on his shoulders on the walk home, dripping ice cream into his hair. The memory almost made me tear up.

"So the rest of this isn't true, either?" Joel opened the magazine and read from an article in the middle. " 'Ethan Jarrett has the reputation, rare in Hollywood, of being a devoted family man. He's been married to the former Brenda Atherton for over thirty years and friends report the couple is still going strong. One unnamed acquaintance said they're as committed as storied Hollywood legends Paul Newman and Joanne Woodward.' "

"That much is true," I said.

"What about this bit where he had an alien encounter on Mulholland Drive after finishing that movie where he played the spaceship captain?"

I shot him a look. Licking a forefinger, he turned the page where grainy photos showed Ethan on a beach somewhere, and the facing page had an article about Anya Vale and *Mafia Mistress*. "She's a hottie," Joel said wistfully, caught by the star's sultry gaze. "It says here she turned down the opportunity to star in the new Kenneth Branagh flick to make *Mafia Mistress*. Keira Knightley got the role Anya was up for, it says, and 'Hollywood insiders who've seen the unedited film think she'll get an Oscar nod.'" Joel looked up from the page and waited for me to comment.

"Ethan's movie will make more money," I said. Although he'd rather have an Oscar than another twenty million dollars, I knew.

"It's not about the fame and money for her," Joel said, defending his crush. "This interviewer says 'Anya Vale wanted the opportunity'—"

"Please, Joel," I interrupted him. "I learned when I was ten that those magazines make stuff up at will. That's when they reported that I had Down syndrome and that my parents were keeping me hidden from the public because they were ashamed of my condition. Actually, I had mono and had to be home-schooled for half a year. Groups that lobbied for people with disabilities called for a boycott of Ethan's movies."

"Okay," Joel conceded. "I see your point. But do you think you could get Ethan to sign this for me?" He slid the fan mag across the desk and I stopped it with my hand.

"Sure." I took a long slurp of my iced tea, and asked, my argument with Ethan still on my mind, "Are you a big movie fan?"

Joel's eyes brightened. "Oh, yeah! I've loved movies and television since I was a kid. I probably see forty or fifty movies a year in the theater and a bunch more on Netflix. I like all kinds. Well, I'm not really into documentaries, but sci fi, rom-com, heavy dramas, action flicks, good horror—I like them all. Everyone in my family gives me movie theater gift cards for Christmas and my birthday."

"I didn't know. What's the best movie you've seen lately?"

He named a film already being called an Oscar contender and seemed prepared to analyze each beat of the script and all the camera work for me. I stopped him with a simple question: "Why?"

"Why what?"

"Why do you like movies?" I crumpled my sandwich wrapper and chips bag into a ball and lobbed them into the trash can.

Giving me a look like I was a simpleton, Joel said, "Because they take you away, don't they? They create a different world and put you in it for a couple of hours. It's almost like time travel or falling through a worm hole or apparating."

Joel had watched far too much science fiction and fantasy.

He took a big bite of his sandwich and chewed as if he needed to fuel his thoughts. He swallowed. "I'm not putting it very well, but at movies it's like I can worry about being eaten by a *T. rex* or crashing my Formula One car or ending up with Jennifer Aniston for a while, instead of worrying about work stuff or if I'll ever be able to afford new wheels. I hate that van."

Joel drove the used family van his parents had given him.

"You can escape from reality for a while."

"Exactly!" He beamed at me as if I were the class dullard who'd finally come up with the right answer.

I guess I'd known that movies, like books, provide an escape from day-to-day realities, but I wasn't much of one for ducking out on reality, so I hadn't really considered that they might offer a welcome, even necessary, break to many people. I bit the inside of my cheek and regretted that I'd taken Ethan's work for granted for so long and focused on the business end of it, since that's what I saw at home, rather than the product he created that gave pleasure to so many. Maybe I should see a movie. I tried to think when I'd last seen one and thought it might have been in Afghanistan.

Time to get back to work. "I know it's not as fast-paced as the latest Ethan Jarrett movie, but have you looked at the footage from our cameras?"

Joel shook his head and mumbled around a mouthful of chips, "Waiting for you."

I motioned for him to cue up the camera data from last night and we watched it. There were no cameras in the bathrooms, of course, and none in the utility hall where there was nothing to shoplift, so we were reduced to studying the passersby in the main corridor who could have turned into that hall, looking for Zoë.

"The cops don't know yet when she was attacked, but I talked to a woman who saw her about six last night, so we can start then," I said. Joel fast-forwarded and we studied the images. They were black-and-white and they moved jerkily since Fernglen's cameras only recorded images every few seconds. Still, we could make out shoppers as they passed, schlepping shopping bags, and teens slumping by, killing time.

"There's a lot of cops," Joel observed after we'd been watching for nearly half an hour with the images hurrying past on fast-forward.

I'd noticed that myself. "Actors," I clarified. The kicker was that they all looked way too much alike on our recording. With the hats they wore, I couldn't even tell which were men and which were women. The Vernonville Police

Department might have technicians who could determine relative heights, if they did some measurements in our halls or studied shadows or something, but I had trouble telling one from another.

"Look, there's Zoë," I said, pointing to a figure on the screen.

Joel paused the video and leaned in, slacks fabric straining across his plump thighs, to study the woman. "Yep," he agreed.

We looked for her for the next ten minutes, but the camera didn't catch her returning to the theater wing. "She had her purse with her," I pointed out. "Maybe she was leaving for the day. Freeze that." I pointed to the clearest picture of Zoë. "She's wearing the same outfit she had on when I found her. She never left the mall last night." I was excited by the realization, wondering if the police had figured that out.

Joel reversed until we found Zoë again and we kept track of the people we saw who could have followed her into the restroom area, if, in fact, she went down that hall. There were a dozen, three of them "cops." Based on the length of time between them walking toward the restroom and then returning from it, we figured that seven of the twelve visited the bathroom. Of course, we didn't even know for sure that they'd turned into the restroom hallway, but it seemed a reasonable guess. The rest of the figures never reappeared, so they either went elsewhere in the mall or left it altogether. It would take hours reviewing images from the other cameras to see if we could spot one or more of those people somewhere else in the mall, or leaving it via one of the two dozen exits. The prospect made me wish for an easy needle-in-the-haystack type of task. The police might have the manpower for it, but I didn't think they'd learn anything useful. Joel tapped his mouse and the images zipped by on fast-forward.

"This is a waste of time," I said. "You'd think that the cameras would be more helpful, wouldn't you?" The cameras were mainly a deterrent to shoplifters and vandals; using them after the fact to try and track down a perpetrator was too manpower- and time-intensive to be practical, especially with their poor resolution and the fact that only two-thirds of the cameras positioned around the mall even recorded. Still, we'd had to look—we could've gotten lucky.

I was turning away from the screen when a figure caught my eye. Leaning forward, I rubbed at an imaginary smudge on the monitor so Joel wouldn't notice my interest. It couldn't be . . . I slid my eyes sideways to see if Joel had noticed, but he was peering into his chip bag to see if he'd overlooked any corn chips. Casually, I stopped the video, noting the time stamp—oh-six-thirty—and popped the DVD out. I didn't know what my mom had been doing at Fernglen so early this morning, but I intended to find out.

Joel would have found it suspicious if I'd rushed out of the office, so I filled him in on what I'd learned from Ethan and Margot Chelius while he used a damp forefinger to pick up the chip crumbs from the bag and transfer them to his tongue.

"She did it," he said immediately, brown eyes alight. "The girlfriend. They fought, she lost it, she followed her to the bathroom and—" He mimed thrusting a knife.

"With the knife she happened to have in her purse?" I said skeptically.

"Hm." Joel looked crestfallen at having his theory shot down so quickly. He thought for a moment and perked up. "Let's say the Margot woman was lying to you. She and Zoë were having trouble. Zoë was cheating on her. She brought the knife with her, waited for her chance, and stabbed her in the bathroom. Then she walked away and left her to die.

Man, that's cold." He shook his head, soft brown curls bobbing.

"It could have happened that way," I conceded, "but we have zero evidence to prove it. It could as easily have been a mugger seizing his chance. Zoë fought back, refused to give up her purse—whatever—and he stabbed her. Or it could have been a rape attempt." That thought silenced me for a moment. "There's no proof to support that, either," I said finally. "We could sit here and make up theories all day long, but until we have some hard evidence, that's all we'll have—theories."

"It's not our job to find evidence," Joel pointed out.

"I know." That fact frustrated me and I pushed my chair back a little too hard as I stood. It teetered and I grabbed it before it fell. Papers fluttered from the desk to the floor and I leaned down to pick them up. The first was the shift schedule for next week, but the second was the manila envelope containing the letter Ethan had brought in yesterday. Without touching it, I slid it out and read it again: "Stop making movies that glorify violence and capitalist materialism or we'll stop you."

Eyes widening, I read it aloud to Joel.

He blinked at me. "You don't think—?"

I didn't know, but I knew the police needed to see this letter. "Back in a mo," I told Joel, halfway out the door to see the detective I already knew would take the opportunity to abuse me for not giving him the letter earlier.

"Why the hell didn't you bring this to me when you first received it?" Detective Helland asked when I tracked him down at the crime scene. A uniformed cop had stopped me from entering, but when Helland gave the okay, he had me sign in on a clipboard and let me through. I'd approached the bathroom cautiously and put on the pair of paper booties Helland indicated before inching into the men's room and handing him the envelope. He stood with his back to the sinks, fluorescent lights glinting on his blond hair, blue booties on his feet taking away a bit from his authoritarian appearance as he read the letter.

"There hadn't been a homicide then," I said, "and you know there's nothing the VPD could have done with no signature or mailroom stamp or specific threat. But you're right: I should have turned it over to the police when Ethan brought it in. He was so dismissive of it, though, that I didn't take it as seriously as I should have. He gets tens of thousands of letters annually, and some of them are from kooks, he says. My mom used to keep a scrapbook of the looniest ones, but she gave that up years ago. Too depressing, she said, to think that there were so many people out there who couldn't differentiate between a movie and reality and who apparently had so little in their lives that they had to obsess about a man they'd never met."

Helland nodded and slipped the letter back into the envelope, the latex gloves making his fingers awkward. "I'll send this to the lab. I doubt we'll get anything useful off it, but you never know. Tell Mr. Jarrett if he gets any more—"

"I will." I looked around the bathroom, trying to figure out what Helland was searching for. Surely, the crime scene team was done, or we wouldn't be standing here, potentially muddying the evidentiary waters.

"Look." Helland bent sideways at the waist, cocked his head, and gestured toward the floor.

I assumed a similar posture and tried to see what he was indicating. The bleach smell was stronger this close to the floor. It took me a moment, but then I saw a swirly pattern on the tile that occupied only a narrow swath of the floor leading from two feet in front of where we stood to the stall where I'd found Zoë.

Helland caught the comprehension in my eyes and nodded. "The murderer tried to clean up. We found bloody paper towels in the bin. He or she stabbed the victim there"—he pointed—"and dragged her into the stall, presumably so she wouldn't be found too quickly. Then he had to erase the blood trail."

The thought of a blood trail nauseated me and I took a deep breath. "Did you find her purse?"

Helland nodded. "Yes, in the trash. Her wallet and cell phone were gone. So it could have been a robbery gone wrong, but I have trouble seeing a garden-variety mugger taking the time to wipe up the blood and set out the 'Closed' signs."

"No, a mugger would have panicked and run for the nearest exit," I agreed. "A rapist?"

"No sign of sexual contact."

My shoulders relaxed. "Did you find anything else?"

Helland gave a disgusted snort. "Too much. It's a public restroom in a mall. We've got enough latents and hairs and miscellaneous body fluids—including a used condom from the trash—"

Ew, I thought. The idea of having sex propped against a urinal made me gag.

"—to keep every crime lab technician in the state employed full time for the rest of the year." Snapping off his latex gloves, he led the way out of the bathroom and I followed, happy to escape the white-tiled tomb.

"I don't think she left the mall last night." I told him what I'd noticed about her clothes on the camera. I didn't mention seeing my mother and didn't even feel guilty about it—well, not very—because I knew my mother didn't have anything to do with Zoë's death, especially if Zoë had died last night, long before the cameras caught Mom headed toward this hall.

He gave me the arched brows I always got from him when he was semi-impressed with my findings. "Good catch. I don't suppose your father mentioned anyone connected with the movie who might have had a grudge against Ms. Winters?" Helland asked a shade too casually as we lingered in the main corridor, watching a young mother push a stroller built for triplets.

I eyed him cynically, understanding now why he had been relatively forthcoming in the restroom. He thought I might have an inside track with the movie people. I told him what I'd learned—not much—from Ethan and threw in what Margot had told me for good measure.

"That matches what she told us," he said. "If you hear anything more—"

Before he could leave, I asked him the question I'd been dying to ask: "Have you talked to Jesse Willard?"

Helland's face closed down. "We're still looking for him."

I bit my lip, not knowing what to say. Jesse not being home, which is how I interpreted Helland's comment, looked bad. Helland's cell phone rang before I could ask what Mr. Willard had said—not that Helland would've told me—and he moved off with a brief nod as he answered it. I stood for a moment, admiring the way his broad shoulders looked under his jacket, before I realized what I was doing and took off a little too fast on my Segway, startling an old gentleman with a walker.

I might find Detective Anders Helland somewhat appealing physically, but that was it. No way was I interested in a relationship with the man. He was too sure of his own abilities, too quick to discount others'. Mine, I admitted. He knew I'd been a military cop until I got injured and medically retired, and yet he persisted in treating me like I was a clueless mall security officer who didn't know the first thing about police procedure. I had to admit that my prideful side would be happy to beat him to the solution on this case, even though, strictly speaking, murder investigations didn't fall into my job jar. Okay, they weren't in my job jar no matter how one viewed it.

But I *was* the mall security office's liaison with the production company and the movie people. And if I *happened* to learn something useful while hanging around the set, liaising . . .

I put the pedal to the metal (figuratively speaking, since the Segway didn't have pedals), and resumed my patrol of the mall. The customers and merchants deserved my usual attention, even though there was a movie being filmed on the premises and a homicide investigation going on. I'd pencil in some hard-core liaising for when I got off shift.

Ten

. . .

When I got off work at three o'clock, the production office was virtually empty, the movie theater wing quiet. Only the thin woman with the clipboard was in the office, stuffing envelopes. Cardboard boxes stacked two deep surrounded her on three sides, and an open box gaped on the table in front of her. She looked up when I entered, tucking a section of curly, ginger-colored hair behind her ear. Her gaze scanned me from head to toe. "That uniform's all wrong. If you're looking to be cast as an extra, you need to talk to—"

"I don't want to be in the movie," I said, laughing. "I work here. EJ Ferris." I held out my hand.

She blushed. "Oh, right. Sorry. Iona Moss. I saw you with Ethan yesterday, didn't I?" Hazel eyes appraised me.

"Yes."

She waited for me to elaborate, but I stayed silent. After a moment, she bent and used a box cutter to rip through the tape on another box in one efficient motion. She hauled out a stack of colorful brochures and began slipping them into envelopes. If she had to empty all the boxes, she was in for a long evening.

"I was actually looking for Bree Spurrier," I said, remembering that Ethan had mentioned she was the second assistant director who was in charge of the extras.

"I thought you didn't want to be in the movie," Iona said suspiciously.

"I'm trying to find Tab Gentry."

"Oh. Well, Bree's not here. We had to change the schedule around when they found . . . when Zoë . . . Bree's shooting some short exterior scenes on the Occoquan."

The Occoquan was a scenic river north of here, up I-95, that ran through a picturesque town of the same name. I'd have to wait to talk to her until she got back. "Okay, well—"

"What were you and Ethan talking about anyway?" Iona asked, her curiosity finally getting the better of her. Her eyes flicked up to meet mine for a moment, before she returned her gaze to the envelopes. "I mean, I've worked a couple of movies with him and he's never been one to get chummy with . . ."

She drifted off and I wondered if she was having trouble coming up with a word that wasn't too derogatory. The help? The little people? Non-movie people? Ethan wasn't a snob, but I knew he took his acting seriously and didn't allow himself a lot of distractions when he was working, so Iona was probably right that he didn't usually wander around chatting up strangers on location. I didn't see any harm in assuaging her curiosity. "He got a crank letter he thought he should turn over to us in the security office."

Iona dropped a stack of brochures. "Not another note from that nut-job woman who calls herself 'Truly, Madly, Deeply'? I thought she'd finally given up."

"No," I said. "It wasn't from her. Who is she?"

Iona bent to pick up the brochures, raking them toward herself with long arms. "Oh, I probably shouldn't have said anything. But Delia and I—she was Ethan's assistant until she got married—were friends and she used to show me the notes from this woman. They were always written on pink stationery and went on about how she loved Ethan and she was the only woman who truly appreciated him, and how she couldn't wait until they could be together forever. She always signed them 'Truly, Madly, Deeply,' so we called her TMD for short. Delia said Ethan laughed them off, but they gave me the creeps."

Her description of them gave me the creeps, too; I needed to talk to Ethan about his fan mail. "Thanks for letting me know." I remembered something from yesterday. "You said Gentry was aiming at Mr. Jarrett when the gun went off . . . ?" I let my voice trail up into a question.

Shifting uncomfortably, Iona said, "Well, it seemed like that to me, like he was pointing the gun at Ethan. But he told the police he was only goofing around and hadn't really meant to *aim* at anyone."

"Did he have a problem with Mr. Jarrett?"

Iona shook her head. "Oh, no. Everyone loves Ethan. He's the kindest, most wonderful man. Everyone thinks so." Her eyes shone with the fervor of a disciple.

"Including Zoë Winters?" I tried to keep my voice neutral but apparently didn't succeed.

"Why do you ask it like that?" A slight frown rumpled Iona's brow. "There wasn't anything going on between them, if that's what you're hinting at. Ethan *wouldn't*."

I could have smacked myself for being so obvious. "Good to know."

I turned to leave, and Iona called after me, "If you want

to talk to Tab, I heard the payroll guy tell him he could pick up his paycheck first thing in the morning."

"Could you give me a call if you see him?" I scribbled my name and number on the back of an envelope when she nodded.

I thanked her and left, detouring to Ethan's trailer on my way. I was determined to apologize for this morning's comments. No one answered when I knocked and I figured he might be filming at Occoquan. As I turned away, a familiar figure came out of the wardrobe trailer parked kitty-corner to Ethan's. White hair riffled in the wind. Grandpa Atherton. He was saying something over his shoulder to someone in the trailer and started when he turned around to find me in his path.

"Emma-Joy!"

"What were you doing in there?" I asked.

He gave me a mischievous grin. "Why, getting fitted for my costume, of course."

A feeling of foreboding settled on me. "What costume?"

"Well," he said breezily, hooking his elbow around mine and strolling toward the gate, "I figured that when they fired the poor lad for the gun incident, they would be short one police officer. It seemed to me that it might be useful to cozy up with the people who knew Zoë best if we want to find out who killed her. I had a word with Ethan and he set it up. I look quite dashing in my police uniform, if I do say so myself."

"Nothing happening with Mr. North Korea?" I asked, referring to his recent surveilling of North Korean businessmen for an unnamed agency.

"They pulled the plug on that," Grandpa admitted. "I retrieved the devices early this morning. I can work full time on the murder."

"It's not our job to find out who killed her," I said, conveniently forgetting that I was trying to do exactly that.

"Admit it, Emma-Joy," Grandpa said, "you're jealous because I can go undercover and you can't."

"Who's going to believe in an octogenarian cop?" I said sulkily. He'd hit a bit too close to the truth.

"I wear a hat," Grandpa said, "and there's always makeup. Do you know I still have my Screen Actors Guild card from when I had a bit part in a movie back in the '60s? It was being bankrolled by a German industrialist the Agency was interested in because—well, never mind that. Let's just say that after he met an untimely end—we were filming in Portugal and his car went over a cliff one night—the Agency saw no need for my continued involvement and pulled me out. Now, I've got another shot at fame."

"More like you've got another shot at getting in trouble. And who will Mom blame for that? Me."

"Pish. I'm going to keep my mouth shut and my ears open. If I hear anything useful I'll pass it along. In all probability, I'll film my scenes, listen to a lot of boring Hollywood gossip about who's in rehab or who had their face 'done' recently, collect my paycheck, and that will be that."

"Hm." That was never that when it came to Grandpa. "While you're hanging around, you might also see if you can sound out some folks about a note Ethan got." I recited the text of the "movies and capitalism" threat Ethan had found in his trailer.

"In his trailer, hm?" Grandpa said. "Then maybe someone from the movie had something to do with it."

"Possible," I agreed, "but you can't call this tight security. Anyone could have snuck in." I gestured to the black-shirted guard who was chatting up a buxom girl with a blond ponytail and a braying laugh; the Spanish Armada could have sailed through the gate and he wouldn't have noticed. "Want to get dinner later?" I asked Grandpa.

"Can't. Sorry," he said. "Theresa and I are going to Pilates class and then to a new vegan restaurant the teacher told us about."

Theresa Eshelman owned a day-care center and was currently Grandpa's significant other. He'd met her at the mall. The class was new, however. "Pilates?"

"Great for my core," Grandpa said, patting his flat abdomen. "As for the vegan restaurant . . . I figure I can always pick up a couple of tacos on my way home if the nuts and sprouts don't fill me up."

I laughed, kissed his cheek, and headed for my Miata. Normally I'd have stopped by the Y after work, but today I had another mission: Mom.

Eleven

. . .

When I called Mom and told her I'd like to drop by, she told me she had an appointment set up with a caterer, but that I could meet her there. "You can help me choose what to serve, EJ. We're hosting a dinner Thursday for some of your father's business associates—the boring ones who talk budgets and box office and distribution deals—and the caterer has been sweet enough to meet with me on short notice."

No surprise there. What company was going to turn down the opportunity to cater an event at Ethan Jarrett's house, even if they only received fifteen minutes' notice? When Mom mentioned there'd be samples, I told her I'd meet her at the caterer's place in Alexandria.

The drive took well over an hour, and I was crabby by the time I got out of the Miata. In a light industrial park nowhere near scenic Old Town Alexandria, the caterer's building had all the charm of a warehouse, complete with a garage-type door for loading and unloading vans, I presumed. Mom's Mercedes was already parked in the gravel lot so I hustled in.

The interior was more welcoming, with a sitting area featuring two peach-colored sofas and a large, glass-topped coffee table already piled with various food items. Brown carpet covered the floor—and disguised spills, I bet—and a conference table with flowers blooming from a vase sat behind the cozy tasting area. Twelve or fifteen elaborate wedding cakes—fake, I trusted—rested on a long buffet. I could see a large industrial kitchen through a door that opened to my left, and the whole room smelled deliciously of roasting meat. My mouth watered.

"Sorry I'm late, Mom," I said, bending to kiss her cheek where she sat on a sofa, serene and blond. She smiled, producing crinkles at the corners of her eyes. She'd never had her face "done" like so many of her Hollywood wife counterparts, and I liked that she was comfortable with her aging self. Not that she was aging badly; she worked out with a trainer several times a week so her figure was still shapely, even though she might weigh five or ten pounds more than she had in her twenties. Additionally, she had a genius of a (mega-expensive) hair stylist who kept her shoulder-length tresses highlighted and natural-looking. Still, no one would mistake her for a thirty-year-old and she was fine with that.

"This is Christopher," she said, gesturing to the thirtyish man with male pattern baldness who hovered nearby. He wore a pristine white chef's jacket and I wondered if he wore it to cook or only to schmooze with potential clients. I sat on the sofa opposite my mother as she said, "He recommends the berry tarts, although I like these kiwi ones." She passed me a plate of tiny tarts with perfect fluted edges, filled with kiwi slivers.

I popped one into my mouth. The flaky pastry and the tangy fruit seemed to melt on my tongue. "These ones," I said definitively.

Mom laughed and Christopher half smiled. "Don't you at least want to try the flourless chocolate torte or the green tea sherbet?"

I said yes to the torte and declined the sherbet and talked about nothing very substantial as Mom and Christopher hashed out the menu. When the caterer disappeared into the back again to write up Mom's order and run her credit card, I pounced.

"So, you didn't stop in to say 'hi' when you were at Fernglen," I said.

Her brows arched. "How did you—? I was going to, of course, honey, but they started filming earlier than I expected and then, of course, they found that poor woman—"

"I found her."

Mom gasped. "Oh, honey, are you okay?" She leaned forward to put a hand on my knee.

I wasn't, actually; I kept seeing the dead Zoë on the bathroom floor. "I'm coping. Her name was Zoë Winters. Did you know her?"

Mom seemed to still, then smoothed a hand down her already perfect hair. "Um, I don't think so. Your father may have mentioned her once or twice. She did something with props, right?"

"Exactly." I let the silence lengthen.

"Where could Christopher have gotten to?" Mom asked, shifting as if she was going to go in search of him.

"He's swilling champagne with the kitchen workers to

celebrate your order," I said. "He'll be back. Why were you at the mall so early?" There. I'd asked her straight-on.

She gave me a puzzled look. "What are you getting at, EJ? You know I frequently visit your father on his sets."

True, but. "That doesn't explain why you were *in* the mall instead of in his trailer, or why you went down the very corridor where I found Zoë."

"She was killed in *that* bathroom?" Mom asked, eyes opening wider. "Oh, my."

"The men's room."

"Oh, I was never in—You know, I don't like what you're implying, EJ." Anger and hurt showed in her eyes and tone.

Christopher returned then, handing my mother's credit card to her and reiterating how happy he was to have her business. He held a large white box that contained, he said, an assortment of dessert samples for her to take home. She thanked him graciously and let him walk her to the door. I trailed half a step behind, wondering if she was using the caterer as a shield. I knew she was when she invited him to carry the box to her Mercedes and slide it gently onto the floor.

"Thanks for helping," she said, giving me a quick hug while Christopher held her door open. "Come to dinner tomorrow night. Your father and I will need help eating all these yummy desserts. You know he won't eat more than a morsel when he's filming. Your grandfather's coming, too." Putting on her sunglasses, she slid into the car. "Ciao."

I watched as she drove off. Christopher returned to the building without a word, and I stood alone in the parking lot, chilled by a breeze, unhappily aware that my mother hadn't come clean with me.

Twelve

. . .

Wednesday began with a chance encounter in the mall parking lot. I'd spent a virtually sleepless night, awakened every time I dozed off by images of Zoë on the bathroom floor. Only, in my dreams the floor was coated with wall-to-wall blood. The third time that I drifted into the same dream and dragged myself awake, at four fifteen, I crawled out of bed and huddled in the chair by the window, a blanket draped around my shoulders. Fubar joined me for a while, and I stroked his rusty fur, waiting for morning. I'd spent too many nights like this after returning from Afghanistan, and I hoped that finding Zoë wasn't going to send me back to the ugly place I'd been in then.

As I walked toward the mall entrance, I spotted someone trudging toward a car parked a few rows away. A chilly wind blew, making it feel more like winter than spring, and I huddled into the bomber jacket I was using until I could replace my uniform Windbreaker. I knit my brow, trying to place the man's walk, and then realized it was Mr. Willard, Jesse's father. What in the world was he doing here three hours before mall opening time?

"Mr. Willard!" I hailed him.

He turned, showing me a startled face, but started toward me when he recognized me. His gait was little more than a shuffle and he seemed to have aged since I last saw him two days ago. "Officer Ferris," he said. He tucked a long plaid scarf more securely around his neck.

"Has Jesse turned up?"

He shook his head, the weight of his worry making it sag forward. "No. I was looking for him."

"Here?"

He nodded, and the wind tugged his comb-over loose so his bald spot shone palely. "For some reason, Jesse liked it here. He worked here as a teenager, you know."

I shook my head. "I didn't know that. Where?"

"The food court. He flipped burgers at some place that went out of business a couple years back. I think it was where that Chinese food place is now. He and his friends hung out here a lot. Maybe that's why he keeps coming back now that he's . . . out of the military. The police came to see me, you know. They didn't say it in so many words, but they think he had something to do with that woman's murder." He pressed his thin lips together and gave me a searching look. "They said you saw him."

"Yes. I'm sorry." I wasn't sure what I was apologizing for. Seeing Jesse? Giving his name to the police?

"If he found her, saw her . . . if there was blood, it probably scared him," Mr. Willard said. "He was always squeamish about blood—couldn't stand the sight of a scraped knee as a kid, even—and since the IED . . ."

He didn't need to explain to me how gory the aftermath of an improvised explosive device detonation could be. I'd lived it firsthand. I wasn't remotely squeamish, but I still had nightmares about the explosion, the screams, the smells of burning asphalt and torn metal and dirt.

"He's been walking here every morning," Willard said. "That's why I came now."

The night guard at Fernglen unlocked the main door at four thirty every morning so mall walkers could exercise before starting their commutes to D.C. or Richmond. The few times I'd worked the night shift, I'd been amazed by how many people wanted to racewalk through the mall's halls, especially during the winter when it was dark and cold. "Is that why he was here yesterday—to walk?"

"Um-hm. I dropped him off. He was going to ride the bus home."

"Does he drive? Does he have a car?"

"He's not supposed to," Mr. Willard said. "He's had a couple of seizures as a result of his brain injuries, but he's not incapable of driving, if that's what you're asking. His car is still at home."

"I'll keep an eye out for him," I promised Mr. Willard, impulsively squeezing his hand. "He'll be okay. Even if he's sleeping rough somewhere, the temps aren't going below forty at night."

"I'm not worried about that. The kid's a survivalist—what he didn't learn from the Boy Scouts and books as a lad, the army taught him. No, I'm worried about—" He drew in a deep breath and let it out in a sharp huff. "Can you help him, Officer Ferris?"

He'd startled me. "Help Jesse?"

He bobbed his head rapidly. "Yes. Prove he didn't do it

so he can come home again. He didn't hurt that woman—I know he didn't, but the police suspect him. You're here all the time; you can discover the real killer."

"I can't—"

He ignored my protest. "I'm going to be late. Please call me if you find Jesse."

As I watched him plod toward his car, I thought about his undefined worries. He could be worried about Jesse's mental state if he'd stumbled over the injured Zoë. Or he could have darker, better-left-unexpressed worries about the nature of Jesse's encounter with Zoë, despite his conviction that his son hadn't killed her. Trying to suppress those thoughts myself—I didn't want Jesse to be guilty of harming Zoë—I hurried into the mall's warmth, thinking it would be nice to clear Jesse's name if I could.

I'd completed a circuit of the mall and done some paper-work by nine o'clock when Joel came in. The phone rang as he walked through the door and he dove for it, dropping the handset as he fumbled to take off bulky gloves. I rolled my eyes at him. "Fernglen Galleria Security, Officer Rooney speaking," he said, managing to sound both very young and professional at the same time. He handed me the phone.

"This is Iona Moss," a woman whispered. "You wanted me to let you know when Tab Gentry got here. Well, he's here. And it looks like he wants to cause trouble."

"On my way," I said, hanging up.

Telling Joel where I was headed, I hopped on the Segway and took off for the elevator. Arriving at the movie wing minutes later, I could hear yelling. I dismounted and hurried around the corner. The actor I'd noted yesterday, a man in his midtwenties, tall and handsome in an all-American-boy sort of way, was yelling at a petite woman wearing jeans and a photographer's vest. I realized I'd seen her Monday when I'd escorted Ethan back to the set. She'd wanted to talk to him about some fountain scene. They stood in the doorway of the production office. Three or four onlookers tried to appear as if they weren't paying attention, but their bodies all angled toward the twosome having words.

"All I'm asking for is another chance, Bree," Tab Gentry pleaded.

The petite woman, who must be Bree Spurrier, the second assistant director, shook her head, dark pageboy swaying against her cheeks. "I can't, Tab. Our insurers—"

"Damn the insurers! Did you know the cops came to talk to me yesterday? All but accused me of killing Zoë because she got me fired." He looked around wildly, and ran a hand through his thick, wheat-blond hair.

"Zoë didn't get you—"

"The hell she didn't! No one wanted to fire *her* because Ethan Jarrett, our big star"—he sneered the words—"was cuddling her, telling her it wasn't her fault. It was an accident. No one even got hurt." His voice had changed from accusing to pleading. "I need the work, Bree."

With a shake of her head, the dark-haired woman turned her back on him to enter the office. Gentry's hand flashed out and grabbed her shoulder, jerking her back half a step. Two of the beefy movie security men belatedly realized they should be doing something and started forward even as I came up behind the pair and said, "Mr. Gentry?"

Distracted, he turned and looked at me. "Who are you?"

"My name's EJ Ferris." I offered my hand, and he automatically removed his hand from Bree's shoulder to shake.

Bree scooted into the office and pulled out her cell phone. I had a feeling she was calling the police. The security guys surged forward, about to latch onto Gentry, but I gave them a look that told them to let me handle it. They'd had their chance.

"You really don't want to do this. I know it's disappointing and unfair, but you don't want to make things worse by getting the police involved." I nodded to Bree where she was talking on her phone. "Don't burn your bridges, and they may hire you for another project. Why don't you let me buy you a cup of coffee?"

Gentry looked from me to Bree to the looming security guards. "I don't want any damned coffee," he snarled. He pivoted and half stalked, half jogged toward the mall exit. I let him go, although the security guards followed him to the door.

"You handled that well," a voice behind me said. "Better than I did."

I turned to see that Bree Spurrier had emerged from the office. Crinkles at the corners of her eyes suggested she was older than I'd first thought, maybe in her late forties. Thin lips, slightly chapped, were drawn into a tight smile. Her slight frame seemed weighted down by the bulky vest, even though it looked like the pockets were mostly empty.

I shrugged. "When you've dealt with drunken soldiers, a disappointed actor isn't much to take on. EJ Ferris."

"Bree Spurrier."

We shook hands.

"Drunken soldiers?" she asked.

I gave her the *Reader's Digest* version of my career: "I used to be an air force cop."

"Really?" She looked at me with interest. "Isn't that unusual for a woman?"

"Not these days."

"How do you come to be working in a mall, if you don't

mind my asking?" She tilted her head, reminding me of a grackle eyeing a worm.

I felt uncomfortable with her probing, but said, "I was injured. I'm recuperating."

"Really?" She arched thin brows. "That's very interesting. You know, there've been a couple of movies made about the Iraq/Afghanistan wars, but they've all been from the male point of view. Yeah, I know a woman directed *The Hurt Locker*," she said, as if I were going to object, "but it was about men, the male experience of war. Your story intrigues me. Maybe there's a movie in it. How did you say you got hurt and what, exactly, were the nature of your injuries? Let's get some coffee." She pointed to an urn at the end of a long table laden with Danishes, bagels, and muffins.

"I'm really not movie material," I said, appalled by the idea. "And I've got to get back to work. But thanks for the offer."

I was about to make good my escape when Ethan's voice hailed me from down the hall. "EJ!"

Bree's eyebrows snapped together at his familiarity. "Where do you know—"

"Morning, Bree," Ethan said, as he joined us. He looked rested and ready for filming, made up and costumed. The famous smile lit up the whole hall, and I was relieved that he seemed to have put our last conversation behind him. "Eej—"

"Mr. Jarrett," I said, giving him a look to ward off the hug I saw coming. "I gave that letter you were worried about to the police, but they haven't gotten back to me yet. Have you received another one?"

"Not me," Ethan said, "but some other folks have." He handed me a couple of flyers with the same "stop glorifying violence" message as on Ethan's letter.

Bree's shoulders relaxed at this simple explanation for my being acquainted with one of Hollywood's biggest stars. "I need to talk to you about this morning's scene with Anya," she said to Ethan. "I'm not sure about the kiss—"

"In a minute," Ethan said, throwing one arm over my shoulders and steering me out of earshot.

Before he could say anything, I said, "I'm really sorry about what I said yesterday. I was thoughtless and—"

He interrupted me. "Zoë's murder made us both edgy. Let's forget it. You're coming for dinner tonight, right? We'll send the limo."

I had a feeling that we should continue the conversation we'd started, get our feelings out on the table, but I caved to his "let's forget it" because I hated being at odds with him. "Great," I said.

Ethan moved off to join Bree, and I noticed Iona Moss staring at us through the plate glass window of the store-cum-office. I smiled, but she turned away without responding. Hm. Maybe the light was hitting the window wrong and she hadn't seen me. I Segwayed back to the main part of the mall and spent a couple of hours doing my mall cop thing: I helped a young mother with three toddlers find her car, told a shopper with a Siberian husky that animals weren't allowed in the mall, broke up a loud argument between a man and his wife over his need to own every Craftsman tool ever invented, and summoned maintenance to de-bubble the fountain after some hooligan dumped half a bottle of dish soap into it.

I was about to make tracks for the office when a man stepped in front of my Segway. Detective Helland. I resisted the urge to run him down. Instead, I stopped. "Yes?"

His ice blue eyes surveyed me with a hint of approval. "I hear you defused a tense situation this morning."

"I persuaded Tab Gentry not to tube his chances of ever working in the industry again, if that's what you mean." I shrugged. It had been no big deal.

"The officers who arrived after you left, responding to a call from a Ms. Spurrier, got told how wonderful you were."

I couldn't tell if he was mocking me or complimenting me.

"I wanted to let you know we've given the production company permission to resume filming tomorrow, and you can reopen that bathroom; we're done with it."

I knew it would be a long darn time before I felt comfortable using that particular restroom. Come to think of it, Zoë had been in the men's room, not the women's room, so I wouldn't have to worry about it. I wondered if the fact that she was killed in the men's room meant the killer was a man. Before I could give that any thought, Helland spoke.

"I talked to Mr. Willard again. We still haven't located Jesse."

I stayed silent, not sure why he was telling me this.

"Mr. Willard seems to think Jesse might show up here." Helland met my gaze straight-on and I realized, apropos of nothing, that he was a very unfidgety guy—no tics or habitual gestures. "If he does, you need to remember that he's a murder suspect."

Drawing myself up to my full five foot six, I said coldly, "I'll be sure to let you know immediately if I run into him." I might like Jesse, but I knew I couldn't protect him. "I—"

"I know you will," Helland said, surprising me. "I was expressing concern for your safety. I know you feel some sympathy for the guy—hell, I feel some sympathy for him—but I don't want you trying to talk him into turning himself in or engaging him in any way. He might have killed a woman . . . we don't want to give him the opportunity to make it two." Without giving me a chance to respond, he walked off.

I set the Segway in motion with a jerk and continued on to the office, puzzled by my encounter with Helland. Was he really concerned about me, or was he subtly encouraging me to look for Jesse Willard? Every now and then I thought he found me interesting, even attractive. Then I'd do or say something to make him angry and he'd turn into an iceberg. I couldn't figure the man out.

Thirteen

...

After parking the Segway, I strolled into the security office and stopped. In my year-plus at Fernglen, I'd walked in on Captain Woskowicz hurling the coffeepot at someone, on two officers trading punches over a high school football game (their sons played for rival schools), and, once, on a night shift guard having sex with her boyfriend. I'd never seen anything like this. Joel stood on a chair with Coco crouched in front of him. She was apparently pinning up the hem of the red pants he wore. They had a black stripe down the side and looked very Mountie. The effect was spoiled by the bolero-style jacket and a flat-brimmed hat that looked like something an Argentinean gaucho would wear, complete with a rope that cinched under the chin. Joel shot me a "help me" look and I bit back the giggles that threatened to erupt.

Coco looked over her shoulder when she heard me come in. "Oh, hi, EJ. You're just in time. What do you think?"

She rose, teetering on lavender pumps that matched her silk blouse.

I studied Joel while he blushed crimson with embarrassment. "I think Joel's missing out on a lucrative career as a model." He turned redder, if that was possible, and I took pity on him. "Coco, I think we have more important things to worry about than costumes . . . I mean uniforms."

"But I know I only got hired because I talked about my ideas for new uniforms during the interview," she said, an anxious pucker between her brows.

One of the panel had asked me about uniforms, too; I'd thought she was joking. "I think the interviewers must have noted how your . . . creativity could be an asset to the security office," I said.

Joel gazed at me with admiration and surreptitiously climbed off the desk while Coco was distracted. "Ow!" He bent to remove a straight pin that had jabbed his ankle.

"Really?" Coco looked uncertain.

"Really," I said firmly, refusing to voice my doubts. "How about we talk about how to limit the disruption tomorrow when the movie crew resumes filming? They're shooting that scene where my—where Ethan Jarrett ends up in the fountain."

Joel snuck off to change while I went over some ideas with Coco, who approved them all. We agreed that Harold would man the office and watch the monitors, and our other on-duty officers would be stationed near the mall entrances to ensure that no one unauthorized got in. Coco would be a "floater," moving from station to station and troubleshooting problems that came up. Hopefully, there wouldn't be any because I was pretty sure her troubleshooting abilities began and ended with choosing piping or rickrack as a decorative accent. I would liaise with the movie security people and make sure our efforts meshed with theirs. I told her what little more I knew about the homicide investigation and hinted that she might want to update Curtis Quigley. She went off to do that as Joel came in and sank with a huff into his chair.

"That hat was almost as bad as the pillbox," he said. "I'm serious—I'll quit."

To distract him, I told him about Tab Gentry's run-in with Bree Spurrier.

That perked him up. He swiveled to face me. "Gentry did it!" he announced.

I gave him a look from under my brows. I'd been trying for the better part of a year to get Joel to consider all the evidence before leaping to a conclusion.

"No, think about it," he said before I could object. "This guy Gentry thinks Zoë got him fired. He said so. There's your motive: revenge. He's a man, so he could easily have been in the men's room: opportunity."

"And Zoë happened to wander into the men's room where he whipped out a knife and stabbed her?"

Joel gave that half a second's thought. "He lured her in."

" 'Hey, little girl, you want a piece of candy?' "

"Not like that," Joel said huffily. "Maybe he cried out, like he was sick or something. Or maybe he was coming out, saw her, and dragged her in."

"Barely possible," I conceded. "What about the means?"

He drew fuzzy caterpillar brows together.

"The knife. Did he pull it out of his pants pocket?"

Chewing on his lower lip, Joel paused to think of a plausible reason for Tab Gentry to have a knife on him. "It was part of his costume," he said triumphantly.

"We could check on that," I said. "I don't know why it would be, but we could ask."

Joel crossed his arms over his chest with a satisfied smirk.

Ignoring him, I mused, "It would help if we knew what kind of knife the killer used. Fat chance of Detective Helland sharing that information, though."

In any event, I didn't need Detective Helland to supply the information. Grandpa Atherton came through with it. He flagged me down as I cruised past the movie theater wing on one of my patrols. I didn't recognize him at first in his police costume, and had to admit the makeup experts had done a good job making him look almost plausible as a cop. Either he was wearing a wig or they'd cut his hair to military standards and dyed it brown; a cop's hat covered most of it anyway, as Grandpa had predicted. Tinted glasses fuzzed the deep crow's-feet around his eyes, and a glued-on mustache drew attention away from the grooves bracketing his mouth. A spray tan also contributed to the more youthful effect. He still looked like a cop on the brink of retirement, but at least he didn't look like he'd been drawing a pension in a Florida old-age home for a quarter century.

"Will you be posing for before and after photos?" I asked with mock admiration as I glided to a stop. I put on an announcer's voice: " 'Knock twenty years off your age with Movie Magic Miracle Cream! Only nineteen ninety-five, plus shipping and handling.' "

"I might, at that," he said, unperturbed. "I might have to get me a membership at one of those tanning joints. Spray tans only, of course."

I made gagging noises and he chuckled. "Enough, Emma-Joy. I've got something important to pass along. The police were all over the movie set this morning. With a search warrant."

That sobered me up. "Really? Why?"

"Looking for knives." He wriggled his nose as if his mustache itched. "Switchblades. Apparently, half the thugs in that movie had switchblades to carry as part of their costumes. There's some scene later in the movie where two of 'em have a knife fight."

I whistled softly. "That must mean a switchblade killed Zoë. Did the actors take the knives home with them?"

Grandpa shook his head. "No. I wondered the same thing, so I asked around, discreetly. The knives got turned into Zoë Winters each day after shooting wrapped."

"Were they all accounted for?"

Grandpa shrugged bony shoulders. "Don't know. The police weren't saying. Rumor has it they took all the knives away with them and the director was spitting mad, saying it would delay the filming schedule."

"Who's in charge of the weapons now that Zoë's dead?"

"She had an assistant. Guy named Grayson Bleek. Haven't met him yet, but I will when he gives me my weapon for the next scene." He patted his empty holster.

A garbled call came from the hallway behind us and Grandpa swiveled his head. "Gotta go, Emma-Joy. They're busing us to some warehouse outside Richmond to film a scene this afternoon. I've got all my lines memorized. 'Stop! Police!' and 'You don't want to do that, kid,' and 'Book him, Danno.'"

"You do not say 'Book him, Danno,'" I objected.

He grinned. "I'm chatting up one of the writers, seeing if she can work it in."

I rolled my eyes and rolled away.

Eating a salad back at the security office, I was surprised to see Edgar Ambrose come through the door. He wore a

Green Bay Packers sweatshirt over bike shorts that encased powerful thighs and showed off hairy calves. A sheen of sweat on his midnight-colored scalp made me think he'd been working out. "What are you doing here, Edgar?" I asked. "Isn't it nap time for you?" He was scheduled to work the midshift, which started at eleven p.m., so normally he slept during the day.

"Uh, I have a favor to ask, EJ." He looked uncharacteristically ill at ease.

Joel returned with a full carafe of water for the coffeemaker and gave Edgar a curious look.

"Sure."

"About my shift . . . would you switch?" When I didn't answer immediately, he added, "Just for tonight. It's the movie. I've got my portfolio"—he waved a binder I hadn't noticed—"and I want a shot at showing it to Mr. Vandelinde."

"And you're unlikely to run into him on the midshift."

"Right." He smiled his appreciation of my understanding, showing his gold canine tooth. "He made the Deadly Revenge series in the '90s."

He said it as if Vandelinde had sculpted *The Thinker* or painted the Sistine Chapel. I was tickled by his obsession with acting, because I'd never thought of him as being a performer, so I said, "Sure."

He heaved a sigh of relief. "I owe you."

As he left, I thought through my schedule. I could take a nap after work, before dinner with Mom and Ethan, and then come straight back to the mall. I'd be a little tired, but I'd powered through with less sleep on patrol in Afghanistan, so I knew I could do it. The mall was notoriously quiet at night, so my biggest problem would be staying awake, not like in the desert where I'd had to worry about al-Qaeda ambushing us or the like.

Joel stuck his mug under the stream of coffee pouring from the maker. "Edgar wants to be a movie star?"

"Apparently."

He thought about it a minute. "I can see it, I guess. He's sort of a bigger, tougher-looking Ving Rhames. Isn't he a bit old, though, to be trying to break in? He must be fifty."

"I guess you're never too old to take a stab at doing something you love."

Fourteen

· · ·

I'd thought it more than once, but Fernglen at night feels like a very different place than during the day. It's not the dark so much as the quiet. It was definitely darker, with only a hint of starlight dripping through the glass panels of the ceiling, and strips of low-level lighting—another cost-cutting measure—illuminating the corridors. The lights cast huge plant shadows on the walls, hosta leaf and fern silhouettes making the place feel like a prehistoric jungle. The shops were mostly dark, although a couple of the anchor stores had security lights on that emitted a faint glow from deep in their interiors. I Segwayed through the halls shortly after midnight, feeling the effect of too much good food and wine at my parents' house. If I sat in the security office watching the monitors, I'd be asleep faster than a five-year-old after a day at Disneyland.

Mom had avoided being alone with me in the most unob-trusive way possible after Dad's business associates left. She made sure Ethan or Grandpa was always in the room as she caught us up on my brother Clint's adventures—an investigative reporter, he was on his way to Libya—and mentioned casually that she'd be joining Ethan on the set the next day. Her blond hair shimmered in the candlelight from the forty or so candles of different heights ranged along the middle of the dining room table. One of the staff slid dessert plates in front of us and Mom gave her a quiet, "Thank you."

"Why?" I forked up a mouthful of crème brûlée and let it melt on my tongue.

"It's time to remind everyone that he's a married man." She cast him an affectionate look where he sat talking to Grandpa. "That woman is sending him letters again, and—"

"What woman?"

"I told you about her," Dad broke in. "I don't even read them, but your mom's taken over coping with my fan mail since Delia left, making a big to-do out of nothing." He raised his wineglass to Mom, the cut crystal glinting in the candlelight.

"She's sick, Ethan," Mom said. "And the tone of the letters is getting disturbing. It was one thing when she mooned on about how wonderful you are, how handsome, how talented."

"A discerning woman," Ethan murmured, pouring himself more of the Syrah. I covered my glass when he moved to refill it. I had to go back to work in a couple of hours.

Mom tossed a cloth napkin at Ethan. "Now she's going on about faithfulness."

"I'm the most faithful man in Hollywood." He smiled at Mom.

She returned his smile and reached her hand across the table. "I know that, sweetie. That's why you still have your manhood attached."

Cracking a laugh, he squeezed her hand and released it. I relaxed against the padded seat back, savoring my last inch of wine and thinking how nice it was to have parents who enjoyed each other, even after thirty-four years together. I tried not to let the image of Ethan comforting Zoë, or my mother's evasiveness about her early morning mall visit, intrude.

Grandpa leaned forward, elbows on the table. "Have you given the letters to the police? There are stalking laws."

Ethan nodded. "Delia turned them over to the cops, oh, six or eight months ago. They looked into it, but didn't get very far. Nothing to go on, apparently."

"Where were they mailed from?"

"You'd have to ask Delia." Ethan shrugged his lack of concern.

"Do you still have the note?" Grandpa asked.

"I'll get it." Mom rose in one fluid movement and left the room, returning in a couple of minutes with a piece of pink notepaper. "Funny. There's no envelope with it. When the studio boxes up the fan mail and sends it, they usually clip the envelope to the letter in case you want to reply, hon. Delia sent signed photos to everyone who wrote. Maybe the envelope got lost."

"Or the writer dropped off the note at the studio office— didn't mail it," Grandpa said.

"We should turn it over to the police," I said, reaching for it. "They can compare notes with their colleagues in Malibu."

Grandpa beat me to it, snatching the letter from Mom's hand. "I've got a friend in the FBI who owes me," he said, tucking it into the interior pocket of his navy blazer. "The police can have a go at it when she's done with it."

Since neither Mom nor Ethan objected, I let Grandpa

keep it. "Your mail is certainly more interesting than mine, Ethan." I raised my glass in a silent toast. "I get grocery circulars, Lands' End catalogs, and credit card come-ons. You get love letters from wack-jobs and threats from anti-violence/antimaterialist activists. To the joys of stardom!" I drained my glass.

Now, trundling down the empty corridors, I thought a bit about the note Ethan had gotten in his trailer and wondered if the police had had any luck tracking down the group that must be responsible for it. I sighed. It was unlikely that they'd had anything to do with Zoë's death; it hardly made sense to campaign against violence and then stab someone to make your point. Come to think of it, though, that wasn't too different from what radical abortion foes did when they chanted "pro-life" and then went off and shot doctors. I shouldn't assume the note writer or writers weren't involved.

It struck me that I was letting myself get distracted. Where did every homicide investigation begin? With the victim. I didn't know nearly enough about Zoë Winters. I had no hope of learning more about her death, since Detective Helland wasn't going to let me see the autopsy report or share information about the knives he'd collected on the movie set, but I could probably learn more about Zoë's life: who her friends were, what she did when she wasn't working, whether she had any enemies or supported controversial causes. If I could talk to Margot again, or maybe the guy who was Zoë's assistant . . . What had Grandpa said his name was? Gavin? No, Grayson something. I'd contact—

A *thump* brought my head around. There shouldn't be any thumping in a deserted mall at almost one o'clock in the morning. I stopped and listened. The sound didn't come again. It was probably nothing, but I purred toward the maintenance hall where I'd heard the noise. The only things back here were utility rooms and a large storage area where the mall kept holiday decorations, tables and chairs, a collapsible dais, a portable dance floor and mats for visiting dancers and tumblers, and stacks and boxes of other stuff I'd never investigated. The hall was cement-floored and the walls an institutional gray, scuffed where top-heavy dollies had banged into them. A single fluorescent bulb sputtered overhead, making a sound like a fly buzzing against a window.

I was mainly going through the motions, happy to have something more concrete to do than putt-putt up and down the hall, but that changed when I noticed one of the two doors leading to the storage room was ajar. It should've been closed and locked. Wanting more mobility, I got off the Segway and approached the door, moving silently and wishing I had a Taser, at least, although that would be overkill if the source of the sound turned out to be a rat or a Christmas wreath tumbling off its stack.

"Hello?" I pushed the door wide, standing off to the side.

Scuffling noises came from deep within the storage room and adrenaline flooded through me. Someone was in there! I reached a hand around the door and felt for the light switch, calling, "Fernglen Security." I didn't think that was likely to scare an intruder like "Stop! Police!" would've done. Still, you work with what you've got.

My questing fingers finally found the switch and light flooded the room. Rows of gray metal shelves created a maze, and I heard footsteps from deep within, and then the sound of a door opening and banging shut. Damn. Whoever it was was getting away. The long storage area had a door

on its far end that opened to the outside, to facilitate delivery
and movement of the larger items stored here. Moving as
quickly as I could, I threaded my way through the shelf
maze to the door, finding it solidly closed. I yanked it open
and stared into the dark inlet that allowed access to the
storage room on one side and backed to the Sears loading
dock on the other. A metal Dumpster gaped open, the only
object in sight. Whoever had been in the storage room had
hightailed it out to the main parking lot. I listened for the
sound of a car, but didn't hear anything. He was probably
halfway to the highway by now.

Pulling the door closed, I tested it to ensure it latched
properly. It did. The intruder hadn't gained access this way,
so he must have entered through the doors I'd come in. Had
maintenance left them unlocked? Possible, I supposed. Or
someone could have slipped in and hidden while crews were
moving stuff in and out. I retraced my steps slowly, looking
for something out of place or missing. I couldn't imagine a
thief would find the room's contents interesting: there
couldn't be much market for an inflatable, twenty-foot-tall
jack-o-lantern or the hundred-some-odd American flags the
mall hung up to celebrate the Fourth of July.

Off to one side, a low stack of blue mats, the kind gym-
nasts used, was slightly askew. A flash of red caught my eye.
I approached and found a half-full can of Coke. Had someone from maintenance set it down, maybe days ago, and
forgotten about it? Or . . . I searched around the mats and
saw something lodged between them and the wall. Reaching
into the crevice, I pulled out a jacket. A dark green jacket
like the one I'd seen Jesse Willard wearing yesterday when
he fled the mall. It didn't take me two seconds to realize
Jesse had been hiding here, safe and warm, while his father

and the police searched for him. It took me only a further two seconds to do what I knew I needed to: phone the police.

The unkind side of me had been hoping the operator who took my report would wake Detective Helland and get him out of bed at two in the morning; however, it was a pair of patrol cops who showed up to see where I'd found Jesse Willard and retrieve his jacket.

"We'll search the area," one of them promised me.

I knew they wouldn't find Jesse. In the almost half an hour it had taken the officers to arrive, he could have gotten anywhere in Vernonville or its environs, or driven halfway to Richmond or D.C. if he had a vehicle. "You might check at his house," I suggested.

"Yes, ma'am, we'll do that."

"And make sure Detective Helland knows. Mr. Willard is a sus—a witness in one of his cases."

"I'm sure he'll be by in the morning to talk to you," the skinny cop said, nudging a mat into line with his foot.

They left and I finished my patrol before drifting back to the office. I felt strangely let down. I knew it was the aftereffect of the adrenaline surge and the brief chase. Watching a whole lot of nothing on the monitors, I rubbed my knee, which hadn't liked the twisty-turny running I'd done through the storage room, and felt my eyelids drifting down. I forced myself to get up and make a pot of strong coffee, hoping the caffeine would keep me awake. Writing up the incident in our online logbook kept me occupied for fifteen minutes, but then I started to get sleepy again. I didn't know how Edgar did this night after night.

I glimpsed movement on the cameras and made myself focus. It was a van cruising through the garage. I perked up a little bit. In all probability, it was an early-bird commuter using our garage for a day's free parking while he rode into work with a buddy, but three thirty was a bit early for even the most Type A worker bee. The van motored out of the camera's view and I wondered if it had parked or left the garage. Drug deals on mall property were not unheard of, and I decided that a quick reconnoiter in the brisk morning air was just the ticket for keeping me awake.

I Segwayed to the garage entrance by Macy's and entered the dark space. Even without cars, it felt crowded, with low ceilings and lots of concrete pillars smeared with red and green and blue paint from cars whose drivers had cut a corner too close. Dim lights glowed from over the elevator and the "EXIT" sign near the stairs, and from wall fixtures mounted every fifty feet or so. That still left a lot of room for shadows. I thought I heard an engine growling from the other side of the garage and down a level, so I descended the ramp on my Segway, letting it run at top speed—about twelve miles per hour—enjoying the motion and the feel of the wind tugging at my hair.

A couple of cars sat trunk-in to the wall on the lower level and I felt their hoods as I passed them. Cold. They'd been here for hours. It wasn't unusual for people to leave cars in the garage overnight or for a couple of days, although we didn't encourage the practice. I knew of at least one instance where a man had been meeting his mistress here, leaving his SUV, and driving to her place in her car so no one would spot his ride outside her place or at a motel. I suspected he wasn't the only one using the garage to facilitate illicit rendezvous. I cruised through both levels of the garage, which had exits on the north and south sides, but saw no one. Whoever it was had gone. No biggie.

I emerged into the predawn morning and looked up at a

night sky spattered with stars. We're far enough from D.C. and Richmond to escape most of their light pollution, and I trundled along at a slow pace for some moments, face to the sky. If I tuned out the faint sounds of traffic from nearby streets, it was almost like being in Afghanistan, where the stars seemed so much closer to the earth than they usually do here. Maybe that was because there was no humidity in the desert, imposing a moisture veil between me and the stars. After a few more seconds of stargazing, I started to shiver and reminded myself that I needed to replace my uniform Windbreaker.

Back inside, my fingers tingled from the warmth. It was almost four thirty, and I decided to scoot over to the main entrance where the mall walkers congregated to remind them that we weren't opening that morning because of the filming. We'd posted signs for a couple of weeks, but experience had taught me that there would be people standing outside the doors, inches from the signs, expecting to be let in as usual. Four people stood waiting for me to open the mall and all of them grumbled when I explained that we weren't allowing walkers this morning.

"I can't have a banana chocolate chip muffin with my latte this morning if I don't burn three hundred calories walking first," one woman moaned.

Unless she was eating the world's smallest muffins, she needed to burn at least twice that many calories to work it off, but I didn't mention that. I exercised to stay sane, not to keep my weight in check, and it amazed me how some people go through life making mental calculations about calories in and calories out. How do they enjoy either eating or exercising that way? The thought brought Joel to mind; I'd been trying to help him get started on a regular exercise program because he was trying to lose weight for a woman he liked. He hadn't joined me at the pool in several days and I needed to poke him.

Once the doors were secured again, I returned to the security office, where I found Edgar Ambrose already waiting. He sat at a desk, working a crossword puzzle, but looked up when I came through the doors.

"You're early," I said. It was not quite five o'clock and he wasn't due in for the day shift until seven.

"It's my thank-you," he said, smiling broadly. "For taking my shift. A mid's tough when you're used to days."

"You've got that right," I said, not about to complain about getting off-shift early. "It seems harder than it used to. I must be getting old."

Edgar laughed. "Just wait."

Pulling up the log, I briefed him about chasing an unknown intruder through the storage room. "The police took a report. If Detective Helland stops by, tell him he can call me any time after noon. I'll be sleeping until then." I yawned.

"Will do." Edgar gave me a two-fingered salute.

"Good luck with impressing Vandelinde," I said.

I left Edgar to man the fort and walked to my Miata, parked in its usual spot outside Macy's. After unlocking it, I dumped my gym bag in the passenger seat and slid onto my seat with a sigh. My bed was going to feel good. As I thunked the door closed and started the engine, I glanced in the rearview mirror. A man's head and shoulders rose up at the passenger-side window and I screamed.

Fifteen

. . .

I scrabbled at the door to make sure it was locked, but then processed the man's muffled voice saying something through the window.

"EJ, it's me. Calm down."

I unlocked the door. "Jay?" The relief rushing through me immediately turned to anger as he slid into the seat, wincing. "You scared me to death! What the hell are you doing hiding behind my car?"

I could barely make out his face in the near darkness, but his voice sounded weak when he said, "It's complicated. Can we get out of here and I'll tell you about it at my place? Can you drive me home?"

My faculties returning now that fear wasn't freezing my brain, I shifted until I faced him straight-on. His right arm was wrapped around his midsection, clasping his side, and his face looked pinched and white. "Are you hurt?"

"Let's just go, okay?"

"I'm taking you to a hospital," I said, sliding down in my seat and restarting the engine.

"No!"

A car entered the lot, its headlights glancing over the Miata, and Jay slumped down. "I don't need a doctor," he said in a low voice. "Just take me home. Please?" He gave me an address.

Against my better judgment, I put the car in gear and drove out of the lot. He gave me low-voiced directions and I navigated the quiet, mostly sleeping streets of Vernonville to his condo, a second-floor unit in a large complex built around a swimming pool. "You can park near that truck," Jay said.

Without comment, I parked and opened the door, coming around to help Jay get out. He gave a strangled yelp when I caught his arm, and I saw dark streaks on his shirt. "Are you bleeding?" I asked, regretting not driving him to a doctor.

"Oh, undoubtedly." He managed a weak grin.

The blood seemed to be seeping from along his rib cage, so I hurried to his unhurt side, slipped my arm around his waist, and draped his arm over my shoulders. "Let me help."

Without arguing—which told me he was really in pain—he let me help him up the walk to the heavy wooden door. "Keys . . . pocket," he gasped.

I fumbled in his jeans pocket for his keys, fighting down my embarrassment, and opened the door. I studied the flight of stairs that rose directly in front of us and gave him a look.

"I can do it." He gritted his teeth and put a foot on the first step.

It took us several minutes and a lot of sweat, but we made it to the landing. The dome light attached to the ceiling illuminated the strain in Jay's face. I quickly opened the door to his condo and guided him to the first couch I saw. "Sit."

He sank onto the tan microfiber with a wince. Peeling his arm away from his midsection, he looked at the blood streaking his tee shirt. "Damn."

"Let me see." Without waiting for permission, I carefully rolled the shirt upward, exposing a furrow along his side, skin curling away, blood oozing. I recognized a bullet wound when I saw one—heaven knows I'd seen enough of them in the desert—and I gave him a sharp look. "Busy night?" I asked.

He ignored my sarcasm. "You could say that." He tried to grin, but scrunched his eyes shut in pain.

I headed for the kitchen to fetch hot water, a bowl, scissors from a knife block, and a clean cloth, and then asked, "Bandages?"

"Bathroom. My bedroom," Jay said through gritted teeth.

Normally, I'd have been curious, in an academic sort of way, of course, about his bedroom, but now I marched through it without a glance and opened the medicine chest in his beige-and-white-tiled bathroom. I found gauze pads, stretchy gauze wrap, first-aid tape, antibiotic ointment, alcohol, and a box of butterfly Steri-Strip wound closures. My, the man was either a walking accident or he was prepared for the kind of eventuality that faced us today. I washed my hands thoroughly, gathered up the first-aid paraphernalia, and carried it into the living room.

"Nurse Ratched, I presume?" Jay said.

"You clearly don't want to go to a hospital and have them report the GSW," I said, arranging the stuff on a glass coffee table, "so you're going to have to put up with my efforts. I'll have you know I was never even a Girl Scout, so this is amateur hour at its finest." I cut his tee shirt off, knowing it would hurt too much for him to stretch his arms overhead and shrug it off. "I hope this wasn't your favorite Guns N' Roses shirt."

"Concert. Nineteen ninety-three. Buenos Aires."

I dabbed at the inches-long furrow with an alcohol-dampened pad and Jay caught his breath on a hiss. "You must have had some self-aid and buddy care training in the air force," he said, clearly trying to distract himself from the pain.

"I did, of course," I admitted.

"John Wayne would have a bullet to bite on in this situation."

"And a bottle of whiskey," I agreed, squeezing most of the tube of antibiotic cream directly onto the wound. I used my thumb and forefinger to bring the edges of his skin closer together and secured them every quarter inch with the butterfly bandages. "Sorry," I said when he grunted.

"You're doing great." He lapsed into silence, breathing shallowly.

I worked as quickly as I could, padding the wound area with gauze and then securing the whole with strips of tape that stood out whitely against the tanned skin of his flat abdomen. "Lean forward." When he complied, I fastened the tape around the back of his rib cage, noting a sprinkling of reddish hair and freckles on his back. For some reason, the sight of his bare back made me want to cry and I leaned away from him, saying briskly, "That should hold."

Jay eyed me and for a moment I thought he spotted the almost-tears in my eyes. "Thanks," he said, leaning back carefully against the sofa cushions.

"About that whiskey . . ."

"Pantry, top right shelf." I left him in the living room and found the bottle of Jim Beam in the pantry. Pouring two fingers, I plopped a couple of ice cubes in and brought it back to the living room, along with a glass of water.

Jay reached for the bourbon, but I thrust the water glass into his hand, along with four ibuprofen pills. "Alcohol and painkillers don't mix," I said, taking a long sip of the Jim Beam. It burned its way down my throat and I tried to think if this was the first time I'd drunk whiskey at the crack of dawn.

Jay popped all four pills in his mouth at once and swallowed them with the entire glass of water. I set my whiskey on the table with a crack and collapsed into a barrel chair in the same tan microsuede as the couch. Glancing around for the first time, I noted lots of tan and glass. "This isn't where you really live," I announced. I didn't know how I knew, I just did. The place reflected nothing of Jay.

"No," he admitted with a lopsided smile.

"I think it's time you tell me what's going on," I said, looking him straight in the eyes. His were hazel with long lashes that seemed almost black, in contrast to his dark auburn hair. "Something's happening at my ma—at Fernglen—and I want to know what it is. Who do you work for?"

"I suppose the 'I'm a small businessman trying to make a living selling cookies' line isn't going to work?"

He was stalling, trying to figure out how much to tell me. I shook my head. "Uh-uh."

When he still hesitated, I got to my feet, suddenly angry. "Fine. If you can't trust me, I'll be going. Find someone else to play doctor the next time you get shot."

"Wait, EJ." Jay held out a hand. I remained standing, staring down at him. "I used to be with the FBI," he finally said.

I sat again. "Used to be?"

He nodded, eyes fixed on me, gauging my reaction. "I found the bureaucracy . . . stifling. I'm not a suit-and-tie kind of guy." He gestured to his jeans and the ruined rock concert tee shirt on the sofa.

I suddenly became aware that his chest was bare except for the bandage. "Are you cold?" I asked. "Do you want me to get you a shirt?"

He half smiled, like he realized his bare chest was distracting me. "I'm fine."

"Fine." I crossed my arms over my chest. "You were saying you got tossed out of the FBI . . ."

Chuckling, he said, "I resigned. Turned in my badge. There was this case . . . well, you don't need the gory details. Suffice it to say that I didn't see eye to eye with my superiors on the way it played out. A little boy died." He rolled the water glass between his palms, gazing into it as if it contained the secrets of the universe.

"So, now you work for . . .?"

"Myself." He said it sharply, then looked up at me and softened the word with a twist of his mouth. "I'm a consultant, a contractor."

My brows drew together. "And what are you consulting on that requires you to pretend to be a cookie mogul, live in a prefurnished condo"—I gestured to the room—"and get shot? Somehow, I don't think you're consulting on management practices or software systems."

"No. I'm a recovery agent. Things get lost or stolen and I find them."

My brows soared. He said it as simply as if he'd claimed "I'm a mortgage broker" or "I paint houses." I'd never met anyone who called himself a recovery agent. "What kinds of things? Who do you work for?"

"Insurance companies, usually."

I thought about something my brother Clint had done a story on six months back. "Do you do kidnap recoveries? Are you working for companies who do business in South America, arranging ransom drops when their executives get kidnapped?"

He shook his head. "No, that's a very specialized business. I have no interest in being involved in a kidnapping case ever again."

The way he said it made me think his last FBI case, the one where a boy died, had involved a kidnapping. "Well, then, what?"

He drew a deep breath, then winced at the pressure on his wound. "It varies. This time around, it's diamonds."

"Diamonds? Engagement rings?" I waggled my fourth finger. "Harry Winston and tennis bracelets?"

"Uncut stones."

I studied the grim set of his jaw. "You're serious."

"As a heart attack. My fee is ten percent of the recovery. Since the stones are worth somewhere in the neighborhood of twenty-five mil, my cut—pardon the pun—will be two point five mil. It doesn't get much more serious than that."

I whistled.

He seemed pleased with my reaction. "Exactly."

Needing time to think, I took his empty water glass into the kitchen and refilled it, getting a glass for myself at the same time. I definitely didn't need any more bourbon. Returning to the living room, I asked, "So what are you doing at Fernglen? And who tried to put a bullet into you?"

"I wish I knew the answer to that one," Jay said, accepting the glass. His fingers brushed mine and I felt the slight contact all the way up my arm. I started to return to my chair, but Jay tugged on my wrist and said, "Sit here."

Warily, I settled on the couch. He'd wedged a pillow behind his back and was propped against the armrest, one leg stretched out on the sofa and the other draping off the side.

"I should start at the beginning," Jay resumed his story. "Three months ago, a consignment of diamonds went missing somewhere between Africa and Amsterdam. Jewel-grade stones ranging in size from half a carat to almost thirty carats. Of course, they won't be that big when they're cut."

"Of course not," I said mock-solemnly, like I knew anything about diamonds.

"The corporation who owned them—"

"De Beers?" Okay, so I knew that much about diamonds.

"Confidentiality is important to my clients," Jay said. "Anyway, the company wants their diamonds back. They want them retrieved discreetly, with no fanfare. If word hit the street about the theft, it could play havoc with the price of diamonds on the international market and it might make other thieves take a shot at heisting more of my client's merchandise."

I was too tired to really take in what he was telling me. I returned to the point that most interested me. "So why are you at Fernglen?"

Stretching, he set his foot on my thigh and let it rest there. There was something incredibly intimate in the gesture and it unsettled me. My hand would naturally have fallen to his ankle, but I felt self-conscious about that and instead laid my arm across the sofa back.

"An informant," Jay said. "My client learned the diamonds had been smuggled into the U.S. and that some of them had been cut, set, and sold. Before she was killed—"

I gasped and Jay nodded grimly. "Traffic 'accident.'

Before she was killed, she pointed us at Fernglen. You know the rest. I arranged to take over the Lola's so I could observe the comings and goings at the mall, see if I could figure out who was distributing the diamonds. I thought at first that they must be going through one of the jewelry stores—"

Fernglen had three jewelry stores—one chain store that had been there for years, and two independents, one of which had opened since I'd been at the mall.

"—but now I'm not sure. There're too many diamonds to funnel them all through a single jewelry store, and several of them, rare colored stones, are too distinctive to sell on the open market anyway."

My head was whirling, a combination of Jay's closeness, his story, and my tiredness. "The gunshot wound?"

"You know I've been keeping track of some activity in the garage."

I nodded. I'd more than once stumbled over Jay lurking in the garage at odd hours.

"I was tailing the new partner at Yalenian & Son Jewelers. His bona fides don't quite check out. Anyway, after dinner in Richmond, he drove all the way back here and turned into the garage. I couldn't risk him making me, so I left my car at the Olympus construction site and came over on foot. By the time I got to the garage, he had disappeared. I took the stairs to the second level and as I came through the door, someone shot at me."

"Did you see anything? Get a description?" The cop in me took over.

He shook his head, disgusted with himself. "I never even knew he was there until the gun fired. I dove back through the stairwell door and heard a car take off."

I wondered if it was the van I had seen on the camera. If so, we might be able to determine make and model. I told

Jay that and he perked up. "Let's take a look tomorrow. Anyway, I was losing blood and knew I wouldn't be able to drive myself home, couldn't risk going to the hospital and having the police blow my cover by getting all excited about a GSW, and I'd seen your car in the lot when I arrived, so I hid behind it and waited, hoping you weren't going to work a double shift." He grinned weakly.

"What's your next step?" I asked.

"Take a nap." His eyelids were drooping and I realized I was as tired as he looked.

"Sounds good." I gently lifted his leg and slid out from under it. He barely stirred. Returning to his bedroom, I retrieved the red blanket folded at the foot of his bed and draped it over him. Auburn stubble shadowed his jaw and his lips were slightly parted. Without thinking, I leaned over, intending to kiss him. I stopped with my mouth a hair's breadth from his lips. I was tired. I'd had too much whiskey. This was stupid.

I started to pull back and Jay surprised me by lifting his head so his lips grazed mine. Even that light touch set the blood thrumming in my head—and other places—and I was lost. I leaned toward him and our kiss deepened. Our lips were our only point of contact but the sensation was so intense, the heat that grew in me so all-consuming, that I drew away moments later, shuddering.

Eyes still shut, Jay said softly, "I dare you to try that again when I haven't been shot. In fact"—his eyes snapped open and he didn't look nearly so sleepy—"you should try it again now. It's only a flesh wound after all." He waggled his eyebrows.

Folding my lips in to suppress my smile, I turned away. "Never let it be said I took advantage of an injured man," I said primly, dragging my keys from my pocket. Even though

I really, really wanted to take advantage of this wounded man. The keys clinked in my inexplicably trembling hands.

"I would never say that," he promised, but his eyelids were drooping again and I think he was asleep before I was out the door.

Sixteen

. . .

Back at Fernglen that afternoon in jeans and a sweater, greatly refreshed by six hours of sleep, I searched for Grayson Whoever, the guy who had taken over as weapons master. I was trying not to let my brain worry at Jay's story, and had resisted the urge to casually stroll through each of the mall's jewelry stores, looking for a mother lode of stolen/ smuggled diamonds. As if they'd be displayed in plain sight, I scoffed at myself, or hidden beneath the leaves of a rubber plant in the sales area. The thought of all the criminal activity brought me up short: surely, if the diamonds had been smuggled into the U.S., some law enforcement entity was on the lookout for the diamonds and the thieves. INTER-POL? U.S. Customs? The FBI? My tiredness had fuzzed my brain, keeping me from recognizing all the vague spots in Jay's story.

Focusing on Zoë Winters's death, I asked a guard where I could find Grayson. The guard, used to seeing me around by now, pointed a beefy finger at a trailer parked on the far side of the fenced-in area. Two faux policemen clattered down the stairs as I approached, chatting with each other about an upcoming audition. The door remained open and I knocked lightly before pushing in to the room. A narrow counter topped with a computer and a fat three-ring binder was immediately on my left. Shelves and cubbies made up the rest of the trailer, most filled with what I assumed were props.

"Yes?" A skinny man in his late twenties looked at me over the rims of Harry Potter glasses. Dishwater-colored hair was brushed straight back from a pale, narrow brow, and he looked like he'd have been more at home in an academic library, researching his dissertation, than on a movie set, unloading a box of switchblades. He held one up, pushed a button, and light streaked down the blade as it sprang up.

"Grayson?"

"Grayson Bleek," he acknowledged. "Who are you?"

I introduced myself, letting my gaze wander around the shelf-filled space. I could hardly take in the variety of stuff in the trailer, ranging from staplers and mugs that might go on a desk, to plants and ottomans, and a seven-foot-tall stuffed giraffe. What in the world—? "Is this all the stuff that's in the movie?"

"Good God, no." Bleek looked at me pityingly. "We've rented storage units for most of it."

I blinked. "Being props master must be a complicated job."

"Absolutely." He puffed out his thin chest, covered by a logoed tee shirt under a maroon denim vest. "It requires an exacting eye for detail, the treasure-hunting instincts of Indiana Jones, and the diplomatic skills of Kissinger for coordinating with the set and costume designers, lighting, and the continuity people. I was the assistant props master, but I suppose you've heard about Zoë."

I was relieved he'd brought her name up first. "Had you worked together before?"

"First time. She was one of the best in the biz, though." He propped his skinny rear on a stool and set down the knife. As if that made him aware of it, he patted the box. "The police took all our knives to see if . . . We had to replace them. Had them overnighted. Thank God they got here in time. Van would pop a gasket if we had to delay shooting or rearrange the schedule again tomorrow."

"Do you know if the police found anything on the knives that would help them identify the killer?"

I got the pitying look again. "Do I look like someone the police would confide in? They haven't been back to arrest anyone, as far as I know. I can tell you"—he leaned across the narrow counter—"that we only handed over twelve knives."

"So?"

"So, we started with thirteen." Bleek watched for my reaction.

"Did you keep the knives locked up?"

"The police asked the same question. No. We keep the guns secured"—he jerked his head toward a gun safe behind him—"but the knives didn't get any special treatment. I mean, knives aren't like guns. We've all got one or a dozen in our kitchens, don't we? Guns are different, though. I'm all for strict gun laws. Violence is out of control in this country and we need to do something about it."

"Uh-huh. Would Tab Gentry have had any reason to have a knife for his role?"

"That the extra who got fired?"

I nodded.

"Maybe. I know there's a scene where the cops disarm a couple of the bad guys after a knife fight, but I don't know if this Gentry was one of them."

So Gentry might well have had access to a switchblade. Interesting. I took another tack. "What was Zoë like?"

"A perfectionist," he answered immediately. "One coffeepot out of place, one frame not on the inventory, one stuffed giraffe not on set when it's needed, and *wham!*" He clapped his palms together. "Outa here. Sayonara. Don't let the door hit you on your way out."

"She was tough, huh?"

"Like I said, a perfectionist. It's what made her so good at the job."

"But some people must have resented that." I arched my brows, inviting him to dish the dirt.

His eyes slid from side to side, as if checking to make sure no one had snuck into the trailer while we talked. "Well. I only got on as her assistant because Zoë fired the woman who originally had the job before we ever left California. And one of the actors got fired the other day because he shot off a blank, and—"

Old news.

"—I figure she must have been hard to live with, if you know what I mean?" Ducking his chin, he looked at me over the rims of the Potter glasses.

It took me a moment. "You mean Margot?"

"You didn't hear it here," he said coyly, twiddling a loose button on his vest, "but they had a real catfight the other day. Monday. Right here." He pointed to the trailer floor. "I was in the back, doing inventory, and I don't think they knew I was here. In fact, I know they didn't. And after they started going at it, there was no way I was making a peep." He drew his thumb and forefinger across his lips as if zipping them.

"Wha—" I didn't even have to finish the question.

"Apparently Miss Zoë had been stepping out on her girl-friend," Bleek said, scraping one forefinger the length of the other in a naughty-naughty gesture. "Margot was PO'd. And I mean with a capital P and a capital O. Zoë said something about how they didn't own each other, and Margot said she felt sorry for Zoë because her self-esteem depended on her being able to attract sleazy tramps who didn't have the brainpower or fidelity of a dragonfly. I've got to remember that one. Anyway, that's when Zoë slapped her."

"Zoë hit Margot?"

"Whappa." He mimed a slap in the air. "It was quiet for a good thirty seconds after that and then I heard the door open and close twice, like Margot ran out and then Zoë went after her."

"How do you know Zoë hit Margot and not the other way around?"

I got the pitying look again. "Have you met Margot?" When I nodded, he went on, "Well, there's your answer. Margot wouldn't swat a mosquito. Zoë, on the other hand . . . Margot's lucky the guns were locked up."

I gave him a disbelieving stare.

"Oh, yeah," he nodded. "Zoë was a spitfire. Her being the weapons master was a perfect fit. She was a great shot, had fencing training, and was really into weapons. Suppos-edly has a collection of World War Two guns or some such, but I've never seen it. Me, on the other hand, I'm the last person who should be weapons master because I hardly know which side of the knife to slice a tomato with. But I'm stuck with it until they can hire someone else. I hear they're considering some former SEAL who's right down the road in Annapolis. Better him than me." He pulled a knife from the box, checked something on its handle, and made an entry in an online database.

Turning to get another knife, Bleek brushed against a stack of papers on the counter and they spilled. I bent to retrieve them, freezing when I recognized the top page. "Where did you get this?" I asked, holding up the page on which it said "Stop making movies that glorify violence and capitalist materialism or we'll stop you." Black type on a white page, like Ethan's, with a graphic of a knife dripping red blood. It matched the red of the stapler that had been weighting the pile down.

"That?" He made a dismissive gesture. "It was on the floor, like someone had slipped it under the door, when I came in—what?—day before yesterday. I meant to throw it away."

"Mind if I keep it?"

He hesitated for a moment, as if wondering why I'd want the page, then shrugged. "Knock yourself out."

With a word of thanks and a "nice to meet you," I headed for the door. On the threshold, I stopped. "Uh, the giraffe?" I asked.

Bleek smiled, showing small teeth. "There's a scene in a toy store. The giraffe gets it." He mimed holding a gun in both hands and jerked his hands up. "Boom. The hit man is chasing Ethan but kills the giraffe instead. We bought twelve of them."

Outside the trailer, I paused. It was beginning to look like a large portion of the movie crew had received photocopied "stop making violent movies" notes. Who else had received one? Did it matter? I made a mental note to ask around and to find out from Detective Helland if the police had learned anything from Ethan's note.

Glancing around to make sure no one was watching, I tapped on Ethan's trailer door.

"It's open," he called.

I pushed the door inward and found Ethan and my mom seated at the dinette table, playing cards.

"Thank God you're here, EJ," Ethan said, throwing down his hand. "I owe your mother a million dollars."

"Really?" I kissed Mom's cheek.

"I'm going to collect it in kind," Mom said with a twinkle in her eye. Her blond hair was smoothed off her face in a French braid, and she looked young and vital in blue jeans and an oversized white blouse with the cuffs rolled up. "We're buying season tickets to the San Francisco Opera and your dad's going with me to every production."

Ethan grabbed his throat and made gagging noises. Opera was not his thing.

"Be grateful it's not the ballet," Mom said severely, piling the cards together and sliding them into the box. "What are you up to, darling?" she asked.

Helping myself to a bottled water from the fridge, I told them about almost running into Jesse Willard—I assumed—on the night shift.

"I don't like your working all night," Ethan frowned. "It's dangerous. And it's bad for your health."

"I don't do it often," I said. "And it's not dangerous." If you discounted people getting shot in the garage, as Jay had.

"No filming today?" I asked to change the subject.

"Got a couple scenes in the can this morning. Van's taking a long lunch with the investors. We're resuming later this afternoon—doing a couple of interior scenes. Tomorrow's the big love scene." He shot a mischievous glance at Mom, who smiled, unperturbed.

"Who with?"

"Anya, of course. My character, Hunter, falls for Antonia while protecting her. They have a steamy encounter on an old tugboat that's interrupted when the hit man blows a hole in the boat and it sinks. Once Hunter rescues Antonia and kills the hit man, he agrees to change his name and enter witness protection with her. The last scene is the two of them having the bandages unwrapped from their faces following plastic surgery to have their appearances changed."

"Nothing says 'romance' like getting a new nose for the one you love," I observed.

Mom laughed. Ethan looked a little hurt. "That was my addition to the script," he said.

Oops. A thought crossed my mind. "Where are you filming the love scene?"

"On a tugboat our locations manager spotted somewhere on Chesapeake Bay. He had it brought to Colonial Beach because it's closer," Ethan said. "It's about an hour from here."

"Any chance I could bring a friend along to watch the filming?" I asked, thinking of Edgar. He'd have a better chance of actually talking to Van on a confined set than in the middle of a mall action shoot. Maybe Ethan could finagle him a couple of minutes' conversation with the famous director.

"Sure," Ethan said happily, reading my request as increased interest in the moviemaking business, I was sure. He got down on the dense carpet and began doing sit-ups. "I'll be shirtless tomorrow," he said between crunches. "Gotta work on my six-pack."

Mom gave him an indulgent smile and I escaped from the trailer, knowing I couldn't get anything out of her with Ethan around. I'd catch her alone later and make her tell me whatever she was hiding about Tuesday morning. Not for one second did I think she'd killed Zoë; however, I was darn sure she knew more than she was saying, and I knew that if

Helland identified her on the camera video, he'd have her in a police interrogation room faster than Fubar could catch a mouse.

Telling the dog barking at me from Anya Vale's trailer to hush, I strolled into the mall, thinking I should call Jay to make sure he was still alive. As it turned out, I didn't have to call because when I turned into the food court I spotted him handing cookies to a geriatric couple. He moved a bit stiffly, but otherwise didn't look like someone who'd been shot less than twenty-four hours earlier. As the old couple left the Lola's counter, I hurried over.

"What are you doing here?" I asked in a low voice.

"Hello to you, too," Jay said, his eyes telling me he liked the way my teal sweater contrasted with my chestnut hair.

"Hello. You took a bullet last night."

"It's only a flesh wound," he said in a weird British accent.

I stared at him.

"Monty Python?"

I shook my head, and he sighed as if I'd disappointed him greatly.

"Are you really okay?" I asked.

"Sore," he admitted, "but a handful of ibuprofen every few hours works wonders."

"Why didn't you stay home today?" I bit my tongue; I sounded like a worried girlfriend . . . or worse, his mother.

"We independent small business owners can't afford to be lazing around in bed all day watching *All My Children* and *Ellen*," he said, smiling over my shoulder at a slender woman who looked like she was trying to decide if a chocolate macadamia nut cookie fit into the day's eating plan.

I turned back to him as the woman drifted away, apparently deciding she hadn't spent long enough on the StairMaster that morning to justify a cookie. Before I could say anything else, Kyra appeared, a vision in wide-legged terra-cotta-colored pants with a boat-necked shirt. Her hair was braided at the crown and flowed loose from about ear level and her smile lit up the food court. "My best friend and my favorite cookie man," she greeted us. "I'll have the usual, please."

While Jay fetched her cookie, Kyra looked from me to him and waggled her brows, clearly picking up on some new vibe between us. I frowned her down and had a smile back on my face by the time Jay handed her an oatmeal raisin cookie and a cup of coffee. We chit-chatted about the scene the movie company had filmed that morning—apparently having Ethan splash into the fountain had excited all onlookers, especially when he emerged with his shirt soaked transparent—and then a line formed for cookies and Kyra and I walked off.

"Are you coming to my bout tomorrow evening?" she asked.

Kyra had taken up roller derby a couple years back and I got a kick out of watching her skate. "Wouldn't miss it," I assured her. "Dinner after?"

"Absolutely. I want to hear all about what's going on between you and Mr. Chunky Chocolate Chip."

I felt myself blushing and was furious. "Nothing's going on."

Kyra laughed. "You can't kid a kidder, Eej. How was he?"

"We didn't—There might have been a kiss," I finally admitted.

"A kiss?" She shook her head, grinning. "If he can light you up like this with just a kiss, I can't imagine—"

"Then don't." I'd spent most of the day trying not to imagine, not very successfully. More imaginings finagled their way into my head and I must have blushed again because Kyra shook her head, chuckling. To distract her, I told her about my conversation with Grayson Bleek and my almost-encounter with Jesse Willard.

"I'll bet he's around here somewhere," Kyra said.

She could be right. Clearly, something about the mall made Jesse feel comfortable; either that or it was the only place he could find to sleep at night that was heated. "Keep your eyes open," I suggested.

"Always. Gotta dash." She was gone in a blur of terra-cotta.

I wandered up to the security office to ensure that Joel was going to meet me at the Y after his shift, and check the cameras to see if I could spot anything suspicious around the time Jay was shot. I studied the images from all the garage cameras from fifteen minutes before Jay got shot until fifteen minutes after, but saw nothing but the white van, plate not visible, gliding from the lower level to the top, then out of the garage. Looking for something? Waiting for someone? Whatever it was doing, I didn't see anything that suggested someone in the van was responsible for shooting Jay. In fact, I never even saw Jay, who must have been delib-erately avoiding the cameras. Hm. I headed out to do forty-five minutes of upper-body weight training before Joel arrived at the pool.

When Joel arrived, we swam for half an hour before he begged to stop. He was improving slowly, but still hung onto the end of the pool to rest after every third lap. He hauled himself out of the pool, belly hanging over the waistband of his Hawaiian-print swim trunks, curly hair flattened by water and dripping down his brow. "I saw in the log that you almost caught an intruder in the storeroom last night," he said. "I wish it had been me. Nothing exciting ever hap-pens on my shifts."

I wrapped myself in a towel so it hid my leg. Joel had, of course, seen the scars and twisted muscle before, but I was still self-conscious about it. "It wasn't very exciting." I gave him the details.

"Willard probably did it," he said, shaking his head like a dog and flinging water onto me. "Sorry. I know you like him, but he was *there*."

"It depends on when she got stabbed," I said, keeping my voice low. "If she was attacked in the evening sometime, then I don't see how it could have been Willard. It's not like he would have hung around all night after stabbing her and then run out when I showed up in the morning. If she was attacked in the morning . . ." Jesse Willard looked like a much more viable suspect if Zoë had been stabbed only a short time before I stumbled over her. "But she wasn't. She was wearing the same clothes."

"How can we know when she was stabbed for sure?" Joel asked, his voice a bit too loud so an old gentleman in a Speedo, carrying a kickboard, gave us a funny look.

"We can't," I said, hating that we didn't have access to any forensic data. "The police will know by now, though. Stomach contents will have told them if she ate dinner—"

Joel turned vaguely green at the mention of stomach content analysis, but I kept on, "—and the pathologist might be able to narrow down the time of the attack by how much blood she lost or something." There hadn't been a lot of blood at the scene, maybe because the murderer had cleaned some of it up, but also, I suspected, because most of her bleeding had been internal.

"So she could have been there all night?"

"Um-hm. I think so. She might have been unconscious most of the time, though, and unable to get help." I felt chilled at the idea and huddled into my towel. What a horrible way to die . . . alone, cold, in pain, lying on a tiled floor in the dark.

I shook myself and changed the subject. "How's it going with you and Sunny?"

"Great," he said. "She went to the agility show with me last weekend and was amazed at what the dogs could do. One of the shelties I trained came in third, so it was a great day. He's a smart dog and still young—he'll win the next time out. Sunny's cooking me dinner on Saturday night," he added, the words muffled by the towel he was using to dry his hair.

"Dinner at her place," I teased. "Very significant."

The tops of his ears showed red as he lowered the towel. I took pity on him and asked if he'd watched the filming today. He grew animated describing how great it was when the actor playing the hit man fired at Ethan, blasting him backwards into the fountain. "They did it, like, nine times," Joel said, awed. "And in between times they had to redo Mr. Jarrett's makeup, and dry his hair, and put him into a new uniform. It was really cool. You should have seen the water splash everywhere. Like this."

He stood suddenly and flung himself backwards into the pool, arms spread wide. He landed with a painful splat and the water swelled more than fountained, sloshing over the pool's edge to soak the hem of my towel.

I applauded while another lap swimmer paused to stare at us and the lifeguard blew her whistle.

Seventeen

. . .

The next morning, I arrived at the mall half an hour before my shift started, awakened by nightmares again. I couldn't keep going without sleep, I knew, but I despised the sleep meds my psychiatrist had prescribed soon after my return from the desert and I was reluctant to call him. Downing some of the hot brew in the office coffeepot, I told Edgar that I'd arranged for us to watch the filming on set later that day. He was almost speechless with gratitude, promising to meet me at Colonial Beach at eleven. Joel had agreed to cover for me while I took a long lunch. Coco came in then, a couple hours earlier than usual, and I cleared my absence with her.

"Oh, yeah, sure," she said, seeming a bit distracted. She patted her red hair into place and tucked what looked like a large portfolio more securely under her arm. "I'm . . . I've . . . I'll be out for a while around lunch myself. Um, have the police caught whoever it was that killed that woman yet? Mr. Quigley says I'm supposed to keep him informed and he'd like to hear that the killer's behind bars." She looked at me hopefully.

I was sure we'd all like to hear that, but I didn't think Quigley putting pressure on Coco was going to make it happen. "I haven't heard anything more," I said. "You could ask the detective in charge of the case, though."

"Oh, no," Coco said involuntarily. "He makes me nervous."

"You shouldn't let him intimidate you," I said, feeling some sympathy for her. Helland sometimes intimidated me and I wasn't a newly-graduated-from-college kid working at her first real job. "As the director of security, you certainly have a right to be kept informed about the police investigation."

"Could you ask him?" Coco said.

"Of course. I can go now if you'll watch the monitors."

Moments later, I glided to a stop in front of the storefront the police were using as a temporary command post, smelling a hint of perfume that seeped from beneath the door. I sneezed. The door was shut and locked and no lights glowed within. It *was* still a little before seven, I realized, nodding at a couple of mall walkers as they power walked past me. I'd check back later. As I was turning to go, a woman hurried up. She didn't look like a walker. Dressed in a turquoise pencil skirt and a black bolero jacket, she had burgundy-colored hair, obviously dyed, and wore pointy-toed black heels. I guessed her to be in her late twenties.

"Are you the police?" she asked, eyeing my uniform doubtfully.

I introduced myself. "I'm not sure when the police will

be here today. Do you know where their headquarters is downtown?"

"I don't have time to trek downtown," she said impatiently. "And when I called down there to say I had information about Zoë Winters, whoever I talked to told me the detective in charge was *here*." She had a pointy nose and chin and her face was pinched with either anxiety or irritation. "Can't I talk to you?"

I desperately wanted to hear what this woman had to say about Zoë. "Well . . ."

"It's you or no one," she said, stretching the beaded bracelets on her wrist. "I'm catching a plane in two hours for a weeklong conference in Manchester. England."

"Sure," I capitulated. "Let me call Detective Helland and tell him you're here."

"Fine, but I'm out of here no later than seven-thirty, whether he's here or not."

Dialing Helland's number, I got his voicemail and left a message, sure he would be furious, but unable to think of a better way of handling the situation.

"Any chance of finding some caffeine around here?" the woman asked before I could say anything.

"Sure." I led her toward The Bean Bonanza, which always opened early to accommodate the walkers. It was a smart business strategy, I thought, judging by the short line of people waiting for their caffeine fix. The woman introduced herself as Astrid Jelinek while we waited our turn, and when we had our cups of steaming coffee, we sat at one of the two white-topped bistro tables Suzie put out for customers who wanted to linger over their coffee.

Conscious of Astrid checking her watch, I dove right in. "You know something about Zoë's murder?" I asked.

"Her murder?" She jolted coffee from her cup to the table

and blotted it with a napkin. "God, no. I don't know anything about who killed her or anything like that. I saw the request on the news and I felt I needed to come forward. You know, the one about people with information about Zoë Winters— not that I knew her last name, but I recognized the photo they showed—contacting the police if they'd seen her after six p.m. on Monday."

"You saw her that night?" I leaned forward with anticipation. "Where? What were the circumstances?"

"Well, I work for an investment firm and sometimes after work a few of us stop by Cowgirls for a drink. It's only a couple blocks from the office."

I knew the place by reputation only. It was a lesbian bar run by a woman who used to be a congressional staffer. "You met Zoë there?"

"Uh-huh. My friends were leaving, and I was thinking about going myself, when Zoë walked in." A small smile played around her mouth and, for the first time, I noticed the faint scent of cigarettes that hung about her. She must be a smoker. "The sight of her about knocked me off my bar stool." She met my gaze unflinching. "We went home together. My place."

"What time was that?" I asked, taking notes.

"Eleven, maybe? Before midnight, anyway."

"When did she leave?"

"The next morning. Early. Said she had to be back on the set."

"Do you remember what time?"

"Six-ish? I wasn't really too awake. Told her to help herself to a bagel or a boiled egg and rolled over."

"Were you expecting to see her again?"

Astrid shrugged. "You know how it is."

I didn't, but I let it go. "What did you talk about? Did she say anything that made you think she was worried about something, scared of someone?"

Astrid's pointy pink tongue poked out to lick her lips. "We talked about the usual stuff. 'What's a nice girl like you doing in a place like this?' 'What do you do?' You know." She smiled crookedly, as if making fun of the whole pickup thing.

Astrid kept crediting me with knowledge I didn't have. "Did she mention her girlfriend?"

"Marlo? Yeah. She came up."

"Margot. In what context?"

"Zoë said they'd had a fight, that she felt smothered, misunderstood, didn't know if she wanted to stay with Margot. I took it all with a grain of salt, figured it was the martinis talking. She put away three or four before we ever left Cowgirls, and then we fixed another pitcher at my place. Speaking of which . . ." She shook three aspirin out of a container from her purse and drank them down with a swallow of coffee. "Can't say I'm looking forward to a transatlantic flight today. Anyway, now you know everything I know about Zoë's last night"—her smile faltered—"and you can relay it to Detective Whoever. He can give me a call when I get back from England if he's got any other questions. I'd appreciate it if he'd contact me at work, though," she said, handing over a business card, "since my partner wouldn't understand about Zoë."

I opened my eyes wider. "Any chance she knows about Zoë?" I imagined a scenario where Astrid's lover encountered Zoë leaving their house and followed her to the mall . . .

"He. None. He's waiting for me in England."

Smiling wryly, she stood to go, just as Detective Helland came striding over, face impassive. "You must be the detective," Astrid said, giving him an appreciative once-over. "Sorry I can't stay to chat, but I've got a plane to catch." Nodding toward me, she said, "She knows everything I know." She whisked away before Helland could stop her.

"Don't say anything," I said before Helland could unload on me. "It was let her talk to me or lose out on her information."

"I gathered that from your phone message," he said mildly. "I was going to thank you."

"Oh. Well, you're welcome." Tension drained out of me as I realized he wasn't going to lambaste me for tampering with a witness or sticking my nose where it didn't belong.

A smile lurked in his eyes, making me suspect he knew what I was thinking.

"What did she say?"

I gave him a detailed report on Astrid's encounter with Zoë as we walked back toward his temporary office. "So, it looks like she wasn't killed until Tuesday morning," I said. That put Jesse Willard back in the frame and I didn't like that.

"We knew that. She had a bagel with cream cheese for breakfast no more than half an hour before she died."

"With the timeline narrowed down like that, we can go over all the camera data and see when she arrived at the mall," I said.

"Already done." He offered no further details.

Of course. He had the manpower available to look at data from all the cameras. "And did you also figure out who else was in the mall that early?"

"Way too many people," he said, clearly not happy about it. "Just about everyone on the movie crew since they were filming so early."

"Ah."

We continued in silence until arriving at the former perfume shop. I remembered to hand over Astrid's business card. "Oh, I almost forgot. I talked with Grayson Bleek yesterday—he's now the props master in addition to being the weapons master—and he told me about overhearing a fight between Zoë and Margot the afternoon before she died. In addition, he had one of the flyers like Ethan Jarrett got, the one from the antiviolence, anti-mall faction."

"Lots of people got those, maybe everyone on the movie crew," he said. "The lab's turned up nothing. They're photocopied on standard paper with nothing distinctive about them. We've been unable to link the message to anything similar from any known group. Unless they put out another communiqué or identify themselves in some way, we're at a dead end there. Tell me what Bleek said."

I filled him in and the corners of his mouth pulled down. "We'll have to interview Mr. Bleek. He didn't mention the fight to us, as far as I know. Thanks, EJ."

"Anytime."

We parted more amicably than usual and I returned to the office and Coco. She was on the phone when I walked in, saying, "Yes, I'll be there right at twelve thirty. Thank you for the opportunity to interview—" She caught sight of me and her eyes widened. She hung up hurriedly.

So, Coco was already looking for another job? Her stint as director of security hadn't lasted long. Not that I blamed her; it was clear she wasn't cut out for security work. It wasn't my business so I didn't say anything. "Detective Helland didn't have anything new to offer," I told her, "except the information that Zoë was killed in the morning."

"Oh, uh, thanks for checking, EJ," Coco said, gathering up her portfolio and smoothing down the apricot-colored skirt that hugged her hips tightly and flared when it hit her

knees, ending slightly above her ankles. Tan peep-toe, platform boots reached almost to the skirt's hem. Not good for
chasing perps was my reaction to the outfit, even though I
was sure it must be the height of fashion. I admitted to a
twinge of envy over the high-heeled boots, however. I'd
always enjoyed shoes, but my knee couldn't stand the pressure and instability of heels anymore.

Coco caught me staring. "My own design," she said, pir-
ouetting for me.

"It's distinctive," I said and she beamed.

"I hope you won't tell anyone," she said, lowering her
voice, "but I'm interviewing for a job at a fashion house
today. I know you overheard me on the phone. I don't know
if I'll get it—the competition will be *brutal*—so I don't want
to upset the apple cart here, okay?"

"Sure," I said. Who was I to throw stones at her for interviewing for jobs that suited her better? I'd filled out four
more applications with police departments around the country this past weekend. "I won't say anything."

Looking relieved, she hurried back to her office, probably
to practice answers to potential interview questions: "My
design influences? Chanel—I was named for her, after all,
and Frank Lloyd Wright. The most important advance in
the fashion industry? Polyester, definitely." I smiled at my
own whimsy and headed across the hall to brief Quigley on
the non-progress in the murder investigation. As I pushed
open the glass doors to the mall operations office, I knew
I'd picked a bad time. Quigley stood in front of the aerial
photograph of Fernglen Galleria that hung over a blue sofa
in the waiting area. Fiddling with his cuff links, he looked
dapper but very uncomfortable as an on-air reporter stuck
a microphone in his face. A cameraman stood several feet
away, camera trained on Quigley.

". . . do you think of reports calling Fernglen Galleria the Death Mall? By our count, there have been four bodies found on the property in under two months."

Quigley sputtered. "It's preposterous. I want to assure the shopping public that Fernglen is an absolutely safe place to shop. When people indulge in dangerous, illegal practices or associate themselves with gangs—"

He was talking about the young man found dead of a drug overdose in our garage during a previous murder investigation, and the gangbanger killed elsewhere and left outside the mall a few weeks back.

"—their deaths are not unexpected and cannot in any way be construed as being related to Fernglen. I shop here myself. If I had a wife or a daughter, I'd encourage her—them—to shop here. Fernglen Galleria is a perfectly safe shopping destination for all your home and fashion needs."

Pooja, Quigley's assistant, watched from her desk, brown eyes gleaming. She caught my eye and bit back a smile.

The reporter, a slick-looking young man with blond hair falling across his forehead and a suit that almost outdappered Quigley, asked, "What steps are you taking to protect the customers brave enough to shop at Fernglen?"

"We're, uh—" Quigley looked around wildly and his gaze landed on me. Despite my head shakes, he beckoned me forward. "EJ Ferris is a senior member of our security force and a former military police officer. Why don't we let her answer that question?"

The reporter turned toward me, holding out the mike, and the camera swiveled my way. Taking advantage of being out of the limelight for a moment, Quigley pulled a handkerchief from his pocket and swabbed his forehead. Even though I was furious with Quigley for putting me on the spot, I answered calmly, "Fernglen's security practices are solid, modeled on cutting-edge techniques and using completely adequate technology." Okay, our camera system was practically antique, and only a fraction of the cameras were hooked up, but I knew Quigley would can me if I in any way suggested to the television audience that Fernglen could benefit from security upgrades.

"We have a well-trained staff of security officers dedicated to providing a safe shopping experience. Would the producers of *Mafia Mistress* be filming here this week if Fernglen were unsafe?"

Quigley gave me a big thumbs-up behind the reporter's back for mentioning the movie.

"I notice you're not wearing a weapon, Miss, uh, Officer, uh—"

"Officer Ferris."

He edged closer. "Right. What's up with that? Wouldn't the public be safer if the security force was armed?"

Little did he know how much more in danger the public would be if Coco and Joel and some of our other officers carried guns.

"Our lack of weapons is a testament to how safe Fernglen is," I improvised. "But that's a policy issued by the corporation that owns Fernglen, so Mr. Quigley is the best one to address that."

I blew out a long breath as the reporter and camera turned to Quigley once again. Mouthing "later" at Pooja, I ducked out and caught my breath in the hall. I hated being on camera. I didn't have a performing gene in my body, much to Ethan's dismay. The one time I'd tried out for a school play to make him happy, I'd been more wooden than the stage floor.

Wary of Quigley pulling me back into the office to answer more questions, I jumped on the Segway and left on my patrols. Having the movie company more or less in residence was distracting people from the murder and I heard more conversation about Ethan and *Mafia Mistress* than about poor Zoë. I deliberately Segwayed down utility corridors and into off-the-beaten-path nooks and byways, keeping an eye out for Jesse. It'd been a blow to learn Zoë died Tuesday morning because it made Jesse a more viable suspect. He came early to walk, ran into her, something set him off, and . . . The scenario was too plausible for my comfort. If only Jesse would come forward, give his side of the story. The morning zipped by and it was time to leave for the set and the filming of the big love scene before I knew it. Radioing Joel to make sure he was still okay with covering for me, I hurried to the parking lot and my Miata and headed for the boat dock.

Eighteen

. . .

Colonial Beach is a small beach town east of Vernonville on the Potomac River, not too far up from where it empties into Chesapeake Bay. During the summer, the small, sandy beach is crowded with umbrellas, sun worshipers, and kids paddling in the water. On a brisk spring day, the river gleamed more stainless steel than blue, and the only people in sight were huddled into fleeces and Windbreakers, obviously hoping to catch a glimpse of someone famous. Gulls wheeled overhead, keening, and I spotted a blue heron hunched by the water's edge as I swung into the parking lot. Trees leafed out in soft spring green bounded the lot, and gravel crunched underfoot as I made my way to the dock where the dumpy tugboat knocked gently against tire bumpers.

The black-shirted guards kept the small crowd back as the movie crew set up for the shoot, which was taking place on the deck of the tugboat, ostensibly on a pile of sails, although I couldn't figure out why a tugboat would have sails on board in the first place. Not my worry, I decided, spotting Mom in a webbed chair at the edge of the dock. She invariably showed up on the set when Ethan filmed love scenes. I'd once asked her if the love scenes bothered her, but she shook her head. "It's so unromantic, so unsexy," she said. "All those people around, cameras practically in the actors' faces sometimes. And it's so cold on the set." She shivered. "Your father doesn't do full nudity, either, although he loves showing off his six-pack."

I gave my name to the guards and they checked a clipboard before letting me through. I crossed the uneven terrain to Mom, wishing I'd taken the time to change out of my uniform. "What's that?" I asked, nodding toward the length of sky blue trailing from her needles. The knitting was new—she'd taken a few lessons in the winter and now took her latest project with her any time she anticipated having to wait around.

"A blanket, I think," she said, inspecting her work.

"You think?"

"Well, so far I can only do rectangles or squares, so if it's long and skinny it's a scarf, but if it's long and wide it's a blanket. This is my third one; I'm donating them to the hospital where we helped fund the neonatal ward."

A gasp and a murmur went up from the crowd and I looked over to see that Ethan had appeared on the tugboat deck, surrounded by a shifting swarm of makeup artists, lighting people, and others. "Don't they usually do love scenes in private, on closed sets?" I asked Mom, sinking to the grass at her feet.

"Only if there's nudity," Mom said, apparently unruffled at the thought of her husband making out with one of the most beautiful women in the world. "Your father has to take off his shirt, though; I wouldn't want to do that on a brisk day like today."

She was right. The wind had picked up and it was chillier here at the water's edge than it was in Vernonville. I tried to imagine how the makeup people would camouflage goose bumps.

"Yo, EJ!"

Edgar's voice pulled my head around and I spotted him behind the barriers holding back the crowd. He towered over the security guards as they checked a clipboard and then let him in. He trundled toward us and I introduced him to Mom, taking care to refer to her as Mrs. Jarrett.

She greeted him warmly and invited him to join us. He beamed when he caught sight of her knitting and said, "Great blanket." She excused herself a moment later and wandered down to the set to exchange a few words with Ethan. She did nothing crass like kiss him in public, but the way they interacted made their intimacy obvious. Go, Mom, I thought, as Anya Vale came onto the set, dressed in a summery dress that was ripped and torn, showing a lot of leg and cleavage. I guess your clothes take a beating when you're on the run from a contract killer and miscellaneous gangbangers and mafia thugs. Margot Chelius, denim skirt flapping around her legs, pencil tucked behind her ear, fussed with the way Anya's tattered skirt fell, tugging at the garment until she was satisfied.

Mom retraced her steps, someone yelled for quiet, and the filming began. I'd seen it all before, so I got more of a kick out of watching Edgar's reaction than the scene itself. His head swiveled from the acting, to the camera people, to Vandelinde who leaned forward from a classic director's chair, watching as Ethan swung Anya onto the boat seemingly without effort, and she clung to him, bosom heaving in finest bodice-ripper-novel style. There was a moment of meaningful eye contact and cameras on the boat's deck moved in closer. It always amazed me that actors could summon up any vestige of seeming intimacy with dozens of people on set, doing their jobs or hanging around.

Anya's upturned face, beautiful and vulnerable, full of yearning, invited Ethan's kiss and . . . yada-yada. I found it vaguely embarrassing to be watching my father caress a woman in public, especially when she stripped away his shirt, displaying his muscled back and six-pack in all their glory. Her hand trailed down his chest. I looked around, spotting Iona Moss not far from the action, clipboard hugged to her chest, gaze fixed on the stars as they tumbled awkwardly onto the nest of sails. She made a note about something. My gaze also snagged on Grayson Bleek conferring with the movie's villain, handing him a revolver moments before he fired at Ethan and Anya from a vantage point on the tug's cabin. Grayson nodded, as if pleased with how the actor handled himself, or with how the revolver worked.

Vandelinde yelled, "Cut!" and makeup and wardrobe people moved in to prep the stars before they did another take.

"You're sure you want to do this?" I asked Edgar. "It's a lot of 'hurry up and wait,' and then a lot of repetition." I wouldn't be able to stand all the inaction associated with acting; I noted the irony with an inward smile.

Edgar nodded, firming his mouth and thrusting his chin out a hair. "I love acting," he said.

I resolved to get Ethan to find a way to hook Edgar up with Vandelinde.

They filmed the love scene five more times before finally moving on to the next scene. When the shots rang out this time, Ethan scooped Anya into his arms and dumped her unceremoniously over the side of the tugboat before diving in after her. Onlookers gasped as the stars disappeared into the water with a splash. I shivered sympathetically; I wouldn't want to take a dip in the Potomac in April . . . brrr. The finished movie would have the pair drifting down river, eluding the killer before coming ashore on the opposite bank. Today, they were supposed to climb right out of the river.

The seconds ticked by, but Ethan and Anya didn't reappear. I began to get antsy and edged toward the river, as did my mother. Elias Vandelinde stood and scanned the water. None of us could see beyond the tugboat. Everyone headed toward the Potomac, all of us moving faster the nearer we got, like the flowing water held a magnetic charge that pulled us in. Where was Ethan? Had he hit his head or injured himself diving in? It had been too long. I was going in. I slipped off my shoes, conscious of Mom beside me, fingers pressed to her lips. A cameraman on the boat, who was hanging over the railings on the water side, pointed. "There they are."

I sagged with relief as Ethan appeared, slogging his way around the stern in waist-deep water, carrying Anya. Cameras whirred as reporters captured the image. People hesitated at the water's edge, but I lunged forward to help. My knee buckled and I caught myself with a hand on the damp grass. Edgar plunged past me into the river, taking the burden of Anya away from Ethan. Clearly conscious, she moved away from Edgar as soon as he set her on the riverbank. Six people stood ready with towels, and Anya and Ethan disappeared behind a wall of fluffy combed cotton. Edgar had to make do with a single towel tossed his way.

Still toweling his hair dry, Ethan came to where Mom stood. "What happened?" she asked, hugging him, not caring that he left a damp imprint on her blouse.

He shrugged. "I think Anya bumped her head when I tossed her overboard. She seemed disoriented, was drifting toward the middle of the river instead of swimming for the shore."

I looked toward Anya where she sat surrounded by crew members. Iona was swabbing a bump on the star's forehead with disinfectant and sticking a small bandage over it. "Nothing makeup won't cover easily," she announced.

Anya shot her a look that suggested she didn't like having her injury dismissed so cavalierly. "I could have drowned," she said in her throaty voice. "Ethan saved my life." Inky hair streamed wetly down her face and lay plastered against the white swell of breasts emerging from her soaked dress. She looked like an exotic mermaid. All she needed was a clamshell brassiere, à la Ariel. The paparazzi seemed captivated and pointed their zoom lenses her way.

Ethan made a face. "No such thing." He shouldered his way into a dry shirt Margot held out for him and thanked her. "You'd have gotten yourself to shore if I hadn't been there."

"Nevertheless." She blew him a kiss. Cameras whirred, flashes strobing, and I knew the morning's headlines would feature the incident.

I looked around for Edgar and spotted him shaking hands with Vandelinde. Maybe the director was thanking him for his help. Relieved that Ethan was okay, I said good-bye to him and my mom, and then waited for Edgar when he signaled to me. He powered up the slight incline and caught up to me, his whole face beaming, wet clothes giving off a dank river odor.

"Van says he thinks he's got a role for me in his next film." Edgar announced it like he'd won a Nobel prize. His gold tooth gleamed. "A bit part, but it's a start. I'm going to Hollywood!"

I high-fived him, thinking he sounded like an *American Idol* hopeful. I hoped he fared better than most of them. "Way to go, Edgar! I hope you like it."

"What's not to like?"

I could have given him an alphabetized and indexed list, starting with "arrogance" and ending with "zombies," but I needed to get back to Fernglen before Coco and Joel decided I was AWOL.

Nineteen

. . .

I ran into Coco in the parking lot. We exchanged semi-guilty glances at having exceeded our lunch hours by so long, and I asked, "How was the interview?"

She held up her hand and twined two fingers together. "Fingers crossed."

I couldn't decide if I wanted Coco to get the job or not. She knew nothing about security, but she wasn't obstructive, like Woskowicz had been, and I was virtually running operations from behind the scenes. On the other hand, if she left, I could compete for the director of security job again, only I wasn't sure I wanted to. Should I take it as a sign that I hadn't gotten the job and consider other options, as Grandpa Atherton had been urging? I pushed the thoughts away, deciding I would deal with them when the time came. I realized I was being selfish and decided I wanted Coco to get the new job, since it was clearly what she wanted.

Unaware of my thoughts, Coco babbled about the interview, detailing how she'd answered each question, as we took the elevator up and walked to the office. "—and when I told them that Coco Chanel was one of my strongest influences, they—"

"What about Frank Lloyd Wright?"

"Who?"

Before I could explain that I was joking, Harold Wasserman looked up from the monitors and told Coco that Curtis Quigley had been looking for her. A nervous expression settled on her face and she scuttled across the hall to the management offices.

"Anything going on?" I asked Harold.

"Not so's you'd notice."

My eyes idly scanned the monitors, noting a gaggle of teens who might bear watching, two tween girls apparently chasing each other on heelies, those annoying shoes where wheels pop out of the soles, and a woman texting as she walked, unaware that she was about to plow into the fountain.

"Excuse me?" A man's voice sounded from the doorway, and Harold and I looked around as the woman banged her shin against the fountain wall and her phone went kerplunk into the basin.

A middle-aged man stood there: medium height and build, balding, khaki slacks with blue shirt.

"Yes?" I asked, moving toward him.

"There's a man, in the first floor bathroom—"

I winced, hoping he wasn't going to say anything inappropriate was going on. We'd had one instance the first week I started working here of a teen being propositioned in one of the men's rooms.

"He's just sitting there, on the floor, crying. I think he might be ill. Mentally." Concern blanketed the man's face as he hovered on the threshold.

"Thank you for letting us know," I said. "Which bathroom?" I asked the question, even though I already knew what he was going to say.

"The one down that little hall past Macy's before you get to the movie theaters," he said, backing out of the door. Clearly, he didn't want to get further involved.

"Thank you, sir," I said sincerely. He nodded and disappeared. "Harold, call the police and tell them Jesse Willard is in the bathroom. I'll try to detain him until they get here."

"What makes you think it's him?" Harold asked, dialing.

"I just know."

Skimming through the halls on the Segway, I wished, not for the first time, that it had lights and a siren to drive people out of my path. Luckily, the mall wasn't too crowded on a Friday afternoon, and in under five minutes I reached the bathroom where I'd found Zoë. A man emerged wiping his hands on his jeaned thighs.

"Excuse me, sir," I stopped him and got off the Segway. "Is there anyone in there?"

He made a disgusted face. "Yeah, some nut job."

Mr. Empathetic. He hurried away before I could ask anything else.

Ignoring the fact that it was a men's room, I pushed into the bathroom and immediately spotted Jesse Willard slumped against the far wall, holding his head and rocking from side to side.

"Jesse?" I called softly.

He lifted his head and I saw his wet cheeks. Anguish darkened his eyes . . . physical or emotional, I couldn't tell.

"Are you okay?"

"Head. Hurts." He bowed his head again and continued rocking. His fingers dug into his scalp and made white divots in the almost-bare flesh. I'd seen soldiers in that kind of pain before and I radioed Harold. "Call for an ambulance, too."

"Right. The police are on their way."

I wished he hadn't mentioned the police on our unsecure radios, but it was too late to do anything about it now. Instead, I dampened a paper towel with cold water and brought it to Jesse, knowing it was woefully inadequate. My back against the wall, I slid to the floor beside him. "Here."

He took the paper towel and pressed it against his forehead, not looking at me.

"An ambulance is coming," I told him. "They'll have medicine to help with the pain."

At that his eyes flitted toward me and he struggled to stand. "They'll put me in jail. They'll think I did it." He was taller than I was, and heavier, but he seemed almost frail as he sought a way out.

"Did what, Jesse?"

"She was bleeding. I tried to stop it, tried to help her . . . it was like when Sergeant Newsome got hit. A piece of metal went right through her vest. All that blood . . . Mortar rounds were going off all around us. One must have hit a gas tank because there was an explosion, a fireball. We could feel the heat. The noise—" He pressed his hands over his ears. After a moment, he looked up, gaze flitting from one corner of the room to the next, and then he froze. "Incoming!" He flung an arm around my shoulders and carried me to the floor with him.

My nose pressed against the cold tile, and the harsh scent of cleanser bit at my nostrils. I fought down a momentary panic at his weight atop me, pressing me down, and tried to calm him. "It's okay, Jesse. We're at the mall. Your dad's on his way. It's going to be okay."

"The mall." He raised himself up on one elbow and

looked around. I sighed with relief as his weight lifted off me. "She was right there." He pointed under the stall door and fell silent.

Struggling to sit up, I saw that his gaze was far away and I didn't know if he was seeing Zoë Winters again, or Sergeant Newsome, the victim of a firefight in the desert, I presumed. "Did you see anyone else that morning?" I asked. "Was there anyone here when you found Zoë in the stall?"

He was shaking his head when the door burst open with such force it banged into the wall. Jesse threw himself on top of me again, mashing me to the floor.

"Hands up," the first officer yelled. I couldn't see him, but I knew from his tone of voice that he had his weapon out. "Get off her."

"I'm okay," I shouted, my voice muffled. "He's protecting me from you." Tremors from Jesse vibrated through me and I felt like crying as I realized how terrified he was. "He's not going to hurt me."

"Hands where I can see them *now*," the cop said as if he hadn't heard a word I'd said.

I wormed out from beneath Jesse, showing my palms to the officer who was barely into his twenties, with pale skin and a long nose.

I was shaking with fury. "That is not necessary," I said, raising my torso by pushing up on my elbows. Jesse shifted his weight and crab-walked backwards until his back was against the wall. He buried his head in his arms. "You're scaring him. He doesn't have a weapon." I was nearly certain. "He needs an ambulance. He's in pain."

Detective Helland appeared behind the young cop, took in the scene at a glance, and holstered his own weapon. "Put it away," he told the other cop.

"But—"

A sharp look from Helland's icy eyes cut him off.

"I've got it," Helland said. "Wait for the ambulance outside." The other officer backed out the door and I heard radios squawking and conversation from several voices. "Jesse Willard, I presume?"

I nodded, biting my lower lip.

"Did he hurt you? Are you okay?"

"I'm fine. He thought he was saving me from incoming mortar rounds." I kept my voice matter-of-fact, but Helland must have heard something because he offered me a hand. After a second's hesitation, I grabbed it and let him pull me to my feet.

His eyes scanned my face, but he only asked, "Is he okay?"

"His head hurts," I said. "I don't know what all—"

Jesse lurched to his feet, hands still clutching his head, and Helland stiffened. I put a hand on Jesse's arm. "Can you walk out of here if I help you?"

I couldn't tell if he heard me because he took two steps toward the stall where I'd found Zoë and pushed the door open. "She's gone," he said sadly.

"Yes."

"So many gone." Without warning, Jesse hauled back and punched the stall door. The force of the punch dented the metal door inward and probably broke a couple bones in his hand. He stood quietly, head drooping, after delivering the one powerful punch.

To his credit, Helland didn't immediately reach for his gun or cuffs. He held a hand up behind him to stop the uniformed cops from storming in. They backed out again, reluctantly. "I think the ambulance is here," he said. "Let's get you some pain meds."

With me on one side and Helland on the other, Jesse

shambled out of the bathroom. The EMTs had arrived and one of them led him away. With a nod of his head, Helland detailed one of the cops to stay with Jesse.

"What will happen to him now?" I asked.

Helland looked down his aquiline nose at me. "When the docs have done their thing, I'll talk to him about Zoë Winters."

"He's confused. He mixes up the present day with things that happened in the war. I think when he found Zoë it freaked him out. He was talking about the blood and getting her mixed up with some sergeant who got hurt—probably killed."

Helland nodded. "He'll need a psych eval." He gave me a considering look. "It's possible, maybe even likely, that he didn't 'find' Zoë, that he was having some sort of PTSD episode there in the bathroom, and she walked in to see if he needed assistance. He mistook her for an enemy soldier, or felt threatened in some way, and he lashed out."

"With the knife he coincidentally had on him? A knife from the movie set?"

Helland paused only a moment before saying, "It's possible Zoë had the knife with her for some reason. She drew it to protect herself, he grabbed it from her and stabbed her. Additionally, the ME's report says the knives we found on the set fit the wound, but it doesn't exclude the possibility that another knife was used. We haven't recovered the murder weapon."

I sucked in a deep breath and blew it out. What he'd said about Zoë maybe having the knife with her blew holes in my belief that Jesse couldn't have committed the crime because he didn't have access to the knives. "May I call his father?"

After a momentary hesitation, Helland nodded. He

started toward the exit, but stopped after a couple of steps and turned. His gaze settled on my face and a slightly rueful smile curved his lips. "You have a good heart."

Without waiting for a reply, he strode briskly to the door and passed through it, letting sunlight into the dim hall. I stared after him, feeling ridiculously warmed by his comment and simultaneously confused. I'd been pretty much convinced that Helland found me a nuisance, maybe even disliked me. Of course, he could think I was kind *and* a nuisance, I supposed; the two weren't mutually exclusive.

Twenty

. . .

I was enjoying a quiet Friday evening at home, dreading another sleepless night but looking forward to a day off, when the phone rang at almost nine o'clock. I debated answering it, not in the mood to suffer through a politician's spiel, but picked it up.

"Turn the news on," Grandpa Atherton's tense voice told me.

"Why?" I asked as I hurried into the living room, Fubar at my heels, and clicked the remote to bring up a local station.

"Your parents—"

I hushed him as a brunette reporter standing in front of a house I recognized said, "—shots fired at Ethan Jarrett's house. Jarrett is the star of the long-running series *Roll Call* and numerous blockbusters, and is here in the metro area filming a new movie. It is unknown whether anyone was injured."

Police officers roamed behind the reporter and I scanned the background, looking for Mom and Dad. The camera panned the four-car garage of their rented mansion, but I didn't see anyone I recognized. I didn't see an ambulance. That didn't mean anything, though; one could have come and gone, rushing one of my parents to the hospital. The reporter flagged down a suited detective and asked, "Can we get more details of the shooting from you, Detective? Is it true there's a contract out on Ethan Jarrett because his latest movie, *Mafia Mistress*, reveals the inner workings of the mob?"

Becoming vaguely aware that Grandpa was talking in my ear, I said, "I'll pick you up on my way. Ten minutes." Banging the phone down, I ripped off my jammies and threw on a pair of jeans, patted Fubar, told him to guard the house, and rushed to my car.

With Grandpa riding shotgun, I barreled up I-95 toward Mount Vernon, ignoring every posted speed limit. An accident on Route 1 slowed us down, but traffic opened up after a mile or two and we shot up to my parents' rental house without further problems. My fingers were tense on the wheel the whole way as I tried to block out thoughts of Mom or Ethan bleeding, in pain, being rushed into surgery. Grandpa called the police, trying to get more information, but they wouldn't tell him anything over the phone, even when he told them he was Mom's father. Grandpa tried to phone Mom for most of the drive, but kept getting sent to her voicemail. He didn't say anything, but his expression was grim and he breathed heavily through his nose, nostrils flaring and then collapsing. I put a hand on his knee. "They're okay," I told him as we pulled up at the gate. They had to be okay.

Carefully checking our IDs and shining a flashlight in our faces, the police officer at the gate radioed to someone at the house and then pushed the button that swung the gates open. He blocked a couple of reporters from sneaking in while I zoomed up the driveway, making Grandpa clutch at the underside of his seat. I skidded to a stop in front of the portico, spewing oyster shells across the barbered lawn, partially illuminated by security lights. Two figures stepped onto the portico, silhouetted by the porch light, and I sagged with relief. Mom and Ethan. They were okay. Tears stung my eyes and my stiff fingers trembled as I uncurled them from the steering wheel.

"I'll drive home," Grandpa announced, unfolding himself from the seat. His voice was almost giddy and I knew he was as relieved as I was. "My life flashed before my eyes at least three times. When you slid by that semi—"

"Some of the scenes from your life would be enough to scare anyone," I tossed over my shoulder as I hurried up the shallow steps and threw my arms around Mom. "You're okay," I breathed. She hugged me convulsively.

"Pretty much." The tightness of her hug told me she was still feeling the aftereffects of being shot at.

Grandpa shook hands, grinning, with Ethan who looked like he was ready for a *Town & Country* photo shoot in an elaborate smoking jacket.

"You didn't have to come, EJ, Ralph," he said, wrapping me in a big hug when Mom released me.

"Right. Like I'm going to stay away when someone's taking potshots at my dear old dad," I said.

Ethan winced. "Don't use the O word, Eej."

"Sorry." I grinned, full of relief to find them bullet hole free, apparently doing fine. "What happened?"

"And why did we have to hear about it on the news?" Grandpa grumbled.

"Are the police still here?" I looked around but didn't spot any officers.

Mom shook her blond hair, which lay loose around her shoulders like she was ready for bed. Her makeup-less eyes were red rimmed as if she'd been crying, and I gave her another squeeze. "No, only the man at the gate. The detective left about half an hour ago."

"Drinks," Ethan announced. "Then we'll give you a sitrep."

I rolled my eyes like I always did when he trotted out military or police jargon he'd picked up from some script or another. Everything was starting to feel very normal again and I rotated my shoulders backwards and then forwards, letting the anxiety drain out of me. Mom shepherded me and Grandpa into one of the living rooms, the comfy one with the cinnamon-colored leather love seats and the stone fireplace that went clear to the ceiling. Gas flames danced behind the glass and gave the room a cheery glow. Settling onto a squashy chair, I shucked my shoes and tucked my feet up under me. Ethan appeared with four mugs of hot chocolate on a tray, surprising me. I felt less surprised when I took a sip and realized it was heavily laced with booze.

"Now," I said after we'd all had a chance to sip the warm brew. "Talk. What happened?"

Mom and Ethan glanced at each other, and then Mom said, "We were coming back from dinner with the Carnicks next door—he's in banking and she does interior design, lovely people—when someone shot at your father."

"We've been over this with the police," Ethan said, holding up a hand, "so before you ask, we didn't get a description—"

"Just a figure in black near the garage," Mom put in.

"—and I thought there were three shots while Brenda counted four. We dropped to the ground and rolled out of the light. Your mom called 911 while I chased the shooter."

"You what?" Grandpa and I said simultaneously.

"He was long gone by the time I even made it to the gate," Ethan said, ignoring us.

"Thank God for small favors," Grandpa muttered.

I silently agreed. Maybe Ethan had been a cop or a starship captain so many times in movies that he actually thought he was capable of tangling with an armed criminal. I shuddered at the thought of what might have happened if he'd caught up with the guy. A nine millimeter did a lot more damage than a light saber. "Did the police recover any bullets?"

"Just part of one that apparently hit the corner of the house and shattered," Mom said, pulling a fawn mohair afghan off the back of the sofa and wrapping it around her shoulders. "I think they're going to search more tomorrow, in the neighbors' yards. I'm pretty sure one bullet went right through my hair." She pulled a hank of blond hair sideways, as if we'd be able to see a bullet hole in the expensively highlighted tresses.

Grandpa rose and went over to plant a kiss on Mom's face. "I'm glad you're okay, Brenda."

She caught his hand and held it a moment.

"What do the police think?" I asked.

The firelight played against the rich gold and royal blue silk of Ethan's smoking jacket, making it look alive. "Robbery. They think the perp was planning to burgle the place but that we came home unexpectedly and scared him. They found the spot where he came over the wall. They made a cast of the footprint, like we used to do on that crime scene investigation series I did."

He sounded proud, like he'd poured out the plaster of paris himself; I wouldn't put it past him to have asked the crime scene techs to let him do it, I thought. A seven-foot stone wall surrounded the property; it would have been easy for anyone reasonably agile to scale, being that the wall was more for decoration than security. "So they don't think the shooter was gunning for you specifically, Ethan?"

He licked a chocolate mustache off his upper lip. "I don't think so. They asked about enemies of course, and whether I'd received any threats—"

"Had you?"

"Not that I know of. Not unless you count that note I brought you the other day, EJ, which pretty much everyone on the set got."

Crossing my arms over my chest, I slumped back and thought. A burglar who opened fire when the homeowners arrived home seemed unlikely. Why not run off, especially since he wasn't even in the house yet? Grandpa caught my eye and I read the same doubts on his face, along with a warning not to worry Mom and Ethan further. "How long is the cop out front hanging around?"

Mom answered. "Just till the morning. Your father's called a security company—"

"Forget them," Grandpa said, pulling out his cell phone. "I know some people." He walked into the adjacent dining room to make his call. When he returned, a smile of satisfaction stretched his face. "Con and his boys will be here at six." He yawned, his jaws cracking, on the last word.

"You and EJ are staying here tonight," Mom said in a voice that brooked no argument. "The beds are already made up in the guest rooms and you'll find everything you need in the bureau drawers and the bathrooms. Sylvia will get your clothes washed before you're even up."

I knew from past experience that I'd find silk pajamas in a variety of sizes in the dresser and expensive toiletries, lotions, and makeup in the bathroom. Mom prided herself on her hospitality. Even though they didn't have live-in staff, preferring their privacy, they had a cook and a housekeeper who arrived about five each morning. I yawned, too, and decided Fubar could fend for himself for a night. He had a cat flap in the back door and spent half the night hunting, anyway.

"Sounds great," I said, rising to give Mom, Ethan, and Grandpa a hug. I went to bed feeling tired and unutterably lucky to be part of such a loving—and unhurt—family. Despite my worry and tension, I slept soundly for the first time since finding Zoë. Go figure.

Twenty-one

...

Saturday afternoon found me playing lookout for Grandpa as he planted listening devices in Margot Chelius's hotel room.

The day started out normally enough, if more luxuriously than I was used to, with eggs Benedict and pecan waffles in my parents' light-filled dining room. My parents themselves were not present, being night owls by nature except when Ethan had an early call, and Grandpa Atherton was conferring with the bodyguards he'd hired, so I had the lovely room, and the newspaper, all to myself. The paper had a brief couple paragraphs about the shooting incident on page three, but didn't offer any details I didn't already know. Ethan's publicist had booked him onto some talk show for later today and warned off other reporters, so we were spared the sight of journalists jabbering at the gate, hoping for an interview.

I was pouring my third cup of coffee into the translucent

bone china, wondering if it had come with the rental or if Mom had shipped it from the California house, when Grandpa Atherton blew into the room, smelling like fresh air and with a look in his eye that told me he was on the warpath.

"Come on, Emma-Joy," he said. "No time for lollygagging. There's work to be done."

Refusing to be budged until I'd finished my coffee, I asked, "Are you satisfied with the security guys?"

"Con and his crew are the best in the business," Grandpa said, nodding out the window to where a man in a camo-patterned tee shirt and black pants patrolled the backyard. "There'll be two men on Brenda and Ethan from here on out, twenty-four/seven. Now, you and I have work to do. No one takes potshots at my daughter and her husband and gets away with it."

It had been a long time since I'd seen Grandpa this revved up and serious. "Okay," I said, dragging myself away from the table reluctantly and wondering if it would be crass to ask for a baggie for the last section of pecan waffle. "What did you have in mind?"

Breaking and entering, as it turned out.

On our way back to Vernonville, Grandpa told me he was convinced that the attack on my folks was tied to Zoë Winters's death in some way. "I don't believe in coincidence," he said, "and I don't believe in burglars who open fire on the homeowners *from outside the house*. A potshot in the bedroom, if a sleeping owner challenges you while you're ransacking the safe—sure. But shooting from beside the garage? I'm not buying it."

"Me, neither." Despite Grandpa's statement last night, I

was driving, mostly adhering to the speed limits on a sunny Saturday morning too early in the season for traffic to be headed to the beaches, thank goodness. "What do you think the connection is?"

"Now, don't take this the wrong way, Emma-Joy," Grandpa said, giving me a sideways look, "but there were some rumors on the set that your father was pretty friendly with Zoë."

My foot slipped from the accelerator to the brake and we both jolted toward the dashboard before I got the car moving at speed again. Anger burned through me. "If anyone's implying they were more than friends, that's ridiculous."

"You think I don't know that? I thought the Agency was full of gossips, but it was nothing compared to a movie crew. Anyway, I'm wondering if Zoë knew something that some-one didn't want getting out and if they're worried that she told Ethan."

"Thin," I pronounced after a moment's thought.

Grandpa huffed. "Well, you come up with a better con-nection, Miss Smarty-Pants."

"Ethan had an early call Tuesday morning, the day Zoë was stabbed. Maybe he saw something."

"And is keeping it to himself why?"

"Because he doesn't realize it was significant," I said with a "so there" look at Grandpa. "The killer is trying to shut him up before he catches on to what he saw or overheard."

"I like that," Grandpa said, nodding. "Okay, so who killed Zoë?"

Batting potential suspects back and forth for the rest of the drive, we finally settled on four as the most likely: Mar-got Chelius because she was jealous of Zoë's affairs, Tab Gentry because he blamed Zoë for his firing, Jesse Willard in a PTSD-induced rage, and Grayson Bleek because he inherited Zoë's job. I argued against including Bleek on the list—who killed someone to move up a notch on the job totem pole?—but Grandpa insisted.

"That Bleek's a strange duck," he said. "Since I've been hanging around the set, I've heard some weird stories about him. Did you know his mother was from Berlin?"

"It's not the Cold War anymore, Grandpa," I reminded him. "So what if she was born in Germany? How does that tie in with Zoë's murder?"

"It was *East* Germany when she was born there," he said.

Not bothering to point out that even if she'd been a die-hard commie it was unlikely that had anything to do with Zoë's death, I merely said, "Fine. Who do we start with?"

Which is how I ended up loitering in the lobby of Margot Chelius's hotel while Grandpa planted listening devices. "State of the art," he'd said when I asked about them. "You couldn't buy these off the Internet." I carefully didn't ask what government agency he'd "borrowed" them from. He didn't say how he was going to gain access to Margot's room and I carefully didn't ask that, either.

I lingered in front of an electronic display that listed what activities and meetings were going on in the hotel's conference center and ballrooms, pretending to search for an event. The spot gave me a clear view of the front doors and the elevators. I kept my finger on the autodial button that would let me call Grandpa if Margot showed up unexpectedly.

"May I help you find your event, ma'am?" a polite voice asked at my shoulder.

I started and jerked my head to see a navy-jacketed hotel employee with a name tag, looking at me in helpful inquiry.

"Uh, okay, yes. I'm here for the Lee wedding reception," I said, pulling up a name from the list I'd been staring at.

He looked puzzled, but directed me to a ballroom down

a hall to my right. With his eyes on me, I couldn't stay where I was, so I hurried down the corridor he'd indicated and slipped through the door. I understood the clerk's puzzlement; I found myself in a room full of Chinese men and women dressed to the nines. My Caucasian face and casual attire stood out like a woman in a miniskirt at a Saudi bazaar. Murmuring excuse me's, I backed out the door and beelined for the restrooms, in case the clerk was still watching me. Once inside, I opened the door a crack and peered out, looking to see if the coast was clear so I could find another spot from which to watch the doors and elevators.

"Excuse me," said an affronted voice behind me, and I moved away from the door so a sixtyish woman could get out of the bathroom.

She gave me a strange look as she passed me and I muttered, "Boyfriend trouble." That made her move even faster, and the hall was soon clear of people. I got back to the lobby in time to see a woman who might've been Margot Chelius get on the elevator. The hair and figure were right, but I couldn't see her face. "Damn."

Not wanting to take any chances, I dialed Grandpa's cell, let it ring once, and immediately hung up. That was our signal for "Margot's on her way up so get your octogenarian butt out of her room ASAP." I left the lobby to wait on the sidewalk out front where I would be less conspicuous. I looked at my watch now and then, as if waiting for a ride, and no one gave me a second glance. I'd been out there two minutes when a police car pulled up with an unmarked sedan behind it. Oh, no! Had Margot walked in on Grandpa and called the police?

My heart beat faster, thudding against my chest wall, and I deliberately took a deep breath and blew it out slowly to calm myself. All that was for naught when Detective

Helland stepped out of the second car and headed for the lobby door. I wished desperately I'd thought to bring a newspaper or something to hide behind, but the best I could manage on the spur of the moment was to bend over and pretend to tie my shoe. He didn't spot me twenty feet to his left as he swept into the hotel, followed by two uniformed officers.

Wild thoughts of running up the stairs and dragging Grandpa out of Margot's room ran through my head. Or maybe I could set off the fire alarm somehow and force an evacuation. Surely Grandpa could escape in the chaos. Before I could set any of my impractical plans into motion, a quiet voice at my elbow said, "Mission accomplished, Emma-Joy."

"Grandpa!" I threw my arms around him and hugged him so hard he rocked back.

He hugged me back, chuckling. "What is this for?"

"I thought the police were going to drag you off to jail."

"The police?" He arched his white brows questioningly.

"I thought I saw Margot go up, and gave you the signal and then came out here to wait. Detective Helland just showed up with a couple of uniforms. I thought they were here for you."

"Nope. I ducked into the stairwell when the elevator door opened. I'm sure she didn't see me."

I wrinkled my brow. "Helland must be here to interview Margot, don't you think?"

Grandpa's bright blue eyes twinkled. "Maybe we should listen in."

I followed him to a far corner of the crowded parking lot where we'd left the tan van he'd borrowed from someone. Grandpa had access to a never-ending variety of cars for missions and surveillance. This one had a florist logo on the door panels and no windows in the back. We clambered in and Grandpa fiddled with a receiver that looked like a small radio. Suddenly, Helland's voice crackled into the van, making me jump.

"—lied about being in your room Monday night."

"No," Margot said, her voice breaking up a little. "I was here all night."

"We have video from the Armacost Towers condo complex that says otherwise."

Grandpa looked a question at me and I shrugged. I had no idea where Armacost Towers was or why Margot would have been there.

Something interfered with the reception for a moment, and then Helland said, "—confronted Zoë Winters in the parking lot at five twenty-two a.m."

Silence hummed in the van for a good thirty seconds before Margot burst out with, "Okay! Okay, I was there. After we argued Monday afternoon, I knew what she'd do. I knew she'd go to a bar and find someone to go home with." I heard tears in her voice. "I wanted to know who. I wanted to know if she was prettier than me, if she made more money. I wanted to know what she had that I didn't, what made Zoë want her when she doesn't want me anymore."

Grandpa and I exchanged semiembarrassed looks at eavesdropping on Margot's anguish.

"So you confronted her at her lover's condo, then followed her to the mall and stabbed her."

"No! Oh, no!" Margot's voice sounded muffled and I wondered if she'd put her hands over her mouth. "I didn't. I couldn't hurt Zoë. I loved her. I confronted her at that woman's place, and we argued again. She said I was smothering her. I said she was breaking my heart. She said . . . she said we were finished, that my spying on her was the last straw." Margot's voice had dropped to a whisper. "I didn't follow her. I sat in my car and cried. I didn't get to the set until half an hour past when I should have been there. Surely someone saw me drive up."

Helland didn't reassure her. "Who inherits Zoë's estate?" he asked.

"Me, probably. We made out wills in each other's favor when we had our commitment ceremony six years ago. I haven't changed mine and I doubt that she changed hers." Margot's voice got a little stronger. "Are you arresting me? Do I need a lawyer?"

Yes, I told her silently.

"We're not arresting you at the moment, Ms. Chelius, but don't leave town," Helland said.

The sound of a door wheezing open was followed by a click and then by sobbing. As if by prior agreement, Grandpa and I said nothing. He turned down the volume so the sobbing faded away and we watched until Detective Helland and the other cops emerged from the lobby door. The sun struck pale gold from Helland's hair as he folded himself into his car.

"Well," I finally said.

"Well," Grandpa agreed.

"Do you think she did it?"

"Odds are. She's the woman scorned, she was angry enough to tail Zoë and confront her at that woman's—"

"Astrid's."

"—place, she had access to the knives, I'm sure, and she could easily have followed Zoë into the mall and waylaid her in the bathroom area. She's big enough that she could have overpowered Zoë without too much trouble."

"I'd love to know where she was last night," I said.

"Amen. How about if I stay here and monitor this

gadget"—he patted the receiver—"and you track down our next suspect?"

"Doesn't it record?"

"Of course."

I eyed Grandpa, noticing how the corners of his mouth tucked in. "You're up to something and you want me out of the way."

He didn't deny it.

"Just don't get yourself arrested or shot," I said, kissing his cheek and getting down from the van. "Mom would never forgive me."

Twenty-two

• • •

Leaving Grandpa with some misgivings—even though he'd been able to escape from Cuba during the missile crisis and had handled himself okay in Eastern Europe during the Cold War, he *was* in his eighties now—I returned to the mall, hoping Iona Moss could tell me where Tab Gentry lived or where he might be working. With my luck, he was from Hollywood and had returned there when he was fired.

"No," Iona assured me when I asked. I'd found her in the production office, looking like she'd stayed up all night; her complexion was pasty, and putty-colored circles puddled beneath her eyes. "He was a local hire." She pushed a hank of hair off her face and told a passing gaffer to be careful when he bumped the Oscar statue perched atop a pile of *Mafia Mistress* posters. She grabbed it up and cradled it in her arms.

"Is that a real Oscar?" I asked. I'd never seen one up close; Ethan's movies raked in the bucks, but they weren't the gloomy, arty kind that reeled in Oscar nominations. He said he didn't care that he didn't have an Oscar, but I thought nothing would make him happier than to be recognized by the Academy.

"Van's," Iona said. "He takes it with him on every shoot. Says it's his good luck charm." She polished the golden head with the tail of her shirt and set the little guy on the table she used as a desk. She yawned.

"Rough night?"

Iona nodded wearily. "A few of us got together to hoist one for Zoë. The funeral's going to be in Wisconsin or Wyoming—one of the W states where her folks live—so we put together an impromptu celebration of life, you might say. Which makes it ironic that I feel like death warmed over this morning."

So, while my parents were being shot at, the movie crew had been partying. "Was Margot there?"

Iona wrinkled her brow and winced. "No more tequila shooters for me. Early on. But then she got weepy and went up to her room."

Then Margot was unaccounted for when someone used my parents for target practice. "Was the cast there, too?"

"No. It was mostly crew who have worked with her on a few films. Me. Grayson for a while, but he said something about a toothache and took off. A toothache? Please. Margot, like I said. Bree was there to start with." She named a few others I didn't recognize. "Oh, and a couple of agricultural machinery salesmen from Dubuque horned in around midnight." Her hazel eyes lit up. "Hey, did you hear what happened at the Jarretts? Someone shot at them."

"I heard."

Leaning closer, she murmured, "Publicity stunt is what

I think. That and the whole river incident where Ethan had to 'rescue' Anya." She winked. "Not that Ethan wouldn't pull someone from a burning building, if need be, but this was a little too convenient, don't you think, with all the photogs standing by?"

I stared at her, taken aback by the idea. "You think—?"

She smirked. "Happens all the time in Hollywood. Anyway, to answer your question about Tab, I don't know where he's working now, but he might have gone back to King's Dominion. Someone said that's where he was working before he got cast in *Mafia Mistress*."

King's Dominion was a theme park this side of Richmond. They had shows of some kind, I vaguely remembered, in addition to the standard amusement park fare of roller coasters, rides, junk food, and crowds. This time of year, they were only open on the weekends, but since this was Saturday, I figured Tab might be at work. "You don't happen to know the name of the show he's in?"

"Sorry," Iona shrugged.

I thanked her and was turning away when I heard Kyra's voice call my name. I turned to see my friend bearing down on me, beaming. She looked more like a movie star than a mall store manager with her dark hair floating loose down her back, her height and splendid figure, and a bronze blouse casting a flattering glow on her complexion. "I was actually looking for Ethan," Kyra said. "I haven't laid eyes on the man and I want him to know that my feelings are hurt. He's been hanging out in this mall for a week and he hasn't come up to say hi."

That earned her a stare from Iona. "You know Ethan Jarrett?"

Before Kyra could explain how she knew Ethan, which

would give away our relationship, I burst in with introductions. "Iona, this is Kyra Valentine. Kyra, Iona Moss." The women shook hands, Iona still looking puzzled.

"How do you know—?"

At that moment, Ethan strode in wearing his cop costume, accompanied by what looked like half the movie crew: Van, Anya Vale, Bree Spurrier, Margot Chelius (who must have left the hotel almost immediately after I did), Grayson Bleek, the actor playing the hit man, and various others, including Ethan's new bodyguard.

Ethan's face lit up when he saw me and Kyra. "Kyra!"

In her usual dramatic way, she flung herself at him and they exchanged a big hug and affectionate kiss while the entourage looked on with varying degrees of disapproval. A makeup woman bustled in nanoseconds after Ethan released Kyra and touched up his lips, frowning her annoyance. Ethan asked Kyra how she liked running the store and she made a face. Margot, looking subdued and red-eyed, adjusted the collar of his shirt, and Van announced, "Time is money." He strode away and Ethan ignored him, busy catching up with Kyra.

After a few minutes, Ethan hooked his arm through Kyra's and said, "Come watch this scene. You'll like it. Bradley"—he nodded at the actor playing the hit man, who grinned back at him, looking much less villainous than during filming—"and I exchange shots in a stuffed-animal store and the animals get it. Stuffing everywhere. The special effects guys already have them rigged."

Kyra made some noises about needing to get back to Merlin's Cave, but went along with him, calling over her shoulder, "Don't forget roller derby tonight. The Vernonville Vengeance is going to roll!"

I laughed, waved, and left the mall, intent on tracking down one recently unemployed actor: Tab Gentry.

Two hours of trekking around King's Dominion reminded me why I hate amusement parks. I felt like the Grinch every time I even thought it, but it was true. They were beastly expensive—I could have paid my cable bill for two months for what it cost me to get in—and they were crowded and noisy. Tinny carousel music made me wish for earplugs. I wasn't into the rides; I'd never been much of one for manufactured thrills. The food was too salty, too sugary, too fatty, and too expensive, and I hated being confronted with the opportunity to buy pricey souvenirs at every turn. The water park looked like it might be fun in midsummer, but I was unlikely to find Tab floating on an inner tube at this time of year. I sighed. I was turning into a curmudgeon and I was barely thirty-one. I resolved to at least try to enjoy the next show I went to. I'd already seen two of them, having to sit through the whole performances in case Tab came on stage at the very end.

I crunched to a seat, crushing popcorn and peanut shells underfoot in the covered but open-air venue. I was close enough to the stage to see the features of the performers clearly, but not so close they'd be sweating on me. I left that pleasure to a line of tween girls who were bouncing up and down in front of the stage, eager for the show to begin. Making sure there was nothing sticky on my chair, I settled in and wished I could take a nap. The couple arguing in the row behind me made that impossible, and I learned a whole lot more than I wanted to about Earl's mother and the way she took over family holidays.

Tab Gentry was the first performer to take the stage in

some sort of medley of pop songs. He had a decent voice and some good moves, and the tween girls in the half-full theater were going gaga over him. He had the appeal of a more grown-up Justin Bieber, I decided, then wondered if it was possible to use the words "grown-up" and "Justin Bieber" in the same sentence. I found myself bebopping to the infectious beat of the songs and was almost sorry when the show ended and I could fight my way through the exiting fans to the stage in an attempt to catch Tab Gentry.

"Gentry," I called as he signed a twelve-year-old's autograph book.

He turned my way with a half smile, ready to sign anything I wanted him to, I suspected. Harsh stage lights glittered on the clear sequins sewn onto his open-to-the-navel shirt. As I drew closer, his smile faded and a line appeared between his brows. I knew exactly when he placed me because his eyes narrowed and the line became a full-fledged scowl. "You're the mall cop," he said. "You threw me out of the mall."

"I did not. I offered to buy you coffee and you left."

"Same thing."

Someone cut the stage lights and my face relaxed now that I didn't have to squint. I made note of the fact that Gentry apparently remembered events in the way that best suited him.

"What are you doing here?" Curiosity won out over annoyance. Before I could answer, his face lit up. "Do they want me back? Did Bree send you to find me?"

I hated to burst his bubble, but I shook my head. I couldn't imagine a scenario in which the assistant director would ask me to track down an actor, but I didn't point that out. "No. Actually, I wanted to talk to you about something else."

"If it's a bachelorette party, forget it," he said, leaping

easily down from the stage. "Since I left Chippendales, I don't do gigs like that. I'm serious about my acting and my agent says that the bachelorette parties undermine my credibility as an actor."

He said it like he was booked to play King Lear on Broadway next month and I bit back a smile. "It's nothing like that," I assured him, struggling not to imagine what "that" had involved and wishing Kyra were here; she'd be getting a huge kick out of this interview and would probably have insisted that Gentry give us details of his girls' night out routine . . . or demo it.

"Then what?"

"Can you tell me where you were last night?"

"Why should I?" His tone was more sullen than hostile, but I could tell he wasn't going to cooperate even before his eyes widened. "Last night . . . that's when someone shot Ethan Jarrett!"

"Shot *at*."

"You think I had something to do with that?" He backed away, hands up like he was warding off an armed mugger. "No way! Why would I want to shoot Jarrett? He was decent to me. You're nutso, lady."

"You got fired—"

"Yeah, well if I was going to shoot someone over that, it'd be—"

He cut himself off, but I finished the sentence for him. "Zoë Winters."

"Well, I didn't shoot her, either, or stab her, so get out of my face."

"Tab?" A young woman had emerged from behind the heavy stage curtain. She wore jeans and a low-cut sweater instead of a spangled cheerleader's skirt, but I thought I recognized her as one of the singers from the show.

"Coming, Leilani," he said as she floated down the stairs and gave me a curious look. "Just a fan wanting an autograph," he told her, his look daring me to dispute it. He gave her a kiss, wrapped his arm around her waist, and they walked up the incline toward the main entrance. Halfway up, he turned back and called out. "Check our performance schedule. I was on stage last night, in front of hundreds of people."

Twenty-three

...

The manager I found backstage confirmed that Gentry had appeared in Friday night's seven fifteen show and couldn't possibly have driven to the Mount Vernon area, shot at my parents, and returned in time to take the stage for the nine o'clock show. It was coming up on four by the time I thanked the manager and hiked back to my Miata. My knee was aching from the unusual amount of walking and standing, and it was a relief to settle into the car and point it north toward Vernonville. I tried to get Grandpa Atherton on the phone as I drove, but he didn't pick up, so I decided to drop by his place on my way into town.

Grandpa lived in a retirement community and had his own patio home with a glossy blue door. Leaving my car at the curb and striding up the short sidewalk, I noticed daffodil leaves poking up from mulched beds beneath the windows. For me, daffodils mean it's really spring, and the first yellow blooms each year make me feel lighter somehow, like I'm taking off a heavy winter coat. Consequently, I wore a big smile when Grandpa opened the door to my knock.

"What are you so happy about?" he asked, gesturing me in. "Did you get something out of Tab Gentry?"

"Only a solid alibi for last night," I said. I followed him into the cozy kitchen, where a pot of Campbell's tomato soup bubbled on the stove. Like many older people, Grandpa preferred to eat early. There was a community dining room where he could have eaten all his meals, but on the evenings he wasn't seeing Theresa Eshelman, his lady friend, he mostly heated himself some soup and ate it alone. I'd thought that was sad until he explained that conversation in the community dining room consisted of comparing colonoscopy results or arguing about which brand of denture adhesive worked better. He told me to shoot him if he ever offered to show anyone the images from his colonoscopy. After that, I completely understood why he preferred to eat at home.

Grandpa turned off the burner, divided the soup into two bowls without asking if I wanted some, and pulled a box of saltines from the small pantry. The tiny dining area off his kitchen was stacked halfway to the ceiling with boxes of gadgets he'd bought online, and two computers, ham radio equipment, and other electronics took up the entire table, so we took our bowls and the crackers into the living room. Filled with the relics of his travels—a hammered-silver wall hanging from Nicaragua, a Hmong quilt, a cricket bat, a display of Soviet military insignia, a piece of a jacket that supposedly belonged to a young Fidel Castro, and more— the room barely had space for a love seat, bookshelves, and a couple of folding tables that we set our bowls on.

I spooned up some soup, realizing I was famished. I didn't even much like tomato soup, but I'd emptied my bowl before Grandpa finished crumbling crackers into his. "What did you find out?" I asked.

He slurped up a spoonful of soup before answering. "Aah. Hits the spot. Margot called a lawyer."

"Smart move."

He nodded. "She told him about Helland's questions and supplied the names of a couple other women that Zoë had apparently been seeing on the side."

"Worser and worser. She could have been stewing about Zoë's infidelities for months and totally lost it when she followed her to Astrid's."

"Agreed."

"Did you talk to Mom today?"

Grandpa finished his soup, stacked our bowls, and set them aside. "I called earlier. She said everything's fine, but she sounded down. I think she's ready to go back to California."

"I can understand that." Living a nomad's existence gets old, even when you can do it in a luxurious manner. It'd been a while since Ethan had taken a role that required him to be on location for so long, and I knew they'd only done it because Grandpa and I were in the area.

"I got the results back from my FBI friend." Grandpa reached for an envelope on an end table and drew out a single sheet of paper.

I drew my brows together. "Results?"

"On that letter your father got."

I remembered . . . the love note on pink paper. "And?"

Slapping the paper against his thigh, he said, "Bupkes. No fingerprints, no DNA since we didn't have the envelope which the sender might have licked. The only thing Francine could tell me was that the stationery was from Crane—sold in stores all over the country—and the perfume was something called Shalini."

"Pricey stuff," I said. I didn't have much of a nose for perfume and never wore the stuff myself, but I'd had friends in high school who were walking cosmetics counters and I knew Shalini was in the Joy and Chanel No. 5 realm when it came to price.

"So our mystery note writer probably has a middle-aged husband who made a fortune in insurance or oil, and she's sitting home, bored with organizing charity galas and shopping, feeling neglected, and watching Ethan Jarrett movies, while her husband works eighteen-hour days to keep their coffers filled."

"That's pretty sexist, Grandpa."

"I'm just going with the odds, Emma-Joy."

I glanced at my watch. "Speaking of going . . . I've got to run or I'll be late for Kyra's bout. I'll catch up with you tomorrow." I gave him a quick kiss on the cheek and dashed, wishing I had time to check on Jay before meeting Kyra. I'd call him later.

The Vernonville Vengeance, the roller derby team Kyra had skated with the past two years, held their bouts at the city auditorium. I pushed through the double doors and a blast of crowd-stirring heavy metal music assaulted me. The bass beat thrummed up through my feet. The scent of old cigarettes, released from the decades-old walls by the day's high humidity, mingled with the sharp smell of new varnish. Crossing the small lobby to the event area, I found a seat on the metal bleachers to my left, a bit above where the Vengeance's skaters were assembled. The oval track was laid out with tape boundaries at a slight angle to the long axis of the hardwood floor. Rope under the tape let the skaters know when they were going out of bounds. A projector flashed the score and the time remaining on a screen over the stage at the auditorium's far end. Big speakers on the stage shook as they continued to blast out a song I didn't know, undoubtedly by a band I'd never heard of. The league had padded the hard edges of risky wall corners and stationed volunteers—grinning young men—at two side entryways as "girl-catchers" to stop off-balance skaters from sliding out of sight and into possible harm.

I spotted Kyra right away—not hard to do since she's a six-foot-tall black woman and was wearing her purple uniform and helmet. I'd been skeptical about roller derby when she first told me she was going to try it, but it wasn't what I expected. The women ranged in age from about twenty to almost forty and, like Kyra, were into it for the fun of skating and being part of a competitive team. Some of the women were bruisers, some were almost waiflike. Many sported tattoos, some didn't. Kyra had explained the game to me and although I was no expert, I knew that each team had a skater called the jammer who tried to complete more laps around the rink than the other team's jammer. Other skaters blocked for their jammer.

The bout kicked off with a rich-voiced announcer calling out the names of the skaters. Each skater adopted a roller derby name. They were long on double entendres and violence: Killer Kitten, Natasha the Smasher, and the like. Kyra was Vengeful Valkyrie. I'd helped her think it up. As the women whizzed around the track, with the jammers trying to lap the opposing team, I admired the way they worked together, the way a skater would scramble up if knocked down. These women weren't whiners, not even when a nose got bloodied, a finger got jammed, or a hip got bruised in a fall.

Along with the other fans, I pounded my feet on the bleachers to make a racket as the Vengeance's jammer racked one lap more than the Danville Demolishers. In the last minutes of the bout, a sprite of a woman on the Danville team hip-checked Kyra out of bounds and into the wall. The skater behind her didn't have time to swerve and the two of them went down in a tangle and it looked like Kyra's head whacked the floor. She popped right back up but the other skater grabbed at her ankle, her face saying she blamed Kyra for the fall. Kyra tried to shake her off, but the other skater scrambled to her feet and smacked a meaty hand flat against Kyra's shoulder. Kyra almost fell, but kept her balance and lunged under the other skater's outstretched arms. Dropping to a squat, Kyra rolled under the arch the woman's body made as she dove toward her. The woman fell splat on her ample stomach. Kyra extended her body and used her strong thighs to power her back onto the track and into the midst of the skaters as they came around again. Her opponent gave a middle finger salute to Kyra's back, and shouted something I couldn't hear over the music and PA system.

The bout ended thirty-four seconds later and I hurried down the bleachers to where Kyra sat, surrounded by teammates who were sad or irate about what turned out to be a loss. The music cut off abruptly and I swiveled my jaw from side to side to pop my abused ears. "Are you okay?" I asked Kyra, moving a pair of skates so I could sit beside her. "You took a hard fall. That woman was seriously pissed at you."

The woman's teammates were leading her toward the locker room, but she twisted away and came toward us. "You did that on purpose. Lexie the Leprechaun doesn't take that crap from anyone. This is what I'm going to do to you." She dropped her red-and-white helmet and kicked it toward the doors. Four of her teammates grabbed her and steered her away. I couldn't imagine anyone less leprechaunish, except maybe Shaquille O'Neal.

"Thank goodness for helmets," Kyra said, removing hers, apparently unperturbed by the threats. She swiveled her head from side to side. "I'll be achy tomorrow, but what's new?"

"Do you feel up to dinner?"

"I could eat a horse. Just let me change." She headed for the locker room.

I remained on the bleacher, thinking through the week's events, as the crowd of a 150 or so cleared out. Soon, I was the only one left in the cavernous room, although I could hear voices from the lobby area. It seemed to be taking Kyra longer than usual and I began to wonder if we'd crossed wires: maybe she thought I was waiting in my car. Poking my head into the locker room, I called her name, but got no response, so I retraced my steps to the entrance.

I said good night to a couple of people loitering in the lobby, apparently waiting for another skater, and pushed through the double doors into the parking lot. It was full dark by now, and I shivered in my sweater, wishing I'd thought to bring a heavier jacket. A sliver of moon didn't cast enough light to outshine a Winnie-the-Pooh night-light, and the two lampposts in the lot created more shadows than they dissipated. A tall figure that had to be Kyra walked toward a car parked on the far side of the lot, not far from where a chain-link fence held back a profusion of dogwood saplings, kudzu, and other shrubs that grew wild in the empty lot that bordered the parking area. In the dark, the mass of vegetation blurred into nothing more than mounded lumps atop the fence.

"Kyra," I called.

She started to turn when a dark figure zipped out from behind a parked car in front of her. It collided with Kyra and my friend went down. Her startled yelp floated to me and then I was running toward them. The assailant's arm rose up and a streak of light on metal gave me a sick feeling in the pit of my stomach as the knife plunged down. My knee sent jabs of pain up my thigh and jolting into my ankle, but I kept moving. I screamed as I ran; I'm not sure I formed any actual words, but I hoped the loudness would summon help and scare the assailant.

I was still twenty yards away when Kyra rolled under her SUV and the attacker scrambled up and ran, vaulting over the low chain-link fence and disappearing into the shadowy woodland beyond. As I came up to Kyra, I heard a motor start in the distance, followed by the squeal of tires as someone drove off quickly.

I dropped to my knees beside the car. "Kyra! Are you okay?"

"Is she gone?"

"Yes," I said, so relieved to hear Kyra's voice that I took in a gulp of air and started hiccupping. "Come out."

Kyra dragged herself out from under the SUV. Her hair snagged on something on the undercarriage and she tugged it free, wincing. I threw my arms around her and hugged her as she struggled to sit up.

"Ow," she said.

I pulled back. "What?"

"My arm. I got cut." She held out her left forearm and I could vaguely make out a darker line against the red of her long-sleeved tee shirt.

"I'm taking you to the hospital," I announced, helping her to her feet.

"It's no big deal. I don't want—"

"I don't care." Guiding her to my car, I beeped open the door and stood there, arms akimbo, until she got into the passenger seat. I'd done my share of wound bandaging for the week; Kyra was going to get a real doctor to sew her up whether she wanted one or not.

When we emerged from the emergency room two and a half hours later, Kyra had ten stitches in her forearm and a neatly applied bandage. We'd told our story of the attack to the cops who responded to my cell phone call and the hospital's report of a knife wound. Our descriptions of the attacker were sketchy at best.

"Shorter than Kyra," I said, closing my eyes to bring up the image of the figure lunging at my friend. "You said it was a woman, Kyra—how did you know?"

"I did?" Kyra carefully kept her eyes on the police officers so she wouldn't see what the physician's assistant was doing to her arm. She's fearless in many ways, but squeamish about needles.

I nodded. "You said 'Is *she* gone?' when I came up to you. Do you think it was the skater—the one who was so pissed off?" I explained to the police about Lexie the Leprechaun and said they could easily find out the woman's real name from the team's roster.

One of the cops took over. "Did you see her face, ma'am, or maybe her hair?"

"I don't think so," Kyra said, wrinkling her brow. "Maybe she felt like a woman? You know, felt lighter than a man that height would or something. I really don't know. She was wearing all black, including a ski cap or something that hid most of her face and her hair. If it really was a her. That's all I can remember. I'm sorry."

"It's okay, ma'am. It happens like this sometimes—your memory shorts out—when folks have had a fright. You might think of something later. If you do, give us a call." The policeman handed Kyra a card.

"Will do," she promised.

There was more than "good citizen" in her voice and I caught her eyeing him speculatively. At six-one or -two with a muscled build and shaved head, he had a certain rough attractiveness that clearly appealed to Kyra. From the appreciative look in his gray eyes, I thought he found her appealing, too. I imagined she'd find some reason to phone him and was relieved that she felt well enough to be scoping out date prospects.

"He was cute," she said as we exited the hospital.

"Mm-hm," I agreed out of habit, taking a deep breath of the fresh night air. It had been too hot in the ER, and hospital scents always make me tense. I'd spent way too much time in the hospital recovering from my leg injuries.

"Do you want me to drop you at home and tuck you into bed?" I asked. "Or do you want something to eat?"

"Definitely food. Getting knifed makes me hungry."

We settled for drive-through burgers and hit the Giant close to Kyra's for pints of ice cream before pulling up at Kyra's cottage. The smell of grilled beef was making my mouth water and I'd taken a bite of my burger before Kyra even got the door unlocked. Since her arm was in a sling, I carried both our dinners and plopped them down in front of the red brick fireplace in Kyra's living room. Actually, it was her aunt Harmony's living room; Kyra had moved into her aunt's house when she agreed to manage the store for a

year. Full of cushy floor pillows, sofas soft enough to swallow you up, and Indian, Persian, and Navajo rugs piled three
deep on the floor, the room was a welcoming space. Pale
blue paint stenciled with a star motif added a note of
whimsy, as did kerosene-style lamps wired for electricity.
Kyra turned one on and it cast a yellow glow.

She wiggled her arm out of the sling and held out a hand.
"Food," she demanded.

I knew better than to comment on her ditching the sling
so soon. "Do the losers frequently lie in wait after a bout to
get revenge?" I asked after we'd munched through most of
our burgers and fries. I peeled the plastic off the top of my
coffee ice cream and scooped up a spoonful.

"Only the psychos."

I thought about it. Lexie had been pissed off. Could she
have waited outside for Kyra to emerge, followed her to her
car, and attacked her? That must have been what happened,
and yet . . . I scrunched my eyes closed to bring the scene
back and replayed it in my mind: Kyra walking toward her
car, the dark figure springing out in front of her. My eyes
popped open and I said with certainty, "She was waiting
for you."

"So she asked someone what my car looked like or where
to find me." Kyra shot me a half-exasperated look. "Don't
go making a federal case out of a simple 'I'm pissed at you'
beating."

"Knifing. Still, you're probably right. The simple explanation is usually the right one." I shook off my uneasy feeling. It had to have been Lexie because who else would want
to hurt Kyra? I couldn't help thinking that if Kyra weren't a
trained athlete, if she didn't have superb reflexes and hadn't
reacted so quickly when the attacker pounced, that she might
have suffered a far worse wound than a cut on her arm.

Twenty-four

...

Fubar woke me the next morning by leaping onto the pillow beside me and thrusting his muzzle into my face. He interrupted another nightmare, this one also featuring the blood-stained bathroom, but this time it was my mom lying dead in the stall. I jerked awake and clasped Fubar convulsively.

"Mrrp," he said. He leaped down again and I opened one eye to see him sitting proudly beside a vole corpse. His mangled ear gave his head a lopsided look, but there was no mistaking the smug look on his face. It was the same expression generations of Hemingwayesque big-game hunters sported in photos with their foot planted on the rib cage of a lion or rhino.

"Good job," I murmured, closing my eyes again. Why had my cat made it his mission to rid the neighborhood of rodents? He got perfectly good cat food in his dish every day, served up by his favorite slave—me—and still he had to bring me little trophies? At least he hadn't plopped this one on the bed, as he had the dead ribbon snake he'd caught a couple weeks earlier.

Convinced that he'd impressed me with his prowess, he picked up the dead critter and trotted out the bedroom door. I was wondering if I should call my shrink about those sleep meds when the doorbell rang. I was wide awake and out of bed before the echoes died down. I guessed I was a little on edge from the dream and Kyra's run-in the previous night. Belting my terry-cloth robe around my waist, I hurried to the front door, hoping it wasn't more bad news.

I peered through the spy hole. Jay Callahan stood on the walkway. I stepped back, astonished and revoltingly pleased to see him. Tightening the robe's belt, I opened the door.

Jay beamed at me and held out a cup of Starbucks coffee. "I've got cinnamon buns in here," he said by way of greeting, rattling the paper bag he held in his hand. He wore a striped cotton shirt with the sleeves rolled up so the corded muscles of his forearm stood out. Pale freckles nestled in the light sprinkling of red-gold hair and I thought inconsequently that he must need gallons of sunblock in the summer.

"That's the magic password." I opened the door wider.

He came in, staring around with open curiosity. I'd owned the home for a bit over a year and I was still working to cover up some of the damage done when it was a rental property, but Jay didn't say anything about the hole in the drywall behind the door or the missing bit of baseboard in the living room. "You play guitar?" he asked, crossing to the instrument and picking it up.

"Yep." I took a swallow of the coffee, watching him strum gently.

"I sing."

"Really?"

"Maybe we can form a duo, make our fortunes in Nashville." He sang a phrase from a Garth Brooks song in a surprisingly deep voice.

I applauded, laughing. "You might be ready for the Grand Ole Opry, but my playing definitely isn't fit for prime time." Taking the guitar from him, I placed it in its case. "How are you feeling?"

Putting a hand to his side, he said, "Pretty good. It twinges when I stretch, but I changed the bandage myself and it's healing okay. No sign of infection. It's the price I pay for getting careless." His eyes narrowed slightly.

"To what do I owe this early morning . . . visit?" I'd almost said "invasion," but I was actually pleased to see him so I decided to forgive his unannounced arrival on my doorstep.

"You're not working today, right?"

I shook my head. I couldn't remember the last time I'd had the actual weekend off, as opposed to a Monday and Tuesday, say, and I was reveling in it. Of course, it'd be a lot more fun if someone hadn't attacked my best friend last night.

"Me either," he said with satisfaction.

"Then who's giving the shoppers their sugar fix, plying them with calorie-laden treats?" I mocked gently.

"I hired a new employee. She looks enough like Mrs. Fields to be her twin; in fact, I have trouble not calling her Mrs. Fields. I've decided she can handle things on her own today."

"Because . . . ?"

"Because I wanted to see you."

Wham! My eyes widened, but before I needed to say something, Fubar provided a welcome distraction by poking his head in to see who had invaded his territory without permission. At the sight of Jay, or, more specifically, Jay's athletic shoes, I'd swear his eyes lit up with glee. He pounced. Fubar's main joy in life, right up there with de-rodenting the world, was shoelaces. He liked nothing better than to tangle shoelaces, and frequently discombobulated the neighbors by jumping out of the low boxwood hedge to wreak havoc on their laces. I knew the man next door had switched to loafers purely to confound Fubar.

"Nice kitty?" Jay said doubtfully, looking at the large, rust-colored cat with the mangled ear and truncated tail who was going to town on his shoelaces. Before I could intervene, he stooped and picked up Fubar, holding him at face level, back legs dangling. "Now, fella, I hope to be spending a fair amount of time here so you and I are going to have to come to an understanding. If I bring you a feather toy or your own set of shoelaces next time I come, will you leave my shoes alone?" Jay didn't look at me, he kept his eyes on Fubar's, but I got the feeling he was talking to me. Not about the laces, but about spending time together. Warmth eased through me and I couldn't help but smile.

Fubar twitched his tail back and forth and Jay took that as agreement. "So we're agreed: shoes are off-limits." He set the cat down. Fubar disappeared into the kitchen and I heard his cat door push outward and flap shut.

"I think that went well," Jay said with a mock-serious nod.

The last strange man through my door had been equally unexpected—Detective Anders Helland—and he, too, had been kind to Fubar. I didn't know why that thought crossed my mind. "Did you say something about cinnamon buns?"

When he handed over the bag, I headed for the kitchen and grabbed two plates out of the cupboard. Jay followed me, ignored the gaps in the tile where my handyman had abandoned the task when Spring Break arrived, and sat at the table. "Is it okay that I'm here?" he asked.

I caught a faint undertone of anxiousness. "Sure," I said casually, not wanting to let on exactly how okay it was.

"Did you have anything planned for today?"

"Just finding out who shot at my dad and knifed Kyra."

"Tell me."

In those two syllables, his voice went from bantering to serious. I gave him details of the shooting at my parents' house which he hadn't heard on the news, and told him about the attack on Kyra last night. He munched his way through a cinnamon bun while I talked, and licked his fingers clean before I could hand him a napkin.

"The attacks must be related," he said when I finished.

"To Zoë's death," I said, ripping off a small section of cinnamon bun and popping it in my mouth. I talked around it. "It's too much coincidence, otherwise, although I suppose the attack on Kyra might be a fluke." I scrunched up my face doubtfully. "She's not connected to the movie at all, like Ethan and Zoë."

"Okay, leaving Kyra out of it for the moment, what do you think the link between Zoë and your dad is?"

"Grandpa and I already talked about that." I told Jay our theory and what we'd learned about Margot Chelius.

"You work fast," he observed with lifted brows. "How did you find all that out?"

He was too damn quick. "Let's just say my grandpa is a handy guy to know when you want to find stuff out."

"A wiretap?"

I shook my head.

"You bugged her?"

"I can neither confirm nor deny."

Jay chuckled and shook his head. "Your grandpop's a piece of work. Do the terms 'felony' and 'jail time' mean nothing to him?"

"Not much," I admitted.

He went back to being serious. "So you've eliminated the actor who got fired. That leaves Jesse Willard, the Bleek guy, and Chelius. If your grandpop's on Chelius, you and I should tackle Willard or Bleek." He pulled a coin out of his pocket. "Heads it's Willard and tails it's Bleek. You call it."

He flipped the quarter into the air and it spun in silver circles. I felt like that coin; my head whirled and I didn't know which side was up. Jay's presence had a lot to do with that, I knew, and it wasn't an altogether unpleasant feeling.

"Tails."

Twenty-five

. . .

A visit to Jesse Willard's house elicited the information that he and his father were at a local park. Mrs. Willard, who gave us the information, was a plain woman two inches taller than either her husband or son, with a rawboned angularity emphasized by an unflattering shirtwaist dress. She eyed us carefully when we knocked on the door, and then called her husband on his cell before telling us where he and Jesse were. She had an air of grim determination about her and as we left I wondered if she'd always been like that or if it was new since Jesse's return from the war.

We pulled up to the park, a city-owned property with several miles of walking/jogging trails, a large pond, and sports fields, currently populated by hardy middle schoolers engaged in a soccer tournament. The day was sunny and springlike, and I was suddenly happy to be out in the fresh air and not wandering the climate-controlled halls of Fernglen. A large, shaggy dog bounded toward us, a

Newfoundland cross of some kind, and I knew from the way Jay crossed his arms at stomach level that he was more bothered by his wound than he let on. The dog didn't leap on us, but contented himself with sniffing our shoes thoroughly. I patted his massive head and he licked my hand as a young woman trotted up with a leash in her hand.

"Sorry," she said, clipping the leash to the dog's collar. "Josh doesn't always listen."

"I've got a cat like that." I smiled.

As she hauled Josh away, Jay pointed to a section of park where men sat hunched over small tables playing chess. "That's where Mrs. Willard said they'd be."

We walked along the lakeside path and I stopped to watch six newly hatched ducklings step into the water, following their mother without hesitation, before continuing on to the chess area. I spotted Jesse immediately. He sat with his head propped on one hand, studying the chessboard as his opponent moved a pawn. As soon as the man's fingers lifted from the piece, Jesse pushed his bishop across the board and slapped the chess clock. He had a cast on his hand—probably from punching the restroom stall door, I thought. Mr. Willard leaned against a low rock wall behind the men, watching his son play. A slight breeze riffled his dishwater-colored comb-over and he looked more relaxed than I'd ever seen him.

"Jesse loves chess," he said in a low voice when Jay and I joined him by the wall.

"And he doesn't have any trouble playing it, since—?"

Willard shook his head. "No. For whatever reason, that part of his brain is completely intact. He plays as well—better—as he ever did. This"—he gestured to the park around us—"is the only time he forgets, I think."

"Have the police cleared him?" I asked. Jay wandered a

couple steps away, watching the chess match, but I knew he was listening to every word.

Willard's hound-dog eyes looked even sadder, if possible, the lower lids drooping to expose a fraction of their red interior. "I don't think so. But they haven't arrested him. They questioned him for hours, but Jesse stuck with his story that he found Zoë in the bathroom, that she was already hurt when he arrived. He tried to stop the bleeding, he said"— Jesse would've been trained in the same self-aid and buddy care techniques the military taught me—"but then I think he experienced a break of some kind, had a flashback, and became convinced his unit was under attack."

"That's maybe when I saw him run out of the bathroom."

"Could be. Anyway, without a weapon or a motive, the police don't have enough to arrest him, our lawyer says, so he's free for now. Jesse doesn't need this, Officer Ferris."

"EJ."

"He's got enough on his plate without the police hounding him. I didn't think he'd even met that woman—"

"Wait—he knew Zoë?"

"Not knew her, knew her," Willard said, clearly unhappy. "He had a run-in with her two days before she was killed."

Jesse glanced up from his game and shot us a look, as if he knew we were discussing him, and then refocused on the chessboard.

"What happened?" I asked, getting a sinking feeling in my stomach. Jesse having a "run-in" with Zoë was not good.

"Apparently he argued with her. She knocked into him with a shopping bag and he allegedly ripped it away from her and flung it across the hall. She yelled at him and he shoved her, apparently. It wasn't a big deal." The way Willard's shoulders drooped said he knew it *was* a big deal. It was potential motive.

I'd never heard so many "apparentlys" and "allegedlys" in one sentence outside a TV courtroom show. "How did the police know about this?"

"She told one of the guys she worked with and he repeated it to the police. They found part of the encounter on the mall video."

Jay and I exchanged glances. "Who did she tell?"

"Some guy named Bleek told the police about it. I remember that because it makes Jesse's situation bleaker," Willard said without a hint of humor. "If only he had a job, I think it would help him. He needs to feel like he's got a purpose in life, that there's a reason to get up in the morning. But prospective employers take one look at him . . ."

Jesse's game must have ended because he leaned across the table to shake hands with his opponent, whose grumpy expression suggested he'd lost, and crossed to where Jay and I stood with his dad. His hand smoothed over the burn and the place where his eyebrow had been, as if trying to cover them up, or maybe the scar pained him. "EJ," he said with a smile. "Good to see you. And—" His brow furrowed when he looked at Jay, as if he knew he should know his name but couldn't come up with it.

"Jay." He shook hands with Jesse.

"Right. The cookies."

"You win?"

Jesse nodded and focused on me again. "Thank you for helping me yesterday. That police guy, the detective, he told me what you did."

I felt myself blushing. "I'm glad the docs were able to do something for your headache."

"Yeah, now if only they could unscramble my brain." The words could have been bitter, but he said them with a wry humor.

"You're getting better every day, Jesse," his father said.

"I know." He stood silently for a moment, looking out across the park, and then turned back to us. "I watched a video of that Congresswoman who was shot in the head in Arizona. I think it was filmed more than a year after she was hurt, and she was still speaking in one-word sentences and her husband—the astronaut—was having to translate. You could see how hard it was and she cried sometimes. She was working at getting better, though. That's me. I'm working at it."

There didn't seem to be anything to say to that that wouldn't sound patronizing or falsely cheerful, so I nodded my agreement. Mr. Willard patted his son's shoulder.

"We're trying hard to find out what really happened to Zoë Winters," I said after a long moment.

"I appreciate that," Jesse said. "It wasn't me. I didn't hurt that woman."

After the Willards left, Jay and I strolled around the lake, close enough that our shoulders brushed. We hadn't talked about it first, but we veered as if by mutual agreement onto the path that wound past stands of cattails and water grasses. An early red-winged blackbird called from atop a plume of grass that seemed too thin to support his weight, and I spotted the ducklings I'd seen earlier, now swimming with confidence in the middle of the pond. The sky was a pure blue unfuzzed by humidity, and a colorful kite shaped like a dragon rose from the far side of the water, towed by a boy of seven or eight.

It seemed almost sacrilegious to spoil this gift of a day with worry, so I deliberately put all thought of Zoë, and the attacks on my parents and Kyra, and Jesse Willard's plight out of my mind. "How did you come to be a recovery agent?" I asked Jay instead. "When the other boys in elementary school were saying they wanted to be firefighters and soccer stars, did you pipe up with, 'I'm going to be a recovery agent'?"

He laughed. "Not quite. I wanted to be a baseball star, actually. I pitched for my high school team—"

"Where?"

"In Oklahoma. I got a scholarship to OSU, but I wrecked my shoulder in an ATV accident two games into my first season. No more baseball." He rotated his shoulder, as if in memory of the pain. "It was probably a good thing," he said, "because I could spend all the time I would've spent practicing baseball on actual studying."

"Did you?"

"Hell, no. I joined a fraternity and studied beer and sorority girls for a couple of years until my folks threatened to stop paying my tuition if I didn't get my grades up. So, I buckled down and got a degree in math. It took an extra semester because of all the goofing off I'd done, but I graduated cum laude."

I tripped over a rough patch on the path and Jay gripped my elbow to steady me. "Thanks." His hand slid down my arm and his fingers interlaced with mine. The feel of his palm against my own made it hard to concentrate on what he was saying.

"Then I looked around and wondered how I was going to make a living. I thought about getting my teaching certificate, but I had a friend who taught in a middle school and she talked me out of that, so I got a loan and went to grad school. Accounting."

"You're a CPA?" I pulled back and stared at him. I couldn't imagine him behind a desk all day, crunching numbers. He had too much energy, seemed too restless, to be happy doing that.

He smiled at my astonishment. "My expertise is in forensic accounting. I joined the FBI straight out of grad school. I thought it was what I was meant to be doing, until . . . Anyway, when I left the FBI, I had enough to live on for a while and I traveled: the Philippines, Ukraine, Tahiti. I saw all sorts of spots that were off the beaten path, places I'd always wanted to visit. In Yemen, I ran into a man who'd been a guest speaker at the FBI Academy. He was working for Lloyd's, looking to recover a yacht that Somali pirates had made off with. I helped him out, we got the yacht back, and I discovered I liked the work." Before I could comment on his colorful history, he said, "What about you? How'd you end up in the military?"

I watched the dragon kite nosedive to the ground before answering. "Nothing nearly as interesting. I grew up in Malibu. Ethan made it big when I was still young, so I was a child of privilege, you might say. No athletic talents or performing abilities. My only competitive sport was power shopping. In high school, I got caught up with the wrong crowd and I woke up hungover after my graduation party and knew I needed something more than shopping, boys, and alcohol in my life. I marched right down to the nearest recruiter and enlisted."

Jay gave me a humorously admiring look. "You took teenage rebellion to new heights. I'll bet your parents reacted the way you hoped—went ballistic."

Frowning, I said, "I wasn't trying to piss them off." Was I? "I just felt I needed to do something more real."

"So you went from the land of make-believe to the realest of the real. The military. War."

"I did," I said slowly, never having thought of it that way before.

Jay stopped walking and tugged on my hand until I was facing him. A slight question in his eyes, he leaned forward and let his lips brush mine. When I leaned into the kiss, he put his arm around my waist, pulled me closer, and kissed me properly. A warmth that was more volcanic than cozy fizzed through me. Jay's chest and thighs felt steady and solid against mine and I wondered if he could feel my heart beating. My arms twined around his neck, but then I drew away with a gasp.

"Your side!"

"It's fine," Jay assured me, trying to pull me into his arms again. "It's feeling better by the second, in fact. Hardly know it's there."

I laughed and gave him a quick kiss. "Still, we don't want to aggravate the wound."

"Yes we do."

A gaggle of teens bicycled past, one of them towing a skateboarder. They gave us knowing looks and one of the girls giggled. Jay released me with a rueful grin, his hazel eyes fixed on mine. "Lunch?"

"Sure. Then we can get back to figuring out who's behind the murder and the attacks."

"That romantic streak of yours is what attracted me in the first place. Let's do it."

Twenty-six

...

It was a great plan, but midway through lunch, I got a call from Coco MacMillan.

"EJ," she wailed, "two officers went home with the stomach flu and I don't know what to do. I think Joel Rooney's the only one at the mall now. They called me before they left, but I'm in Boston for the weekend—my sister's wedding—and I can't—"

"Don't worry about it," I said with an inward sigh. "I'll go in."

Coco sighed her relief. "Thanks, EJ, you're a lifesaver. Did I tell you I designed the bridesmaids' gowns for the wedding? They're lavender silk with an asymmetric neckline and—"

After kissing Jay good-bye and putting on my uniform, I trudged into the mall with less than my usual lukewarm enthusiasm for my job. I had trouble pushing thoughts of Jay out of my head as I walked into the office. Joel, looking rumpled and harassed, gave me a sympathetic look. "I'm sorry, EJ."

"You don't have anything to be sorry for," I said. "It is what it is. At least it's a Sunday so we can go home early."

"Yeah. I called Edgar and he's feeling fine and will be here for the midshift."

"Good thinking." I gave Joel an approving look. "I called Vic Dallabetta on my way over and she should be here any minute. She'll have Josie Rae with her—couldn't get child care at the last minute like this—so I told her she could do dispatch and her daughter can stay here with her in the office while you and I get out and about."

"Fine by me," Joel said. He was always eager to escape from the security office. "We got a call two minutes ago about a guy making a ruckus at the pet shop. Howling like a wolf, or maybe a hyena. The woman wasn't sure. He's scaring the bunnies and gerbils, she said. Want me to check it out?"

"Go." I waved him away. The gesture knocked a stack of papers off my desk and I bent with an exasperated sigh to pick them up. The flyers distributed on the movie set, I noticed: Stop making movies, yada-yada. I shuffled the black-and-white photocopies into a pile and then slid one back out again. This one had red on it, a red drop of blood dripping from the knife. My fingertips tingled. Was this the original? Had someone used this page to make the other photocopies? A memory lurked just out of reach. I thought I knew where this came from. I shut my eyes and an image of a red stapler popped into my head. Bleek! This page had come from the props trailer. I remembered picking it up when it fell, thinking that the red was the same color as the stapler.

I smiled grimly. I was going to have a serious talk with Mr. Grayson Bleek as soon as I could find him. I frowned, reconsidering. I had to tell Detective Helland, I decided reluctantly. If Bleek really had had something to do with Zoë's death or the other attacks, Helland, with the full power of the police behind him, was better equipped to deal with Bleek than I was. Damn it, anyway. Why should Helland get to have all the fun after I'd pieced it together? Nevertheless, I dialed his number.

Helland answered, which surprised me. I'd figured that on a Sunday he'd be out doing whatever he did on a day off. I thought about that for a quick second. Was he into sports? Did he hang out with friends or family? Go to the movies? I knew he was a gifted amateur photographer, but I didn't know much else about his off-duty life. Nor did I want to, I told myself as he said, "Officer Ferris. Don't tell me you've found another body?"

Refusing to rise to the bait, I explained my flyer theory. "So, I think Grayson Bleek distributed them," I said. "Maybe he killed Zoë to make his point when production didn't stop. The note said to quit making the movie 'or we'll stop you.' He had access to the weapons on set, he didn't much like Zoë, and he got her job when she was killed—it all fits. Although," I added, thinking as I talked, "it seems a bit ironic that an antiviolence organization would use murder to make its point."

"Beyond ironic," Helland said drily. "Ludicrous."

I was stung by his tone. "I'm not saying Bleek did it, but I'd think you might want to have another conversation with him."

"However did I do my job before I had you to help me?" Helland asked, but I heard resignation in his voice and the skritch of pen on paper that told me he was making note of my information. "Any idea where he is now?"

"No. He might be in the props trailer in the parking lot, though. While I've got you on the line—" I told him about the attack on Kyra.

"Did you report it?"

"Of course."

Clicking from a computer keyboard filtered through the phone. "Got it." He fell silent for a moment, presumably scanning the report. "No description of the assailant?"

"No, but Kyra thought it was a woman."

"I presume you think this is related to the killing? Any idea why someone would go after her?"

"I don't know," I said, letting my frustration leak into my tone. "I'm not even sure it's connected, but the murder, and then someone shooting at Ethan and my mom, and then the attack on Kyra . . . it's all too weird and unusual *not* to be connected."

"Muggings aren't that unusual, even in Vernonville," Helland said mildly, and I knew he wasn't trying to rile me.

"I suppose not."

"The report says Kyra had an altercation with a member of the other roller derby team and that the woman might have lain in wait for her and attacked her. There's a note here that the investigating officer has been unable to contact the woman yet, presumably because she and the roller derby team were on their way back to Danville. We've asked the Danville police to question her."

"That's something," I said, figuring there was maybe a fifty-fifty chance that the enraged roller derby opponent had knifed Kyra. "That still leaves Zoë's murder and the attack on Ethan. Those have got to be connected. They knew each other, they were both working on *Mafia Mistress*, they both received those antiviolence notes . . ."

"Agreed."

Vic Dallabetta arrived then, along with a youngster in braces. I said good-bye to Helland and hello to Vic and Josie Rae. A short, stocky woman with dark hair, Vic Dallabetta had a chip on her shoulder that I'd worked hard to overcome. As a single mother, she felt discriminated against and I would schedule her for shifts that enabled her to spend the most time with Josie Rae. This was the first time I'd met her daughter and I saw she was eyeing me with the same curiosity I felt toward her. I held out my hand. "You must be Josie Rae. I'm EJ."

She shook my hand gingerly. "Mom talks about you."

Carefully not looking Vic's way, I said, "She talks about you, too. She says you're an artist?"

Josie Rae nodded, dark hair like her mom's swishing against her shoulders. "Sure am. Look." She pulled out a sketchbook and flipped the top open.

"Josie Rae—" Vic began.

"I'd like to see them," I said.

They were mostly manga images of girls with big heads and huge eyes, drawn in pen and colored with markers. I turned the page. Josie Rae hovered over me, peering over my shoulder, smelling faintly of bubble gum when she breathed out. "I like the colors, and the way you do shading."

"I can't do hands very good," Josie Rae said. She scrunched her face and gave a philosophical, one-shoulder shrug.

"Thanks for sharing them with me," I said, handing the sketchbook back. "Will you show me what you draw while you're working here with your mom?"

"Maybe." She turned away as if it didn't matter, but I thought she was pleased at my interest.

Giving Vic a wave, I headed for the Segway and pointed it toward Merlin's Cave. I found Kyra at work as I expected to, the bandage on her arm concealed by a gauzy teal green blouse over a slim-fitting black skirt. "I knew you'd be here," I said, "even though the doctor told you to rest."

"This is resting," Kyra said, gesturing toward the customer-free store with a sigh. "If it gets any more restful I'm going to go insane."

"Have you advertised for an assistant?"

"Not yet. The thought of wading through résumés from hordes of unqualified teens or, worse, overqualified electrical engineers who've been out of a job since they were laid off a year ago makes it not seem worth it."

"What would constitute unqualified?" I asked. "You didn't know diddly-squat about magic or this New Age stuff or any of the merchandise before you took over last year."

Kyra bent a look at me. "Yeah, but I knew how to make change if handed five dollars for a dollar-forty-seven trinket, and I knew how to listen to customers and to say 'You're welcome' instead of 'No problem' when someone says 'Thank you.' Teens these days don't have basic addition and subtraction skills, and sure as hell don't have the kind of manners Mama drilled into me and my brothers."

I grinned. "Oh, you're getting curmudgeonly now that you're headed toward forty."

"Forty! I just turned thirty-two."

"Just sayin'. When someone starts talking about 'teens these days,' it's a sure sign of encroaching senility."

She tossed a stuffed unicorn at me. I dodged it, laughing, and then picked it up and restored it to its shelf. "I talked to Detective Helland and he seems to think last night's attack was a garden-variety mugging. At any rate, it doesn't sound like the police have made any progress in finding your attacker."

"Not surprised," Kyra shrugged.

I told her about Jay and me talking to Jesse Willard at the park and my conviction that he hadn't killed Zoë Winters.

"Jay and you, huh?" Kyra said slyly, completely passing over what I'd said about Jesse. "How did that come about?"

"He showed up on my doorstep this morning," I said airily, pretending to examine a book about Stonehenge in a revolving rack. "We decided—"

"The best thing the two of you could think to do on a first date was interview murder suspects?" Kyra said, disbelieving.

"It wasn't a date. It—"

"He shows up on your doorstep unannounced on a Sunday morning, probably with flowers or—"

"Coffee and cinnamon buns."

"Uh-huh. It was a date."

I hadn't had a date in so long—not since before I went to Afghanistan—that I hadn't even recognized one when I was on it. I let a smile blossom. "I like him," I confessed.

"What's not to like? He's handsome, single—He is single, right?"

I just looked at her. Kyra and I had slightly different views on the acceptability of dating married men. She knew darned well I thought married men were strictly off-limits. A couple years back, when she'd had a brief relationship with a married athlete, I'd asked her what was attractive about a guy willing to lie to his wife and spend time with a mistress instead of his kids.

"Right. He's good-looking, single, owns his own business, and he's head over heels for you."

"You think?"

"Puh-leeze. You don't see him giving me free cookies every time I walk past the food court, do you? Or looking at me like I'm the only light in a dark cave."

"He doesn't." I flushed.

"He does." Taking pity on my discomfort, she changed the subject. "Anyway, you were telling me about Jesse Willard . . . wait a minute." Her brown eyes lit up. "He's looking for a job, isn't he?"

I knew immediately where she was going. "He said so, yes, but I don't know if a customer service—"

"I could at least talk to him about it," Kyra said, overriding my concerns about Jesse's ability to cope with sometimes annoying or frustrating customers. Even those of us without traumatic brain injuries sometimes wanted to bean unreasonable customers over the head or toss them into the food court fountain. "Do you have his phone number?"

I gave it to her and left to continue my patrolling, knowing from long experience that there was no point in trying to talk Kyra out of something she'd decided to do. She could charge through the Rams' offensive line to achieve a goal, which is how she became an Olympic athlete, I guessed. My route took me past Yalenian & Son Jewelers. Jay and I hadn't discussed his search for the diamonds this morning, but the store brought him to mind. Thinking about Jay gave me a tingly feeling and put a smile on my face as I continued around the top level of the mall.

Then a thought brought me to a halt directly in front of a man dragging an Exercycle down the hall. What would happen when Jay found the diamonds? An empty feeling in my stomach gave me the answer: he'd leave. He'd go on to the next recovery job, which might be a yacht in Africa, or a stolen artifact in Colombia, for all I knew.

"Why so grim, Emma-Joy?"

Grandpa Atherton had approached from the side and I hadn't even seen him. I shook off my dismay at the realization that Jay Callahan might move on at any moment. I could think through that later. "Hi, Grandpa. I'm not grim . . . just thinking. What are you up to?"

Wearing his favorite blue blazer over gray flannel slacks and with his white hair combed off his face, he looked ready for a photo shoot for *GQ*, if they did a Golden Years edition. "I heard about Kyra getting knifed last night," he said, white brows drawing together. "Why didn't you tell me?"

"I'm sorry. It's been a busy day. I haven't had a chance. The police think it was a mugging."

Grandpa looked unconvinced but didn't pursue it. "I met your mom for lunch today. She gave me this." He handed over a sheet of pink paper, folded in half.

I held the corner between my thumb and forefinger, reluctant to mess up possible prints. "Should I—"

"My FBI friend's already had a go at it," Grandpa said, motioning for me to open the note. "She put a rush on it for me. No joy. Same stationery as before, same perfume, no prints."

Reassured, I unfolded the page. The floral scent drifted up and made me sneeze. " 'My beloved Ethan,' " I read aloud. " 'Don't think I blame you for your lack of faithfulness to me. I know you feel the same way I do, but you are forced to hide it. I understand, my love. Don't worry. I know who to blame and how to deal with them. Soon, we will be together, forever, free to love as we were meant to love. Truly, Madly, Deeply.' "

I looked up, feeling slightly ill, and Grandpa nodded,

apparently satisfied with my reaction. "Makes you want to throw up, doesn't it?"

"Worse. It scares me."

Grandpa put his hand over mine where it rested on the Segway's steering bar. "Me, too. And your mom."

"Did it come from the studio? Was there an envelope?"

Grandpa looked grim. "This one didn't come from the studio. Someone left it in their mailbox—no envelope or stamp, no return address."

"Their mailbox? That means—"

"That TMD is here. That she knows where Ethan and your mom are staying."

My fingers tightened reflexively on the steering bar. "She must have known there was a better than even chance that Mom would check the mail first and would find her note. She might even have wanted Mom to find it, to think that Ethan was—Maybe she's trying to break up my folks' marriage." The thought made me clench my teeth in anger.

"I think it's worse than that, Emma-Joy," Grandpa said. "When I was talking to your mother this morning, she mentioned again how close the bullets came to her. What if the shooter wasn't aiming at Ethan? What if *she* was gunning for Brenda?"

Twenty-seven

. . .

I leaned back and the Segway rocked. "You really think—? Did you warn Mom?"

"I didn't want to scare her. I put a word in Con's ear; he and his crew will stick to her like burrs on a spaniel."

"We need to give this to the police," I said, indicating the pink note I still held. "I know your FBI friend has already gone over it, but the Vernonville PD needs to be aware. They can alert the cops in the Mount Vernon area to keep an eye on Mom and Ethan's house."

A shopper with an armload of bags bumped Grandpa and I realized the mall corridor was hardly the best place to have this conversation. "Look, Grandpa, I get off work at five today. That's"—I checked my watch—"an hour and twenty minutes. Meet me at my place so we can think this through. Don't do anything until we've talked," I added, not sure what he might get up to, but pretty sure it would be outrageous and possibly felonious.

"Emma-Joy!" He pretended to be hurt, but his eyes sparked with mischief. He sobered almost immediately, the threat to my parents being too real to joke about. "Will do. I'll take the note to the police while you finish up your shift."

I handed him the note and he walked off. I continued my patrol, my mind whirring. A shoplifter could have carted off an elliptical machine from Pete's Sporting Goods right under my nose and I wouldn't have noticed. Having cruised through the entire mall, I returned to the security office. Joel was there, watching the monitors, and he hastily closed out a game of computer solitaire.

I ignored his guilty look. "Where's Vic and Josie Rae?"

"Josie Rae wanted to go on patrol, so Vic asked me if I minded doing dispatch," Joel said. "They're cruising the parking lots."

I wasn't sure having a kid along on patrol was a good idea, but before I could say anything, Joel added, "Vic called Coco and asked her, and Coco said it was okay."

Rolling my eyes, I sat. Chances were, nothing would happen while Vic and her daughter patrolled the parking lots and garages in the security office's green-and-white Chrysler, but I thought letting kids do ride-alongs set a poor precedent. However, I wasn't the boss. Pulling up the online logbook, I hastily typed in a few entries, one eye on the clock, planning to dart through the door the minute the second hand ticked over to five o'clock. I cursed under my breath when I accidently hit the Delete key and had to start over.

"What's up, EJ?" Joel asked after a few minutes.

"Nothing," I snapped.

He retired into wounded silence and I was mad at myself for hurting his feelings. I rolled my chair back a few inches

and faced him. "I'm sorry, Joel," I said. "I'm a bit uptight."
What would it hurt to tell him about the letter? "Ethan got
a fan letter from a fan who doesn't sound like she's playing
with a full deck." I quoted it from memory.

Joel's brown eyes widened. "Wow."

"That's one way to put it."

"Did you ever see the movie *The Fan*?" he asked. "Wes-
ley Snipes is a baseball player and Robert De Niro is his
biggest fan. He sells hunting knives and—"

I stopped him with a wince. "I don't need to hear about
anything that combines knives and deranged fans right
now," I said.

"Sorry." He looked contrite but bounced back a second
later. "So, who do you think it is? I mean, it's got to be
somebody connected with the movie, doesn't it?"

"Why?" I asked, giving it some thought.

"Well, because why else would TMD be here? She must
be involved with the movie."

"Maybe she follows him from location to location," I
said, the thought making my stomach hurt.

Joel leaned forward with his forearms on his pudgy
thighs, not one whit discouraged. "Okay. Right. Then how
did she know where your parents are staying?" He answered
his own question before I could. "I suppose she could have
followed him home from the set. I mean, that limo is pretty
obvious, and it's not like he's the president where there's two
or three decoy cars taking off at the same time to fool
assassins."

"She's not an assassin," I said, fear for Ethan making my
tone sharp.

"Sorry. Of course not. Only . . . do you think she
killed Zoë?"

I drew my breath in with a hiss. "Why would someone obsessed with Ethan kill Zoë?" Even as the words left my mouth, the memory of my dad comforting Zoë popped into my head. He'd had his arm around her, had spent some time reassuring her about her job. Could a woman who thought she loved Ethan, who was convinced they had some sort of relationship, have taken his kindness the wrong way? Have interpreted it as romantic interest in Zoë? It seemed ridiculously far-fetched to me, but I was no expert on stalkers. I knew someone who might be, though . . .

Ignoring Joel's curious look, I pulled out my cell phone, blipped through my stored numbers, and found one I hadn't called in several months. After the IED and the surgeries, during my rehab time, I'd spent time with a shrink who was supposed to help me come to terms with the changes in my body and my life and help with any residual PTSD. We'd had weekly sessions for several months, which had eventually tapered off to biweekly and then monthly as I got better. I hadn't spoken to him since late last year, but his number was still in my phone. I crossed my fingers as I dialed, aware that I probably wouldn't get him on a Sunday unless he'd gotten stuck with the weekend on-call shift at Fort Belvoir's Community Hospital.

I didn't get Dr. Duvvoori on the line; I got an answering service. I left a message, emphasizing that it was *not* a patient emergency, and hung up. Before I could even explain the call to Joel, my phone rang.

"EJ, how are you?" Dr. Duvvoori's smooth, calm voice greeted me. Instantly, I was transported to the comfortable club chair in his office where I'd spent many an hour during my recovery.

"I'm fine," I assured him. "Really well." *Except for the nightmares . . .*

"Your leg?"

"Better and better." I kept my voice cheery and didn't tell him I was worried that my improvement had slowed, maybe even declined in the last few weeks.

"Good, good. Are you still working at the mall?"

"Yes."

"What about your applications for police work? Are you still hoping to join a police force?"

"Absolutely."

There was a miniscule pause before he asked, "So, what can I do for you today?"

"I'm sorry to bother you on a Sunday—you didn't need to call back—"

"I was curious," he said.

"Well, then, I was wondering what you know about stalkers, about what makes them tick and how they might behave."

"Do you think you're in danger, EJ?" Dr. Duvvoori's voice was sharper.

"Me? No! It's . . . it's someone I know. And he might not be in danger himself. It's—"

"Perhaps this would be easier in person," Dr. Duvvoori broke in on my explanation.

"I don't want to interrupt—"

"I'm in my office this afternoon, up to my knees in paperwork. Unless there's an emergency, we should be able to chat without interruption. Shall I expect you in half an hour?"

I looked at the clock and did some quick calculations. Fort Belvoir was about twenty minutes up the road, barring traffic. It was a few minutes to five, but I knew Joel wouldn't mind covering for me, and Vic Dallabetta was still here— somewhere. I could call Grandpa and tell him I was going to be later than expected . . . "Yes," I said. "I'll be there."

• • •

I poked my head into Dr. Duvvoori's open office door thirty-five minutes later. He was bent over a file drawer, with stacks of folders mounded around him. I tapped lightly and he looked up. "There's an upcoming inspection," he said, watching my eyes widen as I took in the extent of the chaos. "I must make sure all my I's are dotted and my T's are crossed." He scrunched his face at the thought of the army inspector general's emphasis on paperwork.

"I must say I don't miss inspections," I said, entering when he beckoned. Being back in the hospital, walking the long, linoleumed corridors sparsely peopled on a Sunday with inpatients in gowns waiting for procedures, the occasional visitor in civvies, and medical personnel in uniforms or scrubs, had made me edgy. My surgery and post-op recovery had been done at Bethesda Naval Hospital, but once I'd moved to Vernonville, I'd done a lot of my PT and follow-ups here at Fort Belvoir. It was here, in Dr. Duvvoori's office, that I'd more or less come to terms with the loss of my military career and my altered physical capabilities.

Dr. Duvvoori rose, arcing his spine to stretch it, and stepped over a tower of folders to shake my hand. "You look well, EJ. Maybe a little tired."

An inch shorter than me at five foot five, and maybe eight or ten years older, he had thick, dark hair parted deep on one side, kindly brown eyes, and toast-colored skin with a heavy five o'clock shadow. His left eyelid drooped a little, giving a misleading impression of sleepiness. His light green uniform shirt was crisply ironed, but a couple of extra creases on his sleeve showed a lack of expertise with an iron, something I found strangely endearing. Silver oak leaves on his shoulder tabs denoted his rank—lieutenant colonel—but he'd always preferred to be addressed as "doctor."

I passed up the opportunity to tell him about the new nightmares. They'd go away, I was sure, when we found Zoë's killer. "You got a new chair," I observed, putting my hand on the back of a faux-leather upholstered wing chair in a dark wine color. "My" chair had been a forest green club chair, worn on the tweedy seat and where hundreds of heads had rested over the years.

"Sit," Dr. Duvvoori invited, settling on a small love seat across from me rather than behind his desk. "Tell me why you're interested in the psychology of stalking."

Leaving nothing out—Dr. Duvvoori knew who my parents were, since it's hard to make progress in therapy if you hold back your entire childhood—I spent fifteen minutes filling him in on what had been happening: the movie company filming at Fernglen, Zoë's death, suspicion falling on Jesse Willard, the antiviolence flyer, the attacks on my parents and Kyra, and finally, the love letters to Ethan.

He was silent for a good minute after I finished, eyes half closed, fingers steepled in a pose I had seen often.

"I'm beginning to think the love letters are at the root of it," I said. "Is it possible? That some woman would imagine that she and Ethan have a relationship and would go to murderous lengths to . . . protect it?" I passed him the copy Grandpa had made for me of the latest letter.

Smoothing it flat on his thigh, Dr. Duvvoori said, "It would be helpful to have the other letters to study, to see the progression from the first to the most recent. But failing that . . ." He pulled a pair of rectangular reading glasses from his pocket and read the letter through several times. Removing the glasses, he gestured with them toward the note.

"After you called, I did a little research on stalking to refresh my memory. I have only once worked with a stalker—a man ordered by the courts to receive counseling as part of his sentencing—and twice with the victims of stalking. Stalkers are predominantly men, but women stalkers are by no means unheard of. David Letterman, I believe, was victimized by a stalker for many years. Some statistics suggest that one in twelve women and one in forty-five men in the U.S. has been stalked or will be stalked."

"That's a lot of people. I had no idea."

Dr. Duvvoori nodded. "Mm-hm. When you add celebrity to the mix, well, the numbers grow significantly."

"Are stalkers violent?"

"Sometimes. Maybe half of all stalkers threaten the object of their obsessions, and that increases the risk of violence."

"Whoever's writing these letters hasn't threatened my father," I said, eager to believe there was no connection.

Tapping one finger on the letter, he said, "Ah, but she has implicitly threatened people—women—with whom your father has relationships, real, or—just as important to the stalker—perceived."

"You say 'perceived.' What would make her think Ethan was having a relationship with someone? I mean, he was only casually acquainted with Zoë through work—she never visited my parents' house or went on trips with Ethan or anything." I shifted in the chair, trying to get comfortable. It occurred to me that it was the topic and not the chair that was making me uncomfortable, and I tried to relax.

"Oh, it wouldn't have to be anything as significant as that," Dr. Duvvoori said with a quick headshake. "A hand-shake that the stalker interpreted as lingering too long, a stray look, any word or gesture could take on completely unintended significance for the stalker. It's my guess that she suffers from a typology known as 'erotomania,' where the stalker believes the object of her obsession loves her in return. She fantasizes that they have or will have a love relationship. When the victim does not respond in the way she wants, she has two choices: to blame him, which might lead to violence directed against the love object, or to blame people surrounding the victim, those she perceives as 'coming between them' or 'keeping them apart.' "

I shivered. "That's sick."

"Exactly." Dr. Duvvoori said it in all seriousness.

"Does the stalker ever . . . lose interest? Move on to another victim, or a real-life lover?"

"That's not impossible, but in this case, where you think the stalker might have already attacked, even killed, women she thought threatened her relationship with Ethan Jarrett—"

"She doesn't have a relationship with him!"

Dr. Duvvoori held up his hands in a calming motion. "You're right, of course. I should have said, 'her imaginary relationship' or 'her perceived relationship.' At any rate, I wouldn't expect her to back off at this point."

His words dislodged a thought. "Does she know him? I mean, has she met him? Or is their 'relationship' a total fabrication, something only in the head of a woman who's seen him in the movies, but never said hello to him?"

"I'd say she knows him. Whether he'd remember the encounter, whether it's ongoing or was a one-time thing . . ." He shrugged. Using one finger, he handed back the letter. "I know that isn't what you wanted to hear."

I didn't tell him how worried it made me for my mom and Ethan. Only the thought that they were surrounded by competent bodyguards kept me from rushing straight to their house. "Will you tell the police what you told me?" I asked.

"Of course. Give them my number."

I nodded and rose. "I will. Thank you. It was good to see you again, Dr. Duvvoori."

"Come anytime, EJ," he said with a smile. "Stay well."

Twenty-eight

...

When I got home, Grandpa Atherton was sitting at my kitchen table, hand feeding Fubar bites torn from a strip of bacon. With the other hand, he was sorting through a pile of mail I hadn't gotten to from the past couple of days.

"Make yourself at home," I said caustically, on edge from my talk with Dr. Duvvoori and the hellacious traffic I'd fought on the way back. I'd called Kyra on my cell phone, too, to warn her that a deranged stalker might have her in her sights, but she'd laughed me off, said she could take care of herself, and that had worried and annoyed me, too.

"I've got chicken pot pies in the oven." Grandpa smiled at me.

The smell of browning puff pastry and rich stock and vegetables took the edge off my mood. "Want to move in?"

Grandpa chuckled. While he rose to peek in the oven, I disappeared into my bedroom to change. Fubar, I noticed, stayed with the bacon provider, rather than coming with me to ask how my day was. Fickle feline. Pulling an old Packers tee shirt over my head and slipping into a pair of holey sweats made me feel much more relaxed.

When I returned to the kitchen, the pot pies steamed from two plates on the table and Grandpa had opened bottles of beer to go with them. "Cheers," he said, clinking his bottle against mine as we sat.

We ate in silence for a moment and Fubar disappeared through his cat flap when it became clear the handouts had dried up. The pot pies catapulted me back to my childhood, when Mom used to put pot pies in the oven for me and Clint whenever she and Ethan were going to be out for the evening. The babysitter du jour had served them up with tall glasses of cold milk once Clint and I were in our jammies. I used to love separating the fluted rim of crust, browned almost to burned, from the gooeyness inside the pie, and saving it for last. I did it again now, even though the gourmet-brand pot pies Grandpa had brought were a far cry from the Swanson's of my childhood.

Gesturing toward one of my letters with his fork, Grandpa flicked some gravy on it. "Oops. Sorry, Emma-Joy." He looked at me from under his brows. "That looks like it's from a police department."

"Did you figure that out from the return address which says 'Omaha Police Department'?" I knew what was coming and it made me testy.

"I thought you'd changed your mind about police work," he said.

"You *want* me to change my mind. That's different."

"I want you to be realistic—"

"Why does your version of 'realistic' mean I have to give up on joining a police force, doing the only kind of work I want to do?"

"Your leg—"

"It's my brain that makes me a good cop and there's nothing wrong with my brain. You're as bad as Ethan!"

Grandpa didn't respond; he merely picked up his empty foil container and stuffed it in the trash can, his lips pressed together. I mashed the last bits of pot pie into goo with my fork, watching from the corners of my eyes as Grandpa sponged the table. The silence grew. Leaning back, I stuffed my foil dish and napkin in the trash. When Grandpa returned to the table, he changed the subject.

"Detective Helland wasn't in, but the detective I gave the note to, a woman named Livingston, took it seriously, I think. I gave her my friend's name at the FBI so they can get the forensic data from her. She wanted copies of the earlier notes and I said we'd try to get them.

"I'll give Delia a call," I said. "Knowing her, she has them sorted and filed by date and subject matter. I know she's on her honeymoon, but I don't think she'd mind a quick phone call, under the circumstances. What time is it in Fiji?"

"Noon tomorrow," Grandpa said.

I stared at him. "How do you—?" Shaking my head, I found my cell phone and called Delia's cell, hoping it worked in Fiji. I figured it would because she'd always been reachable when traveling with Ethan.

After congratulating her again on her marriage, and apologizing for interrupting her honeymoon, I told her what we needed. In her usual efficient way, she said it was no problem and that she'd make a couple calls and arrange to have the file shipped to us via overnight mail.

"We'll have them tomorrow sometime," I told Grandpa.

"Good. Maybe a police psychologist can make something out of them."

"That reminds me . . ." I told him about my conversation

with Dr. Duvvoori. "He thinks it's perfectly possible that the woman who wrote those letters thinks Ethan loves her back and that he's being kept from her by Mom and who knows what other women. Zoë, obviously. Ethan hugged her to make her feel better after that prop gun went off by accident. I think the stalker misinterpreted that." I hoped. I was going to get Mom to spill the beans tomorrow, come hell or high water.

Grandpa's white brows drew together. "Then why Kyra? Or do you think the attack on her wasn't related?"

"No, it was," I said, rising in my excitement to pace the small kitchen. "The day she was attacked, we ran into Ethan on the set. He greeted her like a long-lost friend, threw his arms around her, kissed her. I can absolutely see how someone could misinterpret their relationship. Whoever it was knew Kyra was participating in a roller derby bout that night because we mentioned it several times."

"It wouldn't take a KGB agent to find out when and where," Grandpa said.

"Right. So she drives to the city auditorium, hides, and waits for Kyra to come out." I frowned. "Or maybe she follows Kyra there from the mall. That would explain how she knew which car was Kyra's."

"Pretty ballsy," Grandpa observed. "There were a lot of people around, weren't there?"

I nodded. "Yes. She's losing it, losing control, I think. She's taking bigger and bigger risks."

"What did your shrink say were the chances she'd turn against Ethan eventually, start to blame him?"

I stared at him, appalled that I hadn't thought of something so obvious.

Grandpa smiled grimly. "Make a list of who was there

when Ethan hugged Kyra and Zoë. If we cross-reference the two lists, we should narrow down the suspect pile."

"It was crowded both times. All sorts of movie people were milling around. I don't know half their names. But I'll try." I found a pad of paper by the phone and sat at the kitchen table.

"Concentrate on remembering the women," Grandpa advised.

"Duh," I muttered under my breath. "The straight women," I added, crossing Margot Chelius's name off my list. Or did she swing both ways, like Astrid apparently did? I wrote Margot's name down again and sighed. It took me twenty minutes, and when I was done I knew the lists were flawed and incomplete at best. The list of people who had been present both times looked like this: Anya Vale, Bree Spurrier, Iona Moss, Margot Chelius, Vandelinde, the actor playing the hit man (Brad Something), Grayson Bleek, miscellaneous police extras, crew members, security men.

"This doesn't exactly help us zero in on a single suspect," I said, passing the list to Grandpa.

"It narrows down the field," he said. "I'll get started on background checks on all these people, even the men. Who knows? Maybe the stalker is a gay man."

"Writing on pink stationery sprinkled with Shalini?" I didn't try to hide my skepticism.

"You never know," Grandpa said. He rose to leave, tucking the page into a pocket. He kissed my forehead. "Goodnight, Emma-Joy. I love you."

"Love you, too."

Only when Grandpa had left did a new thought cross my mind. We were basing our whole argument that it was a stalker who killed Zoë on the theory that someone shot at

Mom, trying to eliminate her from Ethan's life. What if Mom got shot at not because she was married to Ethan, but because she saw something the morning Zoë died, something that would identify the murderer? Fubar head-butted my ankle, but I ignored him, thinking it through. In that scenario the attack on Kyra was Lexie the Loon out for revenge or a knife-wielding mugger. I shivered. Mom was in danger either way, and the sooner I found out what she'd been up to Tuesday morning, the safer she'd be.

Although I wanted to hightail it out to see Mom Monday morning, I had to work. My first stop was the old perfume store where Detective Helland's task force had set up shop. The blond detective was giving directions to two officers when I walked in. Finishing with them, he greeted me with a lifted brow.

"Any progress?" I asked.

"Grayson Bleek confessed to creating and distributing the antiviolence flyers," Helland said. "He and his brother Hayden, who's one of the movie's security guards, founded the Anti-Violence Anti-Capitalism Movement two years ago in response to, and I quote, 'the insensitivity of the greater Hollywood community to the deleterious effects of conspicuous consumption and glorification of violence on the American ethos.'" He read from his notebook and looked up at me with a gleam in his eye.

"Catchy," I offered, "although they'd never make it in the military with a clunky acronym like AVACM."

Helland laughed, his gray blue eyes seeming lighter and bluer than usual. "I knew you'd appreciate it. Anyway, he confessed to the sabotage but categorically denies having anything to do with Winters's death or the shots fired at the Jarretts."

"Of course."

"Of course," Helland agreed. "However, he has an airtight alibi for the evening your parents were shot at. He was at the dentist having an emergency crown fitted."

"What about his brother?"

"Filling out insurance paperwork. He drove Grayson to and from the procedure. The dentist's office confirms they were both there. Neither one could have shot at your parents."

"Let me tell you what I found out." Handing him a copy of the latest letter from TMD, which Grandpa had already turned over to Detective Livingston, I went through my conversations with Dr. Duvvoori and Grandpa yesterday, and then handed him Duvvoori's phone number and the list I'd come up with. "I think it's possible the stalker, this TMD, killed Zoë and tried to kill my mom and maybe Kyra," I said. I wasn't willing to tell him my mom had been in the mall last Tuesday.

Helland edged his jaw to the left as he thought. "Let's get some coffee." Ushering me out of the office, he turned toward The Bean Bonanza, bought two cups of coffee, and handed one to me without asking what kind I wanted. I sipped it, grateful for the caffeine after a restless night; I'd dreamed of a *Psycho* shower scene in reverse with a woman stabbing Ethan over and over again through a shower curtain.

"You're worried about your folks."

Helland made it a statement, and I nodded. "Yes. Especially my mom, since the stalker's already tried to kill her. But also my dad. What if the stalker decides Ethan has betrayed her?"

Despite the early hour and the mall not being open for shopping, Fernglen hummed with activity. Mall walkers racewalked or ambled past us, and a few shop owners and managers were already slipping under their stores' grilles to catch up with cash register reconciliation or inventory tasks. A man from the plant service squirted water into the planters from a huge blue tank he towed, and wiped dust off the broad-leafed hostas and rubber plants.

"Doing background checks on all these people will take time," Helland said, "even if we focus on the women."

I sighed with relief, knowing he'd accepted my reasoning. "Grandpa's already started on it."

Helland's look soured. "This is police work," he snapped, "not amateur hour. I appreciate your bringing me this information, but you and your grandfather have got to step back now. You don't want to end up in this killer's sights, or screw up evidence and make it impossible for us to prosecute her."

Every time I started to half like this man, he went out of his way to piss me off.

"And don't bother to tell me you're not amateurs," Helland went on before I could object, "because neither of you carries a badge."

I was debating whether to snap back at him or walk off in a dignified dudgeon, when he added, "I don't want you to get hurt."

Something in his voice defused my anger and I buried my confusion by taking a long sip from my cup. I peeped up at him through the steam drifting off the coffee. Was he worried about me? He met my gaze levelly for a moment and then stared into his brew, as if he'd find an important clue in the aromatic depths. The awkward silence stretched to fifteen seconds before I said, "I guess this means Jesse Willard is no longer a suspect?"

"It doesn't mean anything until we've made an arrest," Helland said disagreeably. "Stay out of it, EJ. It's police work." He crumpled his cup, lobbed it into a trash can ten feet away, and walked off before I could respond.

Fine. I stomped back to the security office, arriving in time to see Coco emerge from her office wearing a navy blue catsuit with a beanie-type hat. Joel sat in front of the monitors, but turned to face her when she said, "Ta-da!" She flung her arms wide. Her red curls bounced. "What do you think?"

"Of?"

"The new uniform, of course." She turned around, displaying curves too fulsome for a spandex-laced knit. "It's very Emma Peel, don't you think? Someone gave my sister and her new hubby a boxed set of *Avengers* DVDs and we watched them after the bachelorette party. I knew immediately that this was the look we needed for our uniforms."

"You're kidding, right?" Joel said, taking the words out of my mouth.

I wondered what they'd had to drink at the bachelorette party, and if there was any chance someone had spiked their drinks with a hallucinogen.

"Not for the men, silly," Coco giggled. "Your uniforms would have the same sort of top, but slacks on the bottom. Skinny ones. And shoes like John Steed wore. I'm modeling this for the FBI board this afternoon. Wish me luck!" She darted back into her office.

"Kill me now," Joel said.

I choked. "Look on the bright side."

He peered at me suspiciously.

"Shoplifters and vandals would be laughing too hard to steal or deface anything here at Fernglen. Think how our crime rate would go down."

"I don't care if it goes to zero," Joel said, spinning his chair in his agitation. "I'm not walking around dressed like some cheesy spy from the sixties. You have to talk to her."

I could've asked "Why me?" but I knew why me: because I had assumed the duties of second-in-command, and because I'd briefly been the acting director of security. The other officers counted on me to provide leadership, even though I got paid what they did and had no official standing. My morning was getting better by the minute.

Inhaling deeply, I walked the short distance to Coco's office and knocked on the door. I cast one last, pained look at Joel, who gave me vigorous head nods and two encouraging thumbs-up, before entering the office in response to Coco's "Yes?"

She was at her desk, fingering one of a pile of fabric swatches. She looked up with a smile. "What's up?" She studied my face for a moment and her smile faded. "Oh, no. Nothing's happened, has it? I mean, nothing bad, like—?"

Taking advantage of her disinclination to name the bad things that might have happened, I dove in. "Coco, it's about the uniforms. We don't really need new uniforms. Even though your designs are great, the security guards—I—think they feel too much like costumes. They'd make us look like we're *playing* at being guards; they'd take away our authority."

Puzzlement crinkled her brow. "I don't understa—"

"The current uniforms are utilitarian. They—"

"Utilitarian?" She gagged on the word as if I'd said "radioactive."

"Yes." I nodded firmly. "Our most important job is keeping people safe. Our customers, the mall merchants, visitors like the movie people. We can't do that if we're fussing with our clothes, or feeling self-conscious, or don't have pockets for notebooks or a place to clip our radios." I gestured at the pocket-free expanse of knit she wore.

"I could add a belt . . ." Her voice trailed off before she finished the thought, and I hoped I'd finally gotten through to her. "I'm not any good at this job, am I?"

"I don't know. You haven't tried it yet."

She gave me a startled look.

I gestured to the sewing machine and mannequin. "You haven't tried being the director of security, I mean. You've been inhabiting this office, but working as a designer."

Her lower lip trembled and I was afraid she was going to start crying. "My mom and my uncle—he's her brother and he got me this job—will be so mad if I quit. My folks didn't want me to study design in the first place, and when I couldn't get a job right after graduation, all I heard was, 'You should have studied accounting' and 'We told you fashion design wouldn't pay your bills.' When Uncle Todd said he could get me a job, working at one of FBI's malls, well, they more or less told me I had to take it or move out and start paying all my own bills."

"You live with your folks?"

She gave a tiny head nod and swiped a finger under her eye. "Yes. I want to move out, but I can't afford—"

I didn't feel qualified to offer Coco any career counseling, and it wasn't really my business, but I blurted, "If you're passionate about design, be a designer, even if you have to be a low-paid intern or some such for a while. If that means your parents kick you out, then get a roommate or two, wait tables, or get some other second job—do whatever it takes to work in a field that excites you. Life's too short."

"So, you're passionate about being a mall cop?"

Coco cocked her head to one side, like she was really interested in my answer, and there was no snark in her tone, but the question still stung. "I'm sorry," she said, when I didn't answer right away. "It's none of my business."

Hoisted on my own petard. "No, it's okay," I said. "I guess I'm doing this because I want to be a cop, but I can't get hired." I slapped my injured leg, none too gently. "I'm still trying. If I can't get police work, I don't know what I'll do instead. I don't think I have another passion." That sounded really sad when I said it aloud; I made a mental note to think about it later. "In the meantime, I'm being the best mall security officer I can be."

"Unlike me, huh?" Coco said. She gave a crooked smile, bringing her dimples into play. "You're right: I need to shape up or ship out."

"I didn't say—"

"Yes, you did. You're right. It's not fair to you or the others, or my uncle or me, to keep on like this." She thrust the fabric swatches into a desk drawer. "I don't know what I'm going to do, but I guess I'd better think about it before the meeting with the board. I promise I won't try to get them to approve a new uniform, even though—I think I'll change." She gestured to the catsuit.

Taking that as dismissal, I left the office, closing the door behind me. Joel greeted me with an anxious look when I got back to my desk.

"So?"

"So, she thinks it would look very sharp in lavender. She said something about how lavender flatters all complexions—"

Joel paled and I laughed. "I'm kidding. She's decided we don't need a new uniform."

"Thank God." Joel sagged with relief. "It's bad enough that I need to lose a few pounds. That uniform would've made me look like a blimp."

"You wouldn't have had the worst of it," I pointed out. "Can you see Edgar in a lavender catsuit?"

Twenty-nine

. . .

I drove up to my parents' rental house after work, skipping my swim with Joel in my anxiousness to talk to Mom. I found her in the back by the pool, wearing a linen tunic, cropped pants, and a broad-brimmed straw hat with a whimsical peony attached at the crown. She sat on a lounger, a glass of iced tea on a table to her left and her knitting bag on her right. She plied the needles with great concentration and I noticed that the blue blanket had grown a couple of feet.

She greeted me with a kiss and an offer of iced tea. "I wasn't expecting you today, EJ," she said a bit nervously, handing me a hat and a bottle of sunblock. I applied it to my bare arms, releasing a coconut smell that I enjoyed.

"I was worried about you," I said. "Until the police catch this stalker . . ."

"You're the third person today to mention a stalker," she said with mild exasperation. "Your grandfather called to warn me and then Detective Helland called to ask if I had any idea who could be sending the notes. 'None,' I told him."

I explained about calling Delia. "Hopefully, we—the police—will be able to figure out who it is once they have the other letters in hand."

"Maybe Kyra should stay with us for a few days," Mom offered, a pucker between her brows. "If you really think some madwoman tried to stab her because Ethan gave her a hug . . ."

"That's thoughtful of you," I said. "I'll let Kyra know." I could hear Kyra in my head, proclaiming that she didn't need a "babysitter," and that she could take care of herself, but I'd relay my mom's offer. "Maybe you should go back to California while Ethan finishes up here. It—"

"Not a chance! You think I'm going to let some two-bit floozy chase me away from my husband? You think I'm going to leave the field clear for her to move in on him?"

"I guess not." I smiled at her indignation. "Sorry, Mom." I hesitated, then plunged in. "Speaking of floozies, was there something going on between Ethan and Zoë?"

She didn't look as surprised by the question as I'd hoped she might. However, she said, "Absolutely not," with conviction.

I waited for her to say more.

Finally, she threw an exasperated look my way and sighed heavily. "Okay, fine. I thought there might be. I overheard a couple people on the set talking about Ethan and Zoë, making it clear they thought they were more than co-workers. I don't usually pay attention to set gossip, but I'm not as young as I used to be and I sometimes worry—"

"Mom, Dad loves you."

"I know, dear," she said with a twist of her lips, "but I've never been movie-star gorgeous and now that I'm coming up on fifty-five . . . Well, it's hard when beautiful, younger women are fawning over your father daily, telling him he's talented and handsome and God's gift to women. All of which is true," she added with a freer smile, "but when you've been married to someone for over thirty years, you complain about their snoring, or get cranky when they leave the toilet seat up, instead of constantly praising and admiring."

"Everyone does, Mom." Not that I'd ever been married, but even a month-long relationship brought to light some of your partner's less desirable qualities.

"And Ethan wouldn't be human if he didn't find that sort of flattery appealing."

Some quality in her voice made me study her profile closely. Her mouth was set, her eyes staring at nothing across the expanse of blue water. I stopped myself from asking if Ethan had ever cheated on her. It wasn't my business, and I wasn't sure I wanted to know. "So you confronted Zoë," I said.

Her gaze snapped back to me. "Yes. I'm not proud of myself, EJ. I should have talked to your dad, but I hated for him to see me as insecure and . . . and needy. You can't be married to an international sex symbol and be needy."

I felt ickily uncomfortable hearing this, even while my heart ached for my mom. "And . . .?"

"I followed her to the ladies' room." She huffed an embarrassed laugh. "Pathetic, huh? Chasing down the 'other woman' in a public restroom."

"What did you say?" I couldn't imagine how you started that kind of conversation. *Are you bonking my husband?* Or, possibly: *It has come to my attention that . . .*

Mom took a long swallow of tea. "I told her that her

friendship with Ethan was causing gossip on the set and I thought she should be aware of it."

"Good one, Mom."

"I was rather proud of that approach myself," she admitted. "It took me days to come up with it. It didn't matter, though—she knew exactly why I was there. She laughed and told me she was a lesbian and that I was foolish for thinking Ethan would ever cheat on me. In one way it was a relief to hear, but the way she said it made me feel like a fool. I don't think she was a particularly nice woman."

I wished Zoë alive again so I could slap her silly for humiliating my mom. "What happened then?"

"I left."

"Was Zoë still in the bathroom?"

Mom nodded. "I caught her before she had a chance to go into the stall."

"Think: Did you see or hear anything, anything at all, when you left the ladies' room?"

My intensity told Mom what I was looking for. "My God, EJ. Do you think the killer was there, that I might have walked past him?"

"I don't know, but it's possible. Did you see anyone?"

She wrinkled her brow, then said, "No. No one except Zoë, not even on my way back to the parking lot."

"Hear anything? Like from the men's room?"

She squinched her eyes closed, clutching her tea glass with both hands. After a few seconds, she opened her eyes and looked at me. "Maybe running water? I can't remember. I was distraught; I ended up back at my car without really knowing how I got there."

I reached over to squeeze her shoulder but didn't say anything. On the one hand, it would've been helpful if she could have provided a description of the killer. On the other hand, I had a feeling Zoë's murderer wouldn't have felt much compunction about killing a witness, so I was glad Mom hadn't run into him or her. The silence between us stretched to several minutes. The breeze riffled the pool's surface and wafted a chlorine odor toward us.

"You know what puzzles me," Mom finally said, sounding perfectly composed again.

"What?"

"If this stalker is attacking women who Ethan's displayed some affection toward, then why in the world hasn't she gone after Anya Vale? After all, Ethan and she were all over each other, half naked, on the boat the other day."

I lifted my brows. "Good question. Maybe she wasn't on set that day?" I tried to remember who'd been present for the filming in Colonial Beach. "Or, maybe their love scene didn't make her jealous because it was all scripted—fake—and she knew it."

Mom gave a considering nod. "That makes sense; in fact, I'm sure you're right. Can you stay for dinner? Van and Leslie—the producer—will be here."

Crinkling my nose, I said, "No, thanks. I know how that conversation will go and I won't have anything to contribute. Besides, I want to get home and see if FedEx has dropped off the packet from Delia."

"Okay, honey." Mom lifted her face and I kissed her cheek. She patted my cheek gently, her palm cool against my sun-flushed skin. "You're a good daughter."

Her comment warmed me and I smiled. "Well, you're a good mom, the best mom *ever*."

Mom laughed in a gratified way and I left, stopping to have a word with a bodyguard on my way out. I was impressed with her alertness and relieved when she reported there'd been no suspicious or threatening activity. She seemed to sense my concern and didn't bridle when I asked her to be extra vigilant. "Don't worry, Ms. Ferris," she said. "I was with Ralph"—my grandfather—"in the Balkans and I wouldn't ever let him down."

"Good to know," I said, wondering about the twinkle in her eye when she mentioned Grandpa. She was maybe in her early forties, and Grandpa was almost double that, so it couldn't be *that*. I'd wager they'd started an insurrection together, or captured a war criminal, or infiltrated a terrorist cell. Who wouldn't have fond memories of life-threatening espionage missions? Shaking my head, I started the Miata and hit the road for Vernonville.

Fubar pounced on my feet as I came up the walk an hour later and clawed at the laces of my athletic shoes. I ignored him and broke into a trot because I had spotted a nine-by-twelve overnight-mail envelope half hidden behind the potted geranium on my stoop. Fubar, not happy with being ignored, or else peeved at being deprived of shoelaces to tangle, almost tripped me as I reached for the envelope. I recovered my balance with a hand against the wall.

"Fubar!"

With an air of puzzled innocence, he preceded me into the house. Not even bothering to close the door, I ripped back the tab that opened the stiff envelope. A disappointingly thin stack of pink paper fell out, and the scent of Shalini filtered into the foyer. I didn't know why, but I'd been expecting dozens of letters. There were only—I thumbed through them—six notes here. I called Grandpa to tell him the letters had arrived and he said he'd be right over. Then, feeling distinctly virtuous, I called the police, got a fax number, and faxed the notes to Detective Helland. He was in a meeting, the desk sergeant said, but wasn't gone for the day, so he should get the pages soon. Fetching a Skyland Red Ale from the kitchen, I took the bottle and the letters out to the front stoop.

The notes had penciled dates on the back—more evidence of Delia's efficiency—and I started with the earliest one, dated two years ago.

"Dearest Ethan, I never believed in love at first sight until now. I can hardly breathe in your presence, and your smile makes me light-headed. I knew instantly that we were meant to be together. Was it the same for you? Give me a sign, my beloved. Truly, Madly, Deeply."

Wondering if her use of the present tense—"can" and "makes"—indicated that she was in Ethan's presence routinely, I read the letter several times. I'd hoped that she was some wacko who had become obsessed with him by watching his movies, but her wording made me think uneasily that she'd met him and saw him with some regularity.

The next note came four months later and filled a page with raptures on Ethan's handsomeness and virility, more avowals of true love, and a thank-you for "letting me know you feel the same way I do." I wondered what "sign" the woman had misinterpreted as proof of Ethan's love for her. She concluded with, "Even though we are apart now, I trust you to find a way for us to be together. I can wait, my love." She signed it the same way, and I acknowledged that the "madly" part was undoubtedly true.

The third note was from January of this year and went on about the life they would live together. It was long on romantic beach walks, explicit sex that convinced me we were looking for a woman and not a gay man—I made a

mental note to point the passages out to Grandpa Atherton—
and suggested the woman wanted to bear Ethan's children,
but didn't give any hints as to her profession, geographical
location, or identity. It told me only that she was imaginative
in the bedroom and was, presumably, of childbearing age.
Great: I had narrowed down the suspect pool to women
between sixteen and fifty. I laid the letter aside.

As I was about to pick up the fourth letter, a clinking
sound made me look up. Grandpa Atherton, a plaid tam-o'-
shanter set at a cocky angle on his head, came briskly down
the stone path, holding two bottles of beer in his right hand.
They clinked together with every step. "You started without
me," he said, gesturing to the beer and the letters.

"Sorry." I scooted over to make room for him, and he
lowered himself stiffly.

"Uncover anything useful?"

"You mean like the name of the stalker?" I shook my
head. "She was pretty cagey about what she wrote. The most
I've been able to figure out is that she knew him, that she
wasn't some fan fantasizing from a lonely seat in the middle
of a movie theater."

"Hm." Twisting the top off the Belgian ale he'd brought,
Grandpa picked up the thin stack of notes I'd already read.

"The earliest one is on the bottom," I said, returning to
the unread notes.

The fourth note came only a couple weeks after the third
one, and the increasing frequency made me frown. That
couldn't be a good sign. "I knew you could do it, my love.
I knew you'd find a way for us to be together. I've never been
so happy." It wasn't signed. A brief flash of pity zipped
through me. It was kind of sad to think of this woman,
no matter how warped she was, writing letters to Ethan,

thinking that she was building a relationship with him, when Delia—and then the police—were the only ones reading them. My dad had never laid eyes on these notes.

"What's the sigh for?" Grandpa asked, looking up from the note he held in both hands.

"Nothing," I said. When he gave me a disbelieving lift of his brows, I added, "It's kind of sad, isn't it?"

"It's warped and sick and manipulative." Grandpa didn't believe in sugarcoating the truth.

"That, too."

We returned to reading. The fifth note was much in the vein of the third one and I skipped over TMD's description of their fantasy sex life because it made me queasy. In the last paragraph, she talked about how she was looking forward to their "reunion" and a warning bell sounded deep in my mind. They'd obviously been separated for some time, and now TMD thought she was likely to spend time with Ethan again. It couldn't be . . .

Leaving the sixth note unread, I scrambled to my feet and darted into the house, looking for the movie fan magazine Joel had pushed on me a while back. I found it at the bottom of my swim bag, slightly damp from being in contact with my clammy suit. Prising the gluey pages apart carefully, I found the article Joel had been reading about Ethan. I skimmed it, and turned the page, but before I could read further, Grandpa called to me.

"Emma-Joy? Detective Helland is here."

Footsteps sounded in the hall, and I poked my head out of the bedroom to see Grandpa offering Detective Helland his second beer. I hurried out, holding the magazine. Helland had shucked his coat and tie and looked amazingly human—and amazingly handsome—with his blond hair slightly disheveled and his shirt unbuttoned at the collar. He sucked down a third of the beer like it had been a long day.

"It's been a damn long day," he confirmed, lowering the bottle. "Hi, EJ. Thanks for faxing those notes. You've read them, I see," he said, his gaze drifting to the sheaf of pink in Grandpa's hand.

"Of course we have," Grandpa said testily. "How else are we supposed to figure out who this nutcase is?"

"I've got a team analyzing the notes, including a linguistics expert. Even if we can't get forensic data—which it looks like we can't—they can analyze word choices and syntax and make an educated guess about—"

I'd let their conversation flow past me as I scanned the article, but now I looked up. "You won't need them. I know who it is."

Thirty

. . .

"You do?" Helland sounded doubtful.

"You do!" Grandpa apparently had more faith in me. "Well, who?"

I took a deep breath. "It's Anya Vale."

Both men goggled at me.

"Emma-Joy . . ." Doubt had crept into Grandpa's voice.

"Why would an internationally famous movie star and sex symbol, one of the hottest women on the planet, a woman who could have any man she wants—"

"Not my father."

"—who makes Scarlett Johansson look like a hag—"

I looked at Helland, a hint of amusement in my gaze, and he ground to a stop. "Like brunettes, do you?" I teased. Not waiting for a response, I held up the magazine. "It's all in here." I was beginning to enjoy myself.

"Emma-Joy, you know they print hogswill in those fan magazines," Grandpa said. "I can't believe you're reading one, much less that you'd believe a single word they said. If one of those magazines told me Christmas was on December twenty-fifth, I'd look at a calendar to make sure."

"Agreed," I said. "But in this case . . . Here. Let me show you." Taking the magazine to the kitchen table, I laid it flat, open to the one-page article about Anya Vale, then took the notes from Grandpa and placed them in chronological order above the magazine. Grandpa sat at the end of the table and Helland stood beside me, his shoulder brushing mine.

"Let's look at the timeline first." I pointed to the earliest note. "This was sent two years ago. The use of present tense makes it sound like she was seeing Ethan somewhat regularly." I underscored a line in the article's sidebar which listed Anya Vale's movies and their release dates. "*Random's Redemption* came out in December of that year, about eight months after this first note."

"So?" A crease appeared between Helland's brows.

"I think I get where you're going, Emma-Joy," Grandpa said slowly. "If the movie came out in December, they were probably filming it about the time the note was sent."

"Exactly!" Drawing the second note toward me, I said, "Look. Here she talks about 'although we are apart now.' " I looked up. "What do you want to bet that that's when filming wrapped on *Random's Redemption*?"

Grandpa's expression told me he was beginning to believe me. Helland, however, looked stubbornly unconvinced. "Coincidence."

I nodded. "Okay. But then we come to the fourth and fifth letters. In this one"—I waggled the fourth letter—"she's ecstatic because Ethan has, supposedly, found a way for them to be together, and in this one"—I tapped the fifth letter—"she talks about their 'reunion.' Look at this." I slid the magazine toward them and indicated the pertinent paragraph.

Helland read aloud: " 'Mercury Wing Productions announced they have signed Anya Vale to appear opposite Ethan Jarrett in the upcoming thriller *Mafia Mistress*. She will play the role of Antonia Mugatti, the mistress of mob boss . . .' blah, blah. 'Other actresses considered for the role included Katie Holmes and Ginnifer Goodwin.' " He looked up from the page. "Who are these people? I've never heard of them."

"Stay on task, Helland," I said. "That announcement was made only a couple of days after TMD sent the fourth letter where she talked about knowing he'd find a way for them to be together," I interrupted him, fairly bouncing with excitement. "And if you read further, you'll see that she says she 'wanted the opportunity to work with Ethan Jarrett again,' " I quoted from memory. " 'He's truly special, so generous and passionate about his craft. I learned a lot from him when we made *Random's Redemption* together.' " I swiveled my head, looking from Grandpa to Helland to see if I'd convinced them. "If that's not enough, ask yourselves why no one attacked Anya Vale after her love scene with Ethan on Friday. Mom and I assumed it was because their lovemaking was scripted and the attacker knew it was fake. I think we were wrong; it was because Anya's behind it all. It's her."

"The timing's interesting," Helland conceded.

"Interesting?" Grandpa scoffed. "It's damning. You figured it out, Emma-Joy," he said, coming around the table to hug me. "It's hard to believe, but I think you're right: Anya Vale is Truly, Madly, Deeply. She's the one who's been stalking Ethan."

I squeaked from the force of his hug. He released me and said, "Question is: What are we going to do about it? You could search for the knife that killed Zoë Winters in Vale's trailer or her hotel room."

"No judge would give me a search warrant on what we have here," Helland said. "We have absolutely no physical evidence connecting her to the crime, no proof that she wrote these letters, and no way of getting any."

I looked them both square in the eye, half defiant because I suspected neither of them would like my plan. "Oh, yes, we do," I said.

It took Helland only a split second to figure it out. His response was unequivocal: "No."

Grandpa was right behind him. "Absolutely not, Emma-Joy."

The men moved closer together, forming a wall of solidarity, I thought, amused despite myself. "Come on. It makes sense. It's the only way we'll draw her into the open, get the proof we need to put her away and keep my mom and dad—and who knows what other innocent women—safe."

Identical mulish expressions settled on the men's faces. Helland's lips barely moved as he said, "I am not letting you set yourself up as bait for a woman who has already killed once—that we know of."

His words caught me off guard. Was it possible Anya Vale had killed before? Had she become jealous of Ethan's relationship with some woman on the set of their first movie and removed her "rival"? I hadn't heard about anything like that, but I could tell from the look on Helland's face that he'd be making a call to the Hollywood police before long.

"We've got an opportunity to stop her," I said. "Like you said, she's already killed once and tried to kill on two other occasions. Who knows when she'll lose patience and decide that Ethan is stringing her along, or that he's betrayed her, and decide to go after him. We need to put her in jail—"

"Or a loony bin," Grandpa cut in.

"—and tomorrow's the last day of filming at Fernglen. I

don't know what the schedule is after that, but we'd lose our chance to control the situation. Her trailer's right across from Ethan's. I'll visit Ethan and make sure to hug him good-bye outside his trailer where Anya will have a good view. Then, it's her move."

"I don't like it," Helland said, drawing a hand down his face. "You're a civilian. We couldn't put backup in close enough to protect you without Vale spotting them."

"I can take care of myself," I said, jutting my jaw forward slightly, "and I'd wear a wire."

"If I decide this is doable, would we brief Mr. Jarrett?"

"No!" I said.

"Hell, no!" Grandpa said. In response to Helland's arched brows, he added, "Ethan would want to play an . . . active role. He was on that cop show, *Roll Call*, too long; he'd want to confront Anya himself, probably arrest her, and—"

"And she'd stab him or shoot him because he's not used to 'perps' who fight back for real. Believe me," I said, "you do not want Ethan involved. Things get unbelievably complicated when Ethan's involved." I could have given him several examples from our family life, like the time we wanted to go on a simple fishing trip to a lake near our home, and Ethan hired someone to stock the lake, hoping to ensure that Clint and I had a good time by catching fish, but the people he hired dumped some sort of non-native fish into the lake and Ethan was briefly arrested for something to do with spreading an invasive species when the men he'd hired told the police he'd paid them to do it. It would take too long to convince Helland that he didn't want Ethan's fingers in this pie, though, so I simply said, "Take my advice: don't tell Ethan."

Helland looked like he thought we were being a bit hard on Ethan, but he acquiesced. "Okay. I'm still not sure—"

I looked him straight in the eye, ignoring Fubar who was butting his head against my ankle. "I'm not asking your permission. I can make my mom and dad safer by luring Anya Vale into the open, and I'm going to do it."

Helland held my gaze for a moment, his eyes flinty, before throwing up one hand in defeat. "Is that the way you talked to your commanding officer?"

Having gotten my way, I grinned. "No, but you're not in my chain of command, Anders." I used his first name deliberately, to emphasize that he wasn't the boss of me. I didn't know why I'd been tiptoeing around it—too much time in the military, calling people by rank or sir and ma'am, I guessed.

"Thank God for small favors."

Grandpa laughed and I glared at both of them. Then we got down to business.

Thirty-one

. . .

Tuesday morning, early, I walked self-consciously
from the mall entrance to Ethan's trailer. The deck-of-cards-
sized transmitter taped to the small of my back itched, and
the teeny microphone secured between my breasts felt as
big and obvious as a saxophone. For the first time since
signing on at Fernglen, I carried a Taser on my belt and a
gun in an ankle holster. I hadn't wanted it, but Jay had
insisted and had supplied me with the .22.

I'd run into him moments after arriving at Fernglen following my crack-of-dawn session with the Vernonville
Police Department's surveillance team who had wired me
up. Jay's eyes lit up when he saw me buying coffee at The
Bean Bonanza, and he greeted me with a smile that brightened my whole day and made me forget for a second that I
was about to go toe to toe with a killer. It took him no time
at all to spot the Taser.

"What's that for?"

I bit my lip, debating the wisdom of telling him about the operation, but then I said, "Not here."

He finished buying his coffee, then led me to Lola's, unlocked the door to the kitchen, and dragged me inside. With no cookies baking and no lights on, the white tile and stainless steel were a bit cheerless and cold-feeling.

"First things first." He pulled me close and kissed me thoroughly. The room warmed up nicely, or maybe it was me. I responded in kind and was in a fair way to forgetting there was a murderer running around Fernglen before he pushed me to arm's length and said, "Now, about that Taser . . ."

I told him everything, and our coffee cups were nearly empty by the time I'd finished. I wasn't too worried; it was still half an hour before my shift was supposed to start. I'd thought Jay would respond like Grandpa and Helland had initially, and protest against my being involved. Instead, he bent and fumbled at his ankle. My eyes widened as he straightened with a .22 and holster in his hand. Grabbing my unresisting hand, he pressed the gun into it.

"Wear this. Helland's people won't be close enough. I want you to be armed. Heaven knows I wouldn't say that to most people for fear they'd be more likely to hurt themselves than an attacker, but you were a cop. You know how to handle a weapon. Don't hesitate, EJ." He gave me an unusually serious look, a strand of dark auburn hair falling across his forehead. "If she gets close enough, if she's got a weapon of any kind, take her down."

"Will do," I said, mostly to make him feel better. I had every confidence that I'd be able to outwit Anya Vale without having to use the gun. She was an actor, for heaven's sake, even if she'd gone to Princeton. She wasn't a trained killer, or a martial arts expert, or an ex-SEAL. If I couldn't handle

Anya Vale, I should give up my dream of returning to police work and carve out a niche for myself as a phone marketer or mattress salesperson. I should have remembered what Nana Jarrett used to say about pride going before a fall, or what Master Sergeant Benitez had drilled into us about never underestimating either the stupidity or the cunning of a perp.

Now, approaching Ethan's trailer, I felt a slight flutter of butterflies in my stomach but ignored them. I was only going to wish Ethan good luck on his last day of filming, I told myself. I knocked. No answer. Damn. We hadn't anticipated this.

"You looking for Ethan?" It was Bree Spurrier, walking past in her standard uniform of photographer's vest and jeans, looking harried. "He's in makeup."

When I bit my lip, debating whether I would have to try this later, she said, "I'm headed that way myself, to talk to Anya. Come on."

Pleased to hear that Anya was with Ethan, I told myself that flexibility was the key to mission success and fell into step beside Bree, figuring I could stage my scene in the makeup trailer instead. Bree looked at me curiously. "It's about that letter he got, I guess? The one you mentioned the other day?"

"In a way."

Her brow puckered. "No one's threatening him, are they? I've noticed he's got a bodyguard now. Celebrity can be a bear. I remember that Gwyneth Paltrow got the most hideous threats when we were on location for *Random's Redemption*. They—"

"Anya Vale was in that, too, right?"

Bree nodded. "It was her first role. How far we've come,

hm?" She gave me a wry look that seemed to convey a bit of disdain for the Hollywood star-making machine, or maybe just for Anya Vale. "We're here." She mounted the shallow steps and entered the trailer. I followed.

Bree beelined for Anya, the top of whose head I could see at the far end of the trailer, half hidden by temporary walls that broke the space into half a dozen separate rooms. Lights blazed, reflected by myriad mirrors, and the room smelled like lipstick wax and powder. It hummed with low-voiced conversation as makeup artists prepared the cast for the day's shoot.

I followed Ethan's voice to a semiprivate cubicle and bumped into a woman with a messy ponytail coming out as I went in. The space was outfitted with a large mirror and a counter where the makeup artist had spread her collection of foundations, brushes, sponge wedges, and other items. Ethan sat in a beauty-shop-style chair, the kind you can raise or lower with a foot pedal, wearing the top half of his cop costume with gray sweatpants. Tissue was tucked around the collar and he was fully made-up. Despite the ridiculous combination of uniform shirt and sweats, and the tissue ruff, he looked superhumanly hot, even to a daughter's eyes. Genetics, I thought, not for the first time, and some magical combination of energy and pheromones.

"EJ!" He swept me into a big hug and I returned it, hoping Anya was paying attention from her "room" on the other side of the panel. A sharp yip told me that the Chinese crested dog was in residence, so I had high hopes Anya had a front-row seat for my performance.

"I don't want to smudge your makeup," I said, breaking free after a minute. The thought of Helland's team listening to my conversations made me feel ridiculously self-conscious and I hoped Ethan didn't notice my stiffness.

"Who cares? I get punched in the face, shot twice, and sprayed with a fire extinguisher in this morning's scene. I'll get made up more times today than a supermodel does in a year.

"What brings you around?" he asked, tugging the paper ruff from around his neck and crumpling it into a trash can.

I propped my butt against the counter and crossed my arms. "Can't I pop in to see you and wish you luck on the day's filming without getting the third degree?" I asked lightly.

His eyes narrowed. "That's pretty close to the same line Amy Adams gave me in *Death Stalks the Night*, right before she tried to gun me down with an AR-15."

"Not one of your best," I said to distract him.

He tried to frown, but his forehead remained suspiciously rigid. I leaned toward him and studied his face from six inches away. "Ethan! Did you get Botoxed again?"

He tried to grimace, but his paralyzed forehead muscles remained smooth. "Dr. Verbenna was having an off day. Van's not very happy about it, says I should have waited until we were done filming."

"I guess so," I said, trying not to laugh. "Won't it look weird that you have facial movements for half the movie, and then suddenly you have no more expression than an android? I've got to get back to the office. Good luck today."

Ethan walked me to the door, past a bunch of people, some of whom eyed us curiously and some of whom went on with their tasks, oblivious. I hoped Anya was among the first group. When Ethan opened the door, I hugged him tightly and kissed him by the corner of his mouth, for Anya's benefit. I felt guilty doing it, like I was deceiving Ethan, and that made me hug him tighter. "Love you," I said, not loud enough for anyone but him to hear.

"I love you, too, sweetheart. I wish we saw more of each other. Are you sure you don't want to work in my production compa—"

"La, la, la," I said, sticking my fingers in my ears to drown out his familiar refrain, and he gave up with a laugh as Iona bustled toward the trailer, her omnipresent clipboard held in a way that meant business.

I greeted her absently and walked away, headed into the mall, trying not to feel like I had a target painted on my back.

Thirty-two

· · ·

I returned to the security office for my Segway, letting the surveillance team know where I was going by the simple expedient of whispering, "On my way to the security office." Helland had insisted I keep them updated on my whereabouts since they wouldn't have line-of-sight on me. I thought it unlikely that Anya would attack me in the office, so I needed to make myself available by being out and about. Unfortunately, Joel was in the office and he immediately spotted the Taser.

"What's that?" He bit into a carrot stick and chewed ferociously, his plump cheeks making him look like a chipmunk.

"Taser," I said lightly.

His face brightened. "Really? Do we all get one?"

Shaking my head so my bangs whisked against my forehead, I said, "This is a test program." I felt bad lying to him, but Joel was transparent: if he ran into Anya Vale, his face would give the game away.

He shrugged philosophically and chomped into another carrot. "I wish I'd had one yesterday, I can tell you. There was a customer outside of Dillard's chewing out his son with the kind of language they probably don't even use in a prison. He could have used a few thousand volts." He stiffened and vibrated as if being jolted by electricity, making his curly hair bob.

"Give me a call if you see him again, and I'll take care of it," I joked, patting the Taser.

"Will do."

Joel gave me a two-finger salute as I retrieved the Segway and headed out on patrol.

As the morning passed and nothing happened, the stiffness in my neck and shoulders eased somewhat. I felt slightly ridiculous giving updates to the unseen listeners on the other end of the wire, like I was talking to an imaginary friend, but it did make me feel marginally safer. Late in the morning, I swung by Merlin's Cave to see how Kyra was doing. I was surprised to find Jesse Willard and his father there, talking to Kyra.

My friend gave me a big grin when I came in. "EJ. Good news. Jesse has agreed to a trial period as my assistant."

I looked from the young soldier to his father, both of whom looked more nervous than gratified, and smiled. "Congratulations. I'm sure you'll do great." I wasn't sure he would, but I'd already expressed my qualms to Kyra and it would serve no purpose to say anything now.

"I'm going to work hard at it," Jesse said fiercely. "I don't know much about the merchandise, except the books, but I can learn. I've read all the Lord of the Rings books at least twice, and I love Madeleine L'Engle's *A Wrinkle in Time* ones. I was really into fantasy when I was in high school. Still am."

"Ms. Valentine has said she can work around his doctor's appointments and therapy schedule," Mr. Willard said. "Since I'm retired, I can be here with Jesse sometimes, too."

Aah. I thought I understood. Mr. Willard was willing to keep an eye on Jesse's performance at Merlin's Cave for a while, make sure his son's erratic emotions didn't get him into trouble. That was probably a good idea; I didn't know if it was Kyra's or Mr. Willard's, but I hoped it worked out for all of them.

Leaving Merlin's Cave and telling my invisible minders, I Segwayed to the elevator and descended to the lower level, looking to see how preparation for the day's shoot was going. The action was taking place in the garage and it had been put off-limits to customers for the day while the movie crew set up and filmed. I didn't know what the exact sequence of events was, but it was the movie's climactic scene and included a car chase inside the garage, a gun battle, and enough dead cops and mafia types to keep a mortuary in business for a year, according to Joel, who had read about the movie's plot in, of course, a fan magazine. The stunt drivers, clad in protective jumpsuits, were walking the course of the chase scene with Van and Bree Spurrier, a cameraman tagging along behind them. Iona Moss took notes on a clipboard as they made measurements and studied the turn from the upper-level garage to the lower-level garage and the exit. If I'd been less tense, I would have found it all surprisingly interesting.

Craning my neck, I looked for Ethan, but didn't see him.

Anya Vale, too, was absent. An extra done up like a mafia thug stood nearby (at least, I hoped he was involved with the movie and wasn't waiting to give some mall denizen a pair of cement shoes), and I asked him when filming was supposed to start.

"An hour ago," he said glumly in an incongruous mid-western accent. "I don't know what the hold-up is. No one tells extras anything. I heard Bree say something about being ready to go in an hour." He sniffed loudly and swiped his nose with the back of his hand.

"Thanks."

Segwaying up the ramp to the upper level of the garage, I did a quick patrol, spotting nothing out of place or suspicious, and returned to the mall on the top floor. "Entering mall, upper level, Dillard's wing," I told my minders in a low voice. Cruising by the bathroom, I turned in, debating whether I needed to tell Helland's team I was answering the call of nature. I'd be in and out in a few seconds, I rationalized, so I didn't need to embarrass myself by mentioning my location. They also didn't need to hear what went on in the stall, so I pressed my hand against the microphone through my shirt to muffle transmissions.

I'd barely settled on the toilet seat when the door to the restroom wheezed open and another woman entered, her high heels clicking on the tiled floor. I heard a skittering sound I couldn't place as water gushed from one of the sinks. Then, four dainty paws pranced into my line of sight, inches outside my stall, and I caught my breath on a sharp intake. Anya Vale's dog.

Thirty-three

. . .

I'd never felt more vulnerable.

Footsteps approached my stall door and my chest tightened. Elegant black pumps appeared in the foot of space between the stall door and the floor. Slim ankles and calves were clad in sheer black hose. Hardly the attire of a murderer, I thought inanely. I half rose, muscles tensed, and fumbled to tuck in my shirt and zip my pants. Oddly, I felt somehow safer with my slacks secured.

A hand struck the door with a hollow thunking sound.

"Occupied," I croaked, watching the feet.

They remained stationary for a split second and then stepped to the right as Anya Vale's voice said, "Sorry." The other stall door opened, then shut with a gentle bang, and the lock shot home.

I looked up, eyeing the partition that separated our stalls, half expecting Anya Vale's face to appear above it. If she had a gun, shooting me in the stall would be easier than plugging goldfish in a bowl. Nothing happened. A moment later the sound of pee hitting the bowl let me relax a bit; she couldn't attack me at the moment. The toilet paper roll rumbled in the other stall. The sounds of flushing and the stall door opening followed.

My brain whirred. Had Vale seen me in the garage and followed me in here? Or, was her presence a coincidence, in which case I might be better off remaining in the stall until she left? I didn't believe in coincidence and I was damned if I was going to hide in a bathroom stall. Flushing the toilet, I emerged.

The Chinese crested dog yipped and growled. Truly an unpleasant dog. Fubar would make mincemeat out of him. With a pointy snout, a ridiculous quiff of hair atop his head, a similar plume on his tail, and a liver-colored, hairless body, he looked like something designed by genetic scientists on April Fools' Day.

"Ssh, Conan," Vale hushed the dog. She stood at the sink, her back to me, clad in an above-the-knee mulberry-colored knit dress that revealed every nuance of her lush curves. Inky hair spilled over her shoulders and she was apparently trying to get something out of her eye because she was holding the right eyelid up with one forefinger and using her pinky to dislodge something from the corner of her eye.

"Aren't you Anya Vale?" I asked, hating to sound like a fan girl, but needing to let Helland and his troops know I was in the presence of the enemy.

"Yes." She smiled at me in the mirror, red lips sliding back from vampire-white teeth, her green eyes meeting mine in the glass. They glittered disturbingly, or maybe that was my imagination on overdrive. I got the feeling I'd been assessed and dismissed, which was perfectly justified if she was cataloging our respective physical attributes. If she was sussing me out as a victim, however, she might find out that she'd taken on a bit more than she anticipated, even though I was a couple of inches shorter and walked with a limp.

Somewhat reluctantly, I approached the sink beside her, stepping over the dog which had come to sniff at my ankles, and turned on the water. A lavender scent bloomed when I squirted soap into my palm. While I hastily washed my hands, my whole attention on the woman beside me, she blinked rapidly several times, and said, "Finally. Amazing how something so tiny can be so irritating, isn't it?" She extended her pinky toward me so I could examine the invisible speck of grit.

"Um-hm," I agreed, every nerve taut. She carried a small leather purse slung over her shoulder; if she had a weapon, it had to be in there because her dress clung tightly enough to make it impossible to conceal a safety pin, never mind a knife or gun.

Even as I had the thought, she reached into her purse. I spun away from the sink, putting a couple feet between us, automatically flexing my knees so I could spring out of harm's way if she pulled a weapon. Vale brought her hand out, holding . . . a pen. "Would you like an autograph?" she asked sweetly.

Pretending I'd been headed for the towel dispenser, I pulled one free and dried my hands, not taking my eyes off her for a moment. "Uh, no thanks," I said. "Autographs aren't really my thing. But thank you."

With a shrug, she returned the pen to her purse and hitched it higher on her shoulder. "I've seen you around the set, haven't I? Aren't you with mall security?" Her sultry voice revealed nothing but casual interest; yet, I felt almost as if she were mocking me.

"Yes. It's been interesting having the movie crew here,"

I said. I tossed the towel toward the trash and it fell short. Damn. No way was I stooping to pick it up with Anya Vale mere feet away.

"Aren't you going to get that?" she asked with a lift of elegant brow.

Before I could answer, Conan pounced on the paper towel and began to shred it, growling like he was disemboweling his archenemy.

"Well, I guess that's what janitors are for," Anya said dismissively, watching as her pet strewed paper towel from one end of the bathroom to the other.

I wondered what Helland was making of this conversation.

"Come, Conan." Anya glided toward the door, then turned toward me. "Be sure to watch the filming this afternoon—we start in a few minutes. It's our last day here and you wouldn't want to miss my big scene. Here." She reached into her purse again, scrawled something on a card, and thrust it at me. "This will get you on the set."

"Thanks," I said, puzzled. She was through the door before I finished speaking, the dog darting after her a hair before the door closed on his jaunty tail.

I waited a few moments and then cautiously pushed the door open, awake to the possibility that she might be waiting in ambush. No one was in the hall. Taking a deep breath, I muttered to the microphone, "She's gone. I don't know what the hell that was all about, but she's gone."

I thought for a moment, then added, "I'm going after her. To the movie set."

The garage was much busier now, humming with activity as technicians set up lights, cameras, and sound equipment for the filming. A scrawny young man in jeans yelled at Margot Chelius near a support pillar and I wondered what that was about. I could read the anger in his face but not decipher his words. Grayson Bleek's replacement was seated at a six-foot table pushed against the wall, a line of extras, both cops and mafia types, in front of him. He handed out guns to cast members who signed for them on a clipboard. Ethan, positioned atop a black SUV, saw me and waved. I waved back, scanning the garage for Anya Vale. I didn't see her. That made me uneasy.

I told myself that she was busy acting, doing her job, that she wouldn't come after me now. I was safe until the filming was done. My body didn't believe my brain, though, because I still had the itchy feeling between my shoulder blades and tension kept my spine stiff. I leaned forward slightly to put the Segway in motion, and glided over to where Iona Moss stood, temporarily alone, watching Vandelinde and Bree Spurrier converse with a couple of cameramen.

"Big day, huh?" I said.

She looked up and pushed a strand of gingery hair behind her ear. "Finally. Not to sound insulting about your mall, but I'm ready to get back to California. Living out of hotels gets old. Just a minute." Snagging a bottle of water out of a nearby cooler, she carried it to where my father now reclined on the hood of the SUV. I couldn't hear their exchange, but she gave him the water, he took it with a smile, sipped from it, and handed it back. She beamed.

"Ethan is such a gentleman," she said when she returned. Her gaze stayed on him, even though she was addressing me.

I wondered briefly if she fancied herself in love with Ethan. She certainly never took her eyes off him, and seemed ready to anticipate his every need or want. Working in the office, she'd have access to his address and other data.

Could Iona—? I frowned. No. I'd analyzed the letters from TMD. The timeline, the expensive perfume—it all added up to Anya Vale. Iona might have a crush on Ethan, but I didn't see her as the stalker driven to murder by jealousy. Somehow, Iona didn't have sufficient *intensity*. I couldn't explain it any better than that.

One of the policemen waiting in line for a weapon gave me a half wave, and I recognized Grandpa Atherton. I smiled involuntarily, ridiculously happy to see him, to know that he was nearby, watching out for me as he always had. That feeling of warmth buoyed me as the set manager yelled, "Positions!" and the chaos resolved itself into a moviemaking enterprise. Grandpa and a handful of other police extras headed for the barrier at the garage entrance. Fernglen didn't have one of those arms that lifts up to allow cars in and out; the set people had installed one especially for this scene, probably to have it splinter as someone drove through it.

Ethan and the SUV disappeared up the ramp to the upper level and a black sedan full of mafia types followed them.

"The script calls for Ethan and his partner to chase the sedan through the garage, trying to stop them from leaving. They've kidnapped Antonia, Anya's character. As they come around the corner"—she gestured with the clipboard—"and start down the ramp, Ethan climbs onto the roof of the SUV to get a better shot at the driver of the sedan. He kills him and the sedan crashes into that pillar." She pointed.

"Sounds great," I said, thinking it sounded cliché. How many thrillers had I seen with garage car chases?

Iona was going to add something else, but the set manager called for quiet and I heard the sounds of shots and squealing tires from the upper level, magnified by the echoing cavern of the garage. The sounds made me cringe, triggering memories of real gun battles. I was glad Jesse Willard wasn't here. Every instinct urged me to intervene, even though I knew it was all staged. The actors on this level tensed and I could feel anticipation in the air. The black sedan careened around the corner and the SUV followed it, with Ethan levering his torso out of the passenger-side window, a look of grim determination on his face as he leveled his gun. He got off a couple of shots, but the sedan kept coming toward us. My grip tightened on the Segway's handlebar as Ethan pulled himself onto the SUV's roof and lay prone, sighting along the barrel of his nine mil. The stunt driver, I thought admiringly, was doing an amazing job of holding the SUV steady; I also suspected there were some kind of handholds on the roof to help Ethan stay on.

He fired and the sedan's driver-side window exploded in a cascade of glass. I wondered how the special effects guys did that. Fake blood—I hoped—squirted onto the windshield and the car rolled into the pillar. The headlight shattered and the passenger's side crumpled inward with a groan of offended metal.

I suddenly realized one of the film's major players didn't seem to have a role in this scene. "Where's Anya?" I asked Iona in a low voice.

She turned an excited face toward me. "Watch. This is where Antonia gets out and plugs Hunter. It's the stinger. Even though she had the fling with Hunter and told him everything about her mafia lover's operations, she's gone back to her former lover and has to kill Hunter so he can't testify against either of them."

On the words, one of Anya's shapely legs emerged from the rear door of the stranded sedan. More cliché, I thought as she stepped out of the car, apparently unfazed by the zinging bullets and the crash. Her hair rippled in the slight breeze generated by a huge fan and her face wore a steely expression as she pivoted to face the approaching SUV, a gun hanging from one hand.

Unease rippled up my spine. "Wait," I said. "I thought the movie ended with Anya's and Ethan's characters running off together and having plastic surgery."

"Too low-key, Van decided. Not enough action. They rewrote it. I think the new ending was Anya's idea, actually."

Understanding crashed onto me. She was going to kill Ethan! For real. That's why she hadn't attacked me in the bathroom, why she'd invited me to the filming. She'd snapped. My clinch with Ethan this morning had made her think he'd betrayed her. She wanted to kill *him*, not me, and she wanted me there to watch. Faster than those thoughts flashed through my mind, I leaned forward and sent the Segway speeding toward her. I couldn't risk using Jay's gun in such crowded quarters.

Gripping her gun in both hands, Anya brought it up, leveling it at Ethan where he rode atop the SUV, for all the world like a figurehead on the bow of a pirate ship. *I'm king of the world.*

"Gun!" I yelled. My voice was raw with fear. Ethan's head slewed toward me. I fumbled for the Taser, but the Segway jounced over a cable and I dropped the weapon. Damn!

Movie people stared at me, confused. I felt their gazes rather than saw them, because I was focused on only one thing: Anya. I saw the moment she became aware of me bearing down on her because she half turned her head. Confusion flitted momentarily across her face before a small, dead smile stretched her lips and she snapped her head straight again, arms tensing with the weight of the gun.

"Ethan, get down!"

Anya's finger tightened on the trigger.

I was almost there . . . Only ten feet separated us . . .

Boom, boom, boom! The gunshots deafened me. I couldn't count them. The sound ricocheted off concrete and bullets *kranged* off metal. The force backed Anya up a half step. Ethan slid the length of the SUV's roof until he was hanging off the rear of the vehicle. I didn't know if he was hurt or was trying to take cover. Movie people dived beneath cars and hid behind concrete pillars as it dawned on them that real bullets were zinging around the garage.

Then I slammed into Anya. The weight of the Segway smashed her against the car, but she didn't let go of the gun. The collision jolted through me, driving the handlebars back and into my solar plexus and knocking the wind out of me.

"What the hell are you doing, you lunatic?" Anya gasped, her face twisted with confusion, pain, and dawning fury. "Security! Help!" She still held the gun. Disentangling myself from the Segway, I let it fall sideways with a crash and lunged to grab her wrist with both my hands.

"I will sue you," she bit out. "Ow!" This came as I banged her hand against the sedan to make her drop the gun. It clattered to the ground. I winced, but it didn't go off. "I think you broke my fingernail. You are certifiable! You belong in an asylum and my lawyers will make sure you're locked up until hell freezes—"

I drew back slightly, puzzled. Anya wasn't reacting right. She was furious, yes, but the way she kept babbling about fingernails and lawyers and suing me . . . She didn't smell perfumey like the notes, either, I realized, breathing in through my nose; she smelled like soap. Maybe we should have given all the suspects a sniff test. But she'd been shooting at Ethan—

Two more shots barked out. I whipped my head around

and saw Bree Spurrier, face set, leveling what looked like a nine millimeter Glock at Ethan where he had just rounded the rear bumper of the SUV he'd been riding on. A look of almost comical astonishment on his face, he dove behind a camera dolly. She stalked toward him. No one else moved, except to huddle more securely behind a pillar or cover their heads with their arms.

Oh, my God. How had I been so wrong? I didn't have time to sift through the evidence and see where I'd misanalyzed the data. Bree Spurrier was trying to kill my father.

"You betrayed me, Ethan," she said, her voice eerily flat. Her deliberate footsteps slapped against the concrete and the gun was rock-steady in her hands.

Where were the police? Oh, no! What if they thought the gunshots were all part of the filming? "*Real* shots fired. Helland, I need backup!" I said toward my chest mike. "It's not Vale. It's Bree Spurrier."

"I didn't, Bree," Ethan called from behind the dolly. He shifted it slightly to keep it between him and the approaching woman. "You're sick. We can get you help."

Whang! A bullet caromed off the dolly's metal superstructure.

Keep her talking, Ethan, I thought as I edged into position behind Bree. Nothing lay between us except a wide expanse of oil-stained concrete.

"There's still a chance for us, Bree," Ethan said. "I'm tired of hiding my feelings for you. I've tried to be faithful to Brenda, but the way I feel about you . . . it can't be denied."

Despite the soap opera quality of the dialogue, the words thrummed with sincerity and I briefly admired Ethan's acting. Was it my imagination, or did Bree hesitate a moment? The gun seemed to sag an inch toward the floor.

"All I wanted was for you to love me like I love you, Ethan," Bree said in a heartbroken voice.

"My passion—" Ethan started.

Taking advantage of Bree's distraction, I lunged, propelling myself toward her back. My knee gave out with a flare of pain and I found myself on the ground, feet away from her. She half turned toward me, bringing the gun up again, and I yanked Jay's .22 out of the ankle holster, sighted, and fired.

The force of two bullets plowing into her shoulder propelled her back a couple of steps, and gave me time to low-crawl forward and latch onto her ankle, bringing her down with a powerful yank. The Glock flew out of her hand as she flailed to keep her balance before thudding painfully to the concrete. Blood seeped from the bullet wounds, but her face practically glowed with fury. I knew adrenaline was keeping her going, despite the pain and blood loss. I'd been there.

"He said he loves you," she grated as I half straddled her to try and stanch the blood. Her uninjured arm flashed up and she raked my face with her nails.

"He's my dad," I said fiercely, watching her eyes widen. "You don't mess with my family." Her snarl of rage warned me and when she reached to claw me again, I socked her. The punch broke her nose and she looked dazed, whether from my statement, my punch, or blood loss, I didn't know. Either way, the fight seemed to have gone out of her.

Suddenly, Joel was there, looking grimmer and more grown-up than I'd ever seen him, and he secured both her wrists while I went back to putting pressure on the shoulder wounds. "Catfights aren't near as sexy as I thought," Joel said, his face reflecting a certain shock at the violence.

Authoritative voices called, "Police! Make way!" and a

sea of dark blue uniforms surrounded us. My hands trembled and I clenched them into fists.

I heard Detective Helland's voice in my ear say, "You're bleeding." He sounded muffled and I knew it was because the close gunshots had temporarily—I hoped—dampened my hearing. I put a hand to my cheek and felt the wetness of blood, but I didn't have time to deal with it now. Pulling away from Helland's hand on my shoulder, I struggled out of the knot of people surrounding Bree. There was no one behind the camera dolly. Where was my dad? Was he okay? A horrible thought slammed into me: Had I hit him when I fired at Bree?

"Ethan," I called.

"Over here." His voice sounded tight and I hurried around the SUV he'd been clinging to, lurching when my knee buckled again. Ignoring the pain, I limped on, almost sobbing with relief when I saw Ethan bent over an overalled man on the floor, using the heels of his hands to compress the man's chest.

"Ethan!"

He glanced at me, blood trickling from a scrape high on his temple. "I think Darren's had a heart attack." His words were choppy from the effort of thrusting at Darren's chest.

I yelled for help and an EMT came at a run and took over for Ethan while his partner set up an IV. I guessed Helland had had an ambulance standing by. When they hoisted Darren onto a gurney, I asked Ethan, "Where did you learn CPR?"

"I was an EMT in that series that only lasted six episodes," he said, raising his brows as if surprised I doubted his ability to revive a dead person. "Remember?"

I shook my head, laughing helplessly from the release of tension, and Ethan crunched me against his chest. "Don't

ever do something like that again, EJ," he commanded, his
voice harsh with fear. "I thought she was going to shoot you."

"I thought she was going to shoot *you*." I pulled back
slightly and smiled up at him.

"That vixen scratched you." His hand hovered near my
cheek.

"I'll need a rabies shot." I tried to laugh but it sounded
suspiciously like a sob. "I'm so sorry," I said, giving up the
battle against tears. They streamed down my face, stinging
where Bree's nails had gouged my flesh. "It's my fault."

"Hush," Ethan said, cradling me against his chest while
I coughed up the story of how we'd planned to trap Anya.

"It's my fault Bree almost killed you," I finished. "If I
hadn't tricked you this morning by coming to the trailer
and hugging you . . . If I hadn't been so sure TMD was
Anya. I should have realized that the timing, what was in
those notes, could have applied to anyone who worked on
Random's Redemption with you, not just Anya. I—"

"You set this up without letting me in on it?" he said. He
sounded more left out than angry.

"I—"

"I could have helped you plan the operation," he said.
"When I played that Secret Service agent in *Affairs of State*,
we had to set up a sting to entice a counterfeiter. We lured
him by . . ."

He walked me over to where an EMT stood by to treat
my cheek, talking the whole time about a better scheme for
tricking Bree into confessing to Zoë's murder. I laughed
weakly. There was no one quite like Ethan.

Thirty-four

. . .

Friday evening found me back at my parents' poolside, hands dug into the pockets of my blue fleece jacket to protect them from the chill. It had been a bright April day, but at sunset a feisty breeze had sprung up and it held a definite nip. My parents had the fire pit going. Mom, Dad, Grandpa, Kyra, and I ringed it, leaning in to steal its warmth. Dusk was quickly morphing into night and we were replete with hamburgers the chef had grilled and topped with blue cheese and a mango-pepper chutney, followed by old-fashioned s'mores we made ourselves, using long skewers to toast the marshmallows in the fire pit.

"We should go in," Mom said, but no one moved.

Kyra leaned back in her lounge chair, stretching her legs in front of her, and said, "I can't believe I let Bree Spurrier stab me." She sounded disgusted. "I probably outweigh her by a third." She'd broached the topic we'd tacitly avoided all evening.

"Never underestimate the strength of obsession," Grandpa said.

"She's a sick woman," Ethan said.

"Well, I, for one, don't think that excuses what she did," Mom said indignantly. "She murdered poor Zoë merely because you put your arm around her—and we can discuss that later, buster—and she tried to kill Kyra and you and EJ. I hope she rots in jail for the rest of her life." She jerked her head downward in an emphatic nod.

"I suspect she will," I murmured, letting the warmth of the flames seep into me. "Detective Helland says the DA is certain they can put her away for a long, long time."

"Even though she clammed up and surrounded herself with expensive lawyers," Ethan said, "Helland—I'm going to use that cold steeliness of his for my next cop role—says they found the knife she used on Zoë in her hotel room with traces of both Zoë's and Kyra's blood—"

"And obviously they've got the gun she used to shoot at you, Ethan," I said. "Her plan was pretty clever. She had it all figured so when Anya fired blanks at you, she—Bree—would fire real bullets and kill you. The police would think it was another accident, she hoped. She even had the smarts to place herself in line with Anya so the angle of entry would be right on the bullet wounds when they autopsied—"

"Let's not talk about an autopsy in relation to this body," Ethan objected, patting his chest.

We all laughed, and Kyra asked, "How did she kill Zoë?"

"The police figure Bree put on a cop costume from wardrobe—they found it in her hotel room—to avoid being identifiable on the mall's cameras, followed Zoë to the restroom, and hid in the men's room, maybe because there was someone else in the ladies' room." I carefully avoided looking at Mom. "They don't know how she lured Zoë into the men's room, but they're certain she waited until the coast was clear and then killed her."

I tried not to think about how close Mom had come to a psychopath in that narrow, out-of-the-way hall. "Part of the reason I was convinced it was Anya was that she didn't get attacked after filming that love scene with you. I guess Mom and I were right the first time when we figured the killer knew the love scene was fake and so didn't care about it. I'm still curious about what happened at Colonial Beach, though. The bit in the river where you had to rescue Anya. What was that about?"

Ethan mumbled something.

"What?"

"Publicity stunt," he said sheepishly. "The publicity team thought it would make a good story. You know: 'Handsome action star risks life to save beautiful actress from drowning.' It worked," he said defensively when we all stared at him with varying degrees of disbelief or amusement. "*Mafia Mistress* was the most googled term the next day. And, ah, speaking of Anya, we're in talks about her doing another movie for my production company, so you needn't worry about her suing you, EJ." He winked at me.

"So you didn't have a clue Bree was so into you, Ethan?" Kyra asked.

He shook his head. "No."

"What he means is," Mom put in drily, "that he's so used to women mooning over him that he takes that sort of behavior for granted."

Ethan winced but said, "Guilty as charged."

"Speaking of mooning," I said, shifting away from the flames, "What's up with Iona Moss? I thought for a while that she was the note writer, Ethan, because of how she was always hanging around you."

"She wants Delia's job," he said. "I think she was trying to show me how efficient she could be."

"Uh." I threw my head back in disgust that I hadn't figured that out. "Are you going to hire her?"

Ethan looked at Mom, who said, "If she passes the background check your grandpa's running on her."

"So far she's clean," Grandpa said. "Boring, in fact. Nothing but a couple of antiabortion marches in college." He sounded disappointed that she didn't spy for the North Koreans or work as a mule for a drug cartel.

We settled into silence for a moment and I heard a water bird call from the Potomac. After a second, Ethan said, "Hey, EJ, why don't you help me clean up?"

I looked around, puzzled. The staff had already cleared the dishes and, I was sure, washed them and put them away. The only things left to clean up were our bamboo skewers and the glasses holding the dregs of our drinks. "Okay," I said, moving away from the fire pit reluctantly. I collected the Godiva wrappers that had held the s'mores chocolate and the half-full bag of marshmallows, and headed for the bright lights of the kitchen as Ethan rounded up the skewers.

When we got into the granite and stainless steel custom kitchen, Ethan chucked the skewers in the trash and I set the marshmallows on the counter beside an open box of milk chocolate bars. Pouring us both glasses of water, Ethan said, "I wanted to talk to you, EJ." His voice was more serious than usual and I arched my brows.

"So, talk," I said, leaning back against the counter.

"I've been thinking about our conversation the other day, what you said about how I don't take you seriously. I'm sorry about that."

Guilt niggled at me and I was glad he'd brought it up. I'd done a lot of thinking since we'd had our argument. "Me,

too, Ethan," I said. "I'm sorry I said what I did about acting.
Movies make people happy, entertain them, take them away
from their cares and worries for a bit. That's every bit as
valuable as what I do. Heaven knows we could all use an
escape now and then from wars and the economy and news
of famine and disasters."

He smiled that famous smile. "I've always thought so."

"So we'll just forget—"

"Hear me out." He held up a hand. "I accept that being
a producer isn't for you, that it wouldn't make you happy,
even though I know you'd do well at it. So, I'd like to offer
you the job of chief of security for Mercury Wing Studio
and Productions. We employ about two hundred security
personnel, give or take. They work at the studio and protect
our movie sites around the world, do employee background
checks . . . all the usual security stuff a medium-sized corporation needs. You'd be the boss. How about it?"

He beamed at me, as if he'd handed me the keys to a
Porsche, instead of a huge dilemma. I couldn't tell him now
that Coco had let me know this afternoon that she was quitting the director of security position to take a job for half
the pay with some NYC designer and she was over the moon
about it. I knew I'd get the head cheese job this time; maybe
they wouldn't even bother advertising the position and holding interviews. As Fernglen's director of security I might
be able to give Jay some real assistance looking for his lost
diamonds.

But I couldn't spurn my father's offer. To tell the truth,
running a security operation that size had some appeal, even
though the thought of moving back to la-la land made me
cringe. Especially now that Jay and I . . . Ethan must have
seen the indecision in my eyes because he said gently, "Don't
give me an answer now. Think about it."

"You know," he continued in a casual tone, "I've been talking to an orthopedic specialist in LA—he's in the same building as my plastic surgeon—and he says there's a new surgery that might help your leg. I've noticed you're limping more. You've always said you're satisfied the military docs know what they're doing, but Dr. Samuelson is the best in the country. He's performed this surgery on Olympic athletes who thought their careers were over, and that football player who broke his leg in three places and ruptured his knee and then went on to get a Super Bowl ring. I won't push you."

I was momentarily stunned that Ethan had noticed my knee was paining me more, but then it made sense. His business was all about appearance and gesture and movement; of course he'd noticed that I was moving less easily.

"Thanks, Ethan," I managed to say. "I will. Think about it."

He looked at the marshmallow bag I'd put on the counter and fumbled a marshmallow out. "Nothing but sugar and gelatin," he said, popping it in his mouth and chewing. "Pure poison. Want one?"

He tossed a puffy white cylinder to me and I caught it automatically. My gaze lit on the leftover chocolate bars. Ethan was apparently thinking along the same lines I was because he said, "Think we could fish those skewers out of the trash and reuse them?"

"Absolutely. The graham crackers are still out there."

Ethan retrieved the skewers, I clutched the marshmallows and chocolate, and we headed back to the pool deck. Throwing an arm around my shoulders, he said, "Did I tell you I've been offered the lead as a homicidal dentist in the new Demme film? I'd be playing against type, of course, and they want me to gain a few pounds, which'll be hard for me—I've put a lot of hours in on this bod—but I've been thinking it's time to stretch myself with less heroic parts. What do you think?"

"You can't help but be a hero, Dad," I said, as we came up to the others near the fire pit. A log split, sending up a column of gold and red embers that grayed to ash and drifted to the deck. Ethan squeezed my shoulders and the flickering flames ruddied his face, revealing a gloss of wetness in his eyes. It was probably an ember, I told myself, knuckling the corner of my eye where I seemed to have a similar problem.

Truth can be deadlier than fiction . . .

ELLERY ADAMS

The Last Word

A BOOKS BY THE BAY MYSTERY

Olivia Limoges and the Bayside Book Writers are excited about Oyster Bay's newest resident: bestselling novelist Nick Plumley, who's come to work on his next book. But when Olivia stops by Plumley's rental she finds that he's been strangled to death. Her instincts tell her that something from the past came back to haunt him, but she never expects that the investigation could spell doom for one of her dearest friends . . .

**"Visit Oyster Bay and you'll long
to return again and again."**
—Lorna Barrett, *New York Times* bestselling author

facebook.com/TheCrimeSceneBooks
penguin.com

FROM *NEW YORK TIMES* BESTSELLING AUTHOR
JENN MCKINLAY

-The Library Lover's Mysteries-

BOOKS CAN BE DECEIVING
DUE OR DIE
BOOK, LINE, AND SINKER

Praise for the Library Lover's Mysteries

"[An] appealing new mystery series."

—Kate Carlisle, *New York Times* bestselling author

"A sparkling setting, lovely characters, books, knitting, and chowder! What more could any reader ask?"

—Lorna Barrett, *New York Times* bestselling author

"Sure to charm cozy readers everywhere."

—Ellery Adams, author of the Books by the Bay Mysteries

facebook.com/TheCrimeSceneBooks
penguin.com